RED ROCK RANCH

LISE GOLD

MADELEINE TAYLOR

For Jose
Thank you for showing me the desert.

Sometimes, you find yourself in the middle of nowhere, and sometimes, in the middle of nowhere, you find yourself.

— UNKNOWN

1

DAKOTA

"Come on, Henry. You can do this." The engine of the old pickup truck protests, and although I'm ever the optimist, something tells me I may not make it to Vegas. The plan was to drive there with my belongings in the back, then sell the truck and buy a smaller, more practical car. All I need is to make it to the city. My friends warned me against arranging the move myself, but Henry's never let me down before, so I thought I'd take a chance and save myself a ton of money.

"Please, Henry," I beg when he stutters again. "Please, please, please. Not here."

I shouldn't have taken a detour, but the desert is supposed to be beautiful during sunset. I wanted to take in the scenery while driving toward my new life, so I made the stupid decision to turn off the desolate highway onto a narrow dirt road.

It was spectacular indeed. The sun, a fiery ball of orange, glowed low on the horizon while the sky was ablaze with color. But then the engine light started blinking, and now my eyes are fixated on the dashboard instead. It's been red for a few weeks, but it never blinked until five minutes ago. I'm miles from the highway, and I haven't seen a car in the past twenty minutes. Why did I go into the desert today of all days? I could've booked a tour from Vegas once I was settled or driven here after I bought a new car.

I turn and head back in the direction I came from. If I break down, the chances of someone passing are much better closer to the highway. Besides regretting my decision to venture off-plan, my eyes feel dry, and my muscles are aching. The thought of stopping for a rest is enticing, but I'm afraid Henry will give up the ghost entirely if I do so. I'm in the middle of nowhere, and I doubt anyone will find me here tonight.

The low sun casts long shadows across the barren landscape, and darkness is falling way faster than I anticipated. My satnav doesn't work here, I have zero bars on my phone, and although it seemed pretty straightforward to navigate the few roads, in the darkening landscape, it's not so simple anymore. Was I driving toward the sunset, or was the sun to my right? Reaching one of the crossroads, I'm confused, and through my growing unease, I can't remember which way to turn.

Think, Dakota.

I turn left, following the road, but I don't recognize anything. I suspect I went the wrong way, as I should have reached the highway by now. Didn't I pass a weird rock formation that looked like an elephant? There was a single shoe in the middle of the road too, but I don't see it. Realizing I've lost all sense of direction and that I have no clue how to get back to the highway, panic takes over.

It's crazy how dark it gets once the sun has set, and even with my lights on, I can barely see anything. Am I still on the road, or am I literally crossing the desert now? I suddenly feel a sharp jolt, and then the truck starts pulling to one side. The steering wheel vibrates while I step on the brakes until we stop. What was that?

Startled and shaky, I turn off the engine and blow out my cheeks. I can hear it through my open windows; there's a hissing sound coming from the right back tire.

Getting out and using the torch on my phone to inspect it, I see it's been ripped or punctured by something and it's completely flat. "Fuck!" I curse out loud, then wince at the sound of my voice cutting through the silence.

I have a spare tire with me, but I never bothered to buy a new jack after a friend borrowed mine. Even if I did have a jack, I've never changed a tire before; I always relied on roadside assistance in California. Would they come all the way out here? And where *is* here, anyway? Even if I could call for help—which I can't, I establish when I check my network again—what would I say when they ask me where I am? Somewhere in the desert near Vegas? It couldn't possibly get any vaguer than that.

"This is bad, Henry," I mutter, then let out a long sigh. Leaning against the pickup, I contemplate what to do. Should I start walking and hope to find a sign of life some-where? Or would that be the worst possible idea? If I lost my truck too, I'd be in serious trouble. At least I have water and blankets in the back, so it's probably wise to stay here until the morning when I can see where I'm going. Besides, it's eerie out here in the dark, and I don't feel safe. The only sound is that of lizards slipping past or the intermittent gusts of wind that send tumbleweeds scurrying across my feet. A vast expanse of nothingness stretches for miles in every direction, only broken up by the occasional cactus or yucca plant, standing tall and proud in the harsh environ-ment. They look like figures, their twisted branches reaching out like arms ready to grab anyone who comes near, and the sight of them is unsettling.

What about coyotes? They live in the desert, don't they? And scorpions? That thought makes my heart race as I glance down at my feet in the flimsy flip-flops I'm wearing. *Rattlesnakes?* I curl my toes and point my torch toward the ground, and within seconds, I'm back in the pickup.

I couldn't have messed up more if I tried. On Monday, I'm supposed to start my new job, and I need time to get settled into my apartment. What if no one finds me over the weekend and I don't show up for my first day at work? What if no one finds me at all? What if I die out here? My stomach tightens, and I remind myself that doom thinking won't get me anywhere. Mom will get worried; I promised to call her when I reached Vegas, and if she doesn't hear from me, she'll alert the police, so hopefully, they'll come looking for me.

I'm going to sit here until it gets light, I decide, and if I climb onto the roof in the morning, I might be able to see the highway. If not, I'll wait until someone comes to the rescue. Yes, that's better. That's a safe plan.

Something flashes in the dark, and I narrow my eyes as I focus on the direction it came from. Did I imagine it? I'm getting pretty tired and suspect my mind is playing tricks on me, but then I see it again, and there are two lights this time.

"Help! Over here!" I yell out of the window. "Help!" The lights seem to change direction, so I turn on the headlights and honk the horn over and over, until the lights—there are at least five now—come closer. They move in a funny way, almost in a swaying, drunk motion, and when their silhouettes come into clear view, I realize they're horseback riders with lights attached to their cowboy hats. Then my relief is replaced by fear. How do I know if I can trust them? Is there such a thing as desert pirates? Could they be bad people? As they near, I see two of them are women, and that brings me some comfort, so I get out and wave at them.

"Hey, ma'am." The woman who rides up front taps her hat. "Are you lost?"

"Yeah, you could say that." I point to my pickup. "And I've got a flat. I must've hit something—I couldn't see much in the dark. I have a spare, but I don't have a jack, and there's something wrong with my engine too."

"Okay..." The woman glances over her shoulder and addresses the group. "Do you guys mind waiting for a minute?" She turns back to me, comes closer, and glances curiously at the full trunk of my pickup. "Were you planning on vacationing out here or something? Because it's prohibited to camp in this part of the desert, and it's also unsafe with all the critters."

"No. I was on my way to Vegas. I'm moving there."

"Oh." She arches a brow. "Why on earth did you go off-road in the dark?"

"I wanted to see the sunset," I say sheepishly and blush when the group chuckles.

"God, you couldn't have fucked up worse." The woman looks amused. "Right. Well, I'm in the middle of something, so I can't help you right now, but if you go and sit in your truck and lock the doors, I'll be back for you in about three hours."

"Thank you." I cross my heart and give her a smile. "Thank you so, so much. I can pay you."

"Don't worry about it. Now stay inside with those open-toed sandals. I don't want to return to find you poisoned or worse." She turns her horse and beckons to her companions to do the same. "Three hours. I promise I'll come back."

2

FRANKIE

*W*hen I return to the stranded pickup after midnight, the woman looks like she'd hug me if I wasn't sitting on a huge stallion.

"Thank you so, so much," she says again, smiling with relief. She has a nice, open smile that lights up her face as she shades her eyes from the bright spotlight on my hat.

"Don't sweat it. Do you have any other shoes in the back? Tennis shoes or something?"

"Yes, I do." She jumps into action, climbing into the back of her pickup that's packed to the brim and roots through her cases. I shine my flashlight on her and take in the contents. Boxes, suitcases, bags, a TV, lamps, and even some furniture are piled up in a way that's definitely not safe for the road. I never questioned her when she said she was moving; she doesn't strike me as a thief or a drifter, but I'm still baffled at the idiocy of her going off-road in the dark. Everyone knows it's a bad idea unless you know the desert inside out, like me.

"Found them!" She triumphantly holds up a pair of white sneakers and socks, then perches on what looks like a nightstand to put them on. "Will my stuff be safe here overnight? My whole life is in the back of this truck."

"I can't promise you that, but I think it will be fine. We'll head out early to change your tire and drive it back to the ranch. I'll have a look at your engine there. It's easier." I grin when she jumps off her truck and stares up at me and then Texas, my loyal companion. "Do you ride?" I ask.

"No." Her eyes widen. "Oh…you want me to get on?"

"Ideally, yes," I say with a chuckle. "It's a long walk to the ranch." Assessing her, I decide she doesn't look heavy and move to the back of my McClellan saddle, then hold out my hand. "Put your left foot in the stirrup and hold on to the saddle with your left hand. I'll lift you up."

"Shouldn't I be at the back?" she asks, clumsily maneuvering while the purse she's slung around her neck dangles from side to side.

"No. It's safer this way." I groan as I pull her up and she lets out a sigh when she positions herself.

"Oh my God, it's so high…"

"Don't worry, we're not going to gallop. Hold on to the saddle and let me know if you want me to slow down." Leaning forward, I look over her shoulder and tap my foot against Texas, who immediately sets off. I sense the woman is nervous, so I try to distract her with conversation. "What's your name?"

"Dakota," she says. "I'm sorry, I totally forgot to introduce myself."

"That's okay. I'm Frankie. So, you're from California?"

"Yes. How did you know?"

"Your license plate," I say humorously. "And your looks. The sun-bleached hair and the tan…you look like you've spent a lot of time on the beach."

"I did. I lived in Newport Beach."

"Fancy. Do you think you'll miss the ocean?"

"For sure," she says. "But a career opportunity came up in Vegas and I felt a little stuck in LA, so I thought I'd give it a go." She instinctively tries to look over her shoulder as she's talking to me and almost loses her balance.

"It's okay, I've got you. Just make sure you look ahead." I take the reins in one hand and curl my other around her waist. She's tense; I can feel her abdomen tighten under the thin fabric of her white tank top. Her hair smells of coconut and a hint of floral perfume wafts from her neck. "I'm sorry, I should have told you to put on something warmer. It can get chilly here at night, even in summer. Are you cold?"

"No, but it's amazing how much the temperature drops." She pauses. "And you?" she asks. "You mentioned a ranch. Is that where you live?"

"Yeah. I run a small ranch hotel and provide horseback riding experiences. Desert excursions, mainly."

"Is that what you were doing tonight?"

"Uh-huh. The desert is beautiful on a clear night. You'll never see as many stars as you see here." I nudge her when she's about to look up. "Not yet. Wait until we get to the ranch. I don't want you to fall off."

"Sure." She chuckles when I speed up a little. "This is fun."

"You think being stranded in the desert with a flat tire and a broken engine is fun?"

"Not that part, but a midnight horseback ride after being rescued by a cowgirl... That doesn't happen to me every day."

A little confused, I furrow my brows. Is she flirting with me?

"Sorry," she continues. "I suppose it's not much fun for you. I really appreciate you coming all the way back for me."

"It's my pleasure. It's not every day I get to rescue a beautiful woman," I shoot back at her, hoping I'm not overstepping. She laughs nervously and I continue quickly to avoid an awkward silence. "The ranch is fully booked, but you can sleep on the couch in my private quarters. It's pretty comfortable."

"That's so kind, but I don't want to be in your way. I thought I could call a taxi from your ranch to take me to a nearby motel and come back early in the morning."

"That's a waste of time. The nearest motel is practically in Vegas, so you might as well stay over or you'll get no sleep at all. Really, it's not a problem."

"Thank you. And your..." Dakota hesitates. "Your husband won't mind? Or your..."

"Partner? No. I'm single." It feels weird to have this kind of conversation without being able to look each other in the eyes. "What about you? Is someone special joining you in Vegas?"

"No. It's just me." Dakota points to the lights in the distance. "Is that your ranch?"

"Yes, that's Red Rock Ranch." I smile with pride. The ranch was renovated a few years ago and it still gets me excited to see how good it looks from a distance.

The main farmhouse stands proud against the starlit sky, its weathered wood siding glowing warmly under the porch lights. It's a sturdy two-story structure with a wide, wraparound porch that I added a few years back. The roof's steep pitch is perfect for shedding the rare desert rain, and the brick chimney hints at the cozy fireplace waiting inside. To the left of the farmhouse, separated by a tidy gravel path lined with desert sage, is the guesthouse. It's a long, single-story building with a covered walkway connecting a series of doors, each leading to a private room. The exterior matches the main house, giving the whole property a cohesive feel. Solar panels glint on the roof, a recent addition I'm particularly pleased with.

The stables and corrals are off to the right, and I can see the shapes of a few horses moving in the moonlight.

"That's quite the ranch you've got there," Dakota says. "Is it family run?"

"It used to be, but since my parents retired, I'm running it. The farm was getting too much for them, so they moved into a condo in Vegas after I took over. I have a brother, but he was never interested in horses. He lives in California and works for a tech company. I have a great team, though. I could never do it all by myself."

When we arrive, I hop off and lead Texas through the gate, then help Dakota off. "Welcome. I'll show you in before I take care of Texas. Do you want to have a shower?"

"That would be amazing." Dakota shoots me a grateful smile and ruffles a hand through her hair. "I'm all sticky and dusty from the long drive." She takes in the premises as she follows me to the main house. "You have a beautiful home," she says when I let her in.

"Thanks. Please, make yourself at home." We head to the bathroom and I hand her a towel. "Wait, let me get you something clean to sleep in."

"Oh, you don't need to do that, I can—" Dakota stops herself and winces. "Actually, that would be great. I'm so sorry to be a pain."

3

DAKOTA

*D*ressed in a pair of grey jersey shorts and an old sweatshirt with the logo of some local diner, I feel a little self-conscious. I love to slouch around in garments like these at home, but I always make sure I look presentable when I'm around other people. The couch in the living room is made up and a delicious smell wafts from the kitchen.

"Are you hungry?" Frankie asks. "I've heated up some leftovers. Figured you must be famished."

"I am," I say, gratefully taking the bowl of pasta she hands me.

"There's a dining table on the porch if you'd like to sit outside." Frankie holds up a half-full bottle of wine. "I'm having a glass of red. Care to join me?" She opens the door to the porch without waiting for an answer and lights a few candles on the table.

"You really don't have to keep me company. It's late and you must be tired."

"I'm fine. I'm used to staying up after the late tours, and the temperature is much nicer at night." She sits and pours us wine. "So...Nevada is a big shift from California. What's the job?"

"I'll be managing a spa in one of the hotels on the strip. The White Salon—it's a chain. I ran their branch in Newport Beach, and now I'll be responsible for the Vegas branch, which is much bigger." I slide onto the bench opposite Frankie and only then really take her in. In a state of near panic and desperate to get somewhere more civilized, I didn't pay much attention in the dark earlier, but she's a very attractive woman.

She's changed from her jeans and shirt into sweatpants and a white tank top, and her arms are toned and tanned. Her hair, previously hidden under her cowboy hat, is short and dark, slicked back like she's just splashed water over her face. She has curious brown eyes, dark lashes, and dark eyebrows that move expressively while she speaks. She strikes me as someone who would tell a good story around a campfire; one of those engaging types who draw people in. She's certainly drawn me in. I don't tend to let people see me with wet hair, especially not a single, tall, attractive woman who undoubtedly plays for my team.

"A spa?" She lowers her gaze to my hands. "Forgive me for generalizing, but I thought all beauticians had long nails." Her voice is a soft whisper, and in the light of the flickering candles, I'm sure I'm detecting a hint of flirtation in her eyes.

"Well, I'm not a beautician, I'm a general manager," I say, stirring my fork through the pasta. "I used to give massages and that requires short nails," I add playfully, hoping she'll take the bait. "But my massage days are over. I'm only focusing on the operational side of the business now."

"Oh?" Her eyebrow shoots up. "What a waste of a talent. Don't you miss using those lovely hands?"

My lips stretch into a grin, and I shake my head as I focus on my food. "Are you flirting with me, cowgirl?" The tomato and basil pasta is delicious, but my body reacts to Frankie in interesting ways, and suddenly I don't feel that hungry anymore. Still, I continue to eat as I don't want to be impolite.

"Would it be so terrible if I was?" she asks.

I pick up my glass and twirl the wine around while I meet her gaze. Her expression is cocky, like she knows she already has me in her pocket, and although I'm normally not this easy to chat up, it feels like too good an opportunity to pass. She's sinfully sexy, and if nothing else, it would make for a great story to tell my friends. *My move to Vegas: Stranded, saved, and seduced by a cowgirl.* It would make a good book title too. "No..." I feel a blush rise to my cheeks but don't shy away from her eyes.

Frankie holds up her glass in a toast and winks. "In that case, you're welcome to share my bed tonight."

Sitting back, I sip my wine and stare at her while a million fantasies rush through my mind. "Is this what you do with all your ranch guests?"

"No. Only some and only occasionally." She tilts her head from side to side. "Most of my guests are couples, and the singles tend to be straight or not my type. It seems like tonight is my lucky night."

"How do you know I'm not straight?"

Frankie frowns and studies me. "You're flirting back and you're not nervous like straight women when they want to experiment." She shrugs. "There have been a few here over the years."

"And your job is to make sure their holiday is memorable?"

"Anything for a five-star review," she jokes. "I could ensure your move to Vegas is memorable too."

"Trust me, it already is." I'm having fun with our playful back-and-forth, and arousal is tugging at me. It's been years since I've had such chemistry with someone, not to mention the opportunity to act on it.

"Can I sit next to you?" Frankie asks. "It's a little lonely on this side and I prefer to face the stars." When I nod, she moves around the table. "That's better," she says, sitting back and draping one arm over the backrest behind me.

"Smooth. Very smooth," I say humorously, but I move a little closer anyway. I feel her body heat against me and I'm pretty sure she tenses at the contact. She's taller than me, and I like how I fit into the crook of her arm. "So, what's your next move? Are we going to look at the stars together?"

"Yes, and you'll love it." Frankie reaches behind her to turn off the porch lights, then blows out the candles. "We'll need total darkness for this." She points to the sky. "Let your eyes adjust for a moment."

I stare into the black, and after a while, millions of twinkling lights become visible. Some are tiny specks, some significantly bigger. Some are clustered together, creating shapes and bright spots.

"Can you see it?"

"Yes. It's beautiful." When I feel her eyes on me, I hold my breath. "I've never seen so many stars," I whisper, turning to her.

"Welcome to the desert." Frankie gives me a lopsided smile while she caresses the back of my neck, and my eyes flutter closed for a beat. Her touch feels electric, and I can hardly believe how such a simple gesture can cause such fire inside me. A flash of heat shoots between my thighs and my gaze lowers to her mouth. Her lips are glistening and inviting, and I feel an overwhelming urge to kiss her.

This is the moment, I think, bracing myself to be swept away. She inches closer, curls her hand around my neck, and pulls me in. I can feel her breath on my face, and it quickens along with my pulse. Just as our lips are about to brush, a loud call pulls us out of the moment.

"Frankie!" A young man comes running up to the house. "Frankie, Sahara is foaling!" He's panting, steadying his hands on his knees, then suddenly narrows his eyes as he spots me. "Oh, sorry. I didn't realize you had company."

"That's okay," Frankie mutters. "Sorry, Dakota. I have to go." She continues to stare at my lips, then gets up with a sigh and shoots me a regretful smile. "You're welcome to join us in the stables. Otherwise, I'll see you in the morning."

4

FRANKIE

I spread more of the fresh hay Lawrence brought in over the stable floor, then stand up to stroke Sahara. My mare has been uncomfortable for hours, and I feel for her. "It's going to be okay, girl. I promise I'll take care of you."

"Dystocia?" Lawrence asks.

"Yes. We'll have to give her a hand."

Dakota is sitting on a haystack in the corner of the stable with her back against the wall. We've been here for a while, and I told her she could go to bed, but she wanted to stay. "Shouldn't you call a vet?" she asks.

"I am a vet." I stroke Sahara's back while I feel inside her. "That's what I thought. It's a malpresentation. It means the foal is positioned incorrectly," I explain to Dakota. "But I think we can fix it."

Lawrence looks like he's about to panic. He's only worked here for four months and has never experienced a birth before. It's been a while since I've witnessed one too. I don't breed my horses, but this rescue turned out to be pregnant.

"Hold her still, Lawrence. Stroke her and try to reassure her," I say.

Sahara is breathing hard as I work my arm inside her birth canal again and try to shift the foal's position. After identifying the misalignment, I gently manipulate the limbs, guiding them for a smooth delivery. "It's okay, girl. We're almost there."

Sahara resists, but she knows I mean no harm. After a few minutes, when I'm confident she'll be safe, I carefully grasp the foal's legs and work in tandem with Sahara's contractions, ensuring the foal's head and front limbs are aligned properly. Sahara is tired, but she pushes through, and finally, the foal comes into the world.

Covered in a glistening coat of amniotic fluid, the newborn looks sleek and damp as its slender legs unfold. Its eyes, wide and curious, hold a beautiful sense of wonder as it takes in the sights and sounds of its new surroundings, and I feel a lump form in my throat. Witnessing new life is always magical, and I almost forget Dakota is here.

"Is it okay?" she asks.

"Yes, it's a girl." I beckon her over. "Come here."

Dakota approaches, and her eyes widen. "Oh, wow... She's so sweet." The foal's ears twitch and her nose trembles as her senses come to life. "This is amazing."

"Pretty special, right?" I watch as Sahara turns and starts nuzzling and licking the foal vigorously. "She's cleaning her," I say. "But the licking also stimulates circulation and encourages the foal to nurse."

"You mean she'll be able to stand soon?"

"Yeah. She'll be on her wobbly legs in a few hours. Lawrence and I have to stay here to make sure that happens, though."

Dakota nods as she takes in the scene. "She's so precious. What are you going to call her?"

"I haven't thought of that yet." I clean my hands under the tap by the stable doors and wipe them on my pants. I'm sweaty and stained and ready for a shower, but I can't leave the stables until the foal nurses. "How about Dakota?"

"Really?" Dakota gasps and slams a hand in front of her mouth. "You want to name her after me?" Her enthusiasm is endearing and makes me laugh.

"Why not? You witnessed her birth, and her mom's not a pedigree horse. Sahara's a rescue, so anything goes. Besides, many of our horses are named after states, so it's perfect."

"That's so cool." Dakota looks a little emotional as she inches closer and crouches to watch Sahara caring for her foal. "Hey, little girl. Welcome to the world. Do you want to be named after me?"

The foal lets out an awkward grunt, and we both chuckle.

"Let's take her first word as a yes," I say, then turn my attention to Lawrence. "Sorry, Lawrence. If it was a stallion, I would have named him after you."

Lawrence grins and shrugs. "I like Dakota. It's a good name for a horse." He starts gathering the hay covered in birth fluids and throws it into a wheelbarrow. Though he's only eighteen years old, he wants to be a veterinarian, and I was happy to give him a part-time job so he can get some work experience. "So, we're up for an all-nighter, are we?"

"Yeah, it looks like it."

"Do you mind if I stay?" Dakota asks.

"Not at all. I just thought you might be tired, and we'll have to leave early to get your pickup. I have to be back when my guests wake up."

"I don't mind," she says. "I'd love to see Dakota take her

21

first steps. I'll never get an opportunity like this again." She's still focused on the nurturing mare. "This may be normal to you, but to me it's..." She hesitates. "Wow. Just wow."

I close the distance between us and remove a sprig of hay from her hair. "Okay. Then how about I make some coffee?" She meets my eyes, and that flirty sparkle is back.

"Coffee sounds good."

"I'm sorry we couldn't finish what we started," I whisper, making sure Lawrence can't hear me. I could have been all over this beautiful stranger by now, but my horses come first. Always.

"Yeah." Dakota smiles. "But honestly, this is a once-in-a-lifetime experience, and I'm having the best night." She lingers for a while, then points to the wheelbarrow. "Can I help?"

5

DAKOTA

"It's still there!" I'm so happy when I spot my pickup from a distance. It's been a long night and dressed in Frankie's clothes, I'm longing to get my hands on something that will make me look decent. We haven't slept yet. By the time the foal stood up and started to nurse, it was time to head out, and Frankie is still wearing her bloodstained tank top.

"Of course it's still there." Frankie chuckles. "Not many people venture into this part of the desert, let alone at six a.m." She parks her Range Rover and looks amused as she takes in the pile of stuff in the back. It didn't look so bad when it was dark, but now I'm embarrassed about the mess. Always leaving everything to the last minute, I packed in a rush, and it shows. When I ran out of suitcases and boxes, I used garbage bags, and I notice some are ripped. Secured with only a few ratchet straps, I suspect some of my belongings managed to escape on the way here, but there's nothing of much value in them.

"That's some impressive packing you did there," Frankie jokes as if reading my mind.

"Yeah, I kind of regret not taking the relocation package now."

She walks around the pickup to inspect the ripped tire. "You said you had a spare?"

"Yes, it's somewhere in the back underneath..." I blow out my cheeks and scratch my head. "Underneath all of that." Knowing Frankie hasn't even slept and I'm wasting her time, I add, "Why don't you go home and get some rest? If you call roadside assistance for me and explain where I am, I'll dig out the spare tire and wait here for them."

"It could take hours before they get here, and it's going to be very warm soon. If your engine isn't working properly, there's no way I'll leave you here in the suffocating heat. It's dangerous." Frankie opens the hatch and starts taking out my cases. "Let's just do it now. Come on, give me a hand."

Two hours later, I wipe the sweat off my brow and take a step back to inspect my new tire. Under Frankie's instructions, I did it myself, so I won't be so helpless next time it happens.

"Good job," she says. "If you're going to live in Nevada, you'll have to learn how to change a tire."

"Thank you." I feel silly for the proud grin on my face, but it feels like an accomplishment. "You've been amazing."

"Don't sweat it." Frankie shoots me a wink and scoots into the driver's seat. "Keys?"

I hand them over and wait while she tries to start the engine. It protests a few times and sounds like it's coughing, but against all expectations, it does run. "I think it's your oil," Frankie says. "If it is, I can fix that for you right now." She opens the hood, hops out, and peers inside.

I indulge in watching her while she bends over my engine. There's something exceptionally sexy about women who know about cars, and Frankie is not only good with engines, she's good with horses too. *How on earth is she still single?*

"Is it the oil?" I ask.

"Your warning lights are all over the place, so let's find out. Do you want another lesson?"

"Yes, please." I smile and wait like an obedient schoolgirl while she fetches a bottle of oil and a roll of paper towels from her Range Rover.

"First," she says, "we have to locate the dipstick." She points to a yellow handle sticking out of the engine. "That's it. See the oil icon?"

"Uh-huh." I look over her shoulder, put an arm around her, and rest my hand on her hip. It's an intimate gesture, but we've practically been flirting since we met, so I don't even think twice. Frankie turns me on, and I just want to be near her.

"Good. Now we're going to clean it." She does so, sticks it back in and pulls it out again. "And now we can check your oil level," she continues. "Which is below the minimum level. See?"

"Yes, that's pretty straightforward," I say, mildly embarrassed I didn't know that. "So we just fill it up?"

"Precisely." She hands me the oil. "It should sit somewhere between the minimum and the maximum level. Pour some and see how you go, but I suspect you might need the whole bottle."

I do as I'm told and test the oil levels again. "It looks fine now." I frown. "So that's it?"

"Yes, that's it." Frankie removes a top off a plastic tank in my engine and peers into it. "You're okay for cooling fluid, so fingers crossed you're good to go. You need to have it serviced, though." When she turns around, we're face-to-face and so close I can feel her chest rise and fall against mine. She shoots me a mischievous smile as we lock eyes, and I've already forgotten what she said. "Do you want to try and start the engine?" she asks in a husky tone. Her gaze lowers to my lips for a beat, but then she casually steps back like she didn't just set my libido on fire.

Tease. Although I'm desperate to get Henry out of here, part of me is enjoying this too much to give up just yet. Reluctantly, I get behind the wheel and I'm a little shaky as I turn the key. "It sounds good," I say, revving it up until the oil has pulled through.

"Perfect. You're safe to drive to Vegas now." Frankie taps the roof of my truck. "Good thing it wasn't more serious."

"I was lucky to meet you." I get out to thank her properly and realize I'm sweaty and tired. I'm not wearing makeup and my hair is a mess, and if this is the last she sees of me, I doubt I'll be on her mind for very long. "I don't know how to thank you."

"No need. I enjoyed your company," she replies. "It's only an hour to Vegas. Are you going to be okay driving, or are you too tired?"

"I'll be fine. I'll get a coffee on the way and crash when I get there."

Frankie nods. "Well, it was nice meeting you, Dakota. Good luck with your new life."

I smile at her and inch a little closer. Frankie's a mess too; she's not wearing her cowboy hat and her hair is sticking out on all sides. Her clothes are stained, and she smells like horses and oil, but somehow that only makes her more attractive. Our chemistry is electric, and I'm contemplating whether to kiss her or not.

Frankie runs a hand through my hair and brings her mouth close to mine, taking the decision for me. She lingers there, her lips curling into a smile as she waits for my permission. "I guess this is goodbye then," she murmurs.

I brush my lips over hers and a soft moan escapes me. The light touch awakens all my senses and sends a flash of heat between my thighs. God, I want her, and I think she feels the same because she cups my face and pushes me against my pickup, then kisses me fiercely. When she parts her lips to claim my mouth, I feel like I'm about to explode, and, lacing my fingers through her hair, I bask in the moment and enjoy every bit of pleasure that pulses through me. Her soft lips, her tongue, her persistent grinding against my pelvis, her hands that lower to my waist and my behind, and squeeze me until I squirm in her grip...

Frankie pulls out of the kiss, leaving me desperate and wanting so much more. "Mmm...you're a great kisser," she whispers, then bites her lip as she looks me over. "If I didn't have a group tour in a few hours, I'd invite you back home, but I should probably have a shower and get changed."

I feel myself blush, and a grin spreads across my face. Frankie seems to know exactly how to press my buttons. "And I need to get to Vegas and get some stuff sorted out before Monday." I hesitate and shuffle on the spot. "Well, I appreciate everything you've done for me, and I hope Dakota grows up to be big and strong and healthy."

"I'm sure she will." Frankie looks a little goofy too, and I wonder if she enjoyed that kiss as much as I did. "Take care of yourself, Dakota." She rubs my arm and heads back to her Range Rover. "To get to the highway, follow this road and take the first right. That's all, you're really close."

There's so much I want to ask her, but it's too late now, and I curse myself for not being more inquisitive. I give her a wave goodbye and drive until she's out of sight, then stop the pickup again, sit back, and let out a long sigh. I want to scream, and I don't know why. There's just so much pent-up energy inside of me that's dying to get out, and I need some time to wind down from that searing kiss or I won't be able to focus on the road. *Fuck.* I bring a hand to my lips and close my eyes. That was spectacular. I've had some one-night stands lately, but nothing came close to what I just felt. Taking a few minutes, I concentrate on my breathing until I feel calm enough to drive. Vegas is waiting.

6

FRANKIE

*A*s the sun sets, Red Rock Canyon glows in the evening light. The beauty of it never fails to amaze me, even though I've been here countless times. I've been riding for an hour, guiding my group through the desert at a gentle pace. Most of them aren't used to horseback riding, and some have never done it before, but my horses are calm and accustomed to strangers who have no clue how to manage them.

Reaching a clearing, I hear gasps and murmurs behind me. People rarely raise their voices in the desert, and I like that. It's as if they instinctively want to keep quiet, afraid to disturb the peace. In front of us is a towering red rock formation, so smooth it looks like it's been carved and sanded by a giant. The landscape here is otherworldly, the way I imagine other planets might look.

"These rocks are made of sandstone that was deposited over two hundred million years ago," I say. "They were formed by erosion—the area was once covered by a shallow sea, and as the sea level dropped, the sediment was exposed to the air and eroded by wind and water, creating the canyons and mesas that we see today. The red color comes from the iron oxide in the sediment." I pause to give my group time to absorb the information. "The canyon is home to over two hundred species of birds, including the endangered California condor, and the Red Rock Canyon National Conservation Area is also home to a variety of rare reptiles, such as the chuckwalla, the Gila monster, and the desert tortoise." The words roll off my tongue easily. I do two sunset tours, two morning tours, and two stargazing tours a week and try to keep it engaging so I don't sound like a robot spitting out facts. "Have any of you heard of the Gila monster?"

"Isn't it poisonous?" a woman asks.

"That's right. It's the only venomous lizard in North America, and it can grow quite big. It bites quickly and can hold on tenaciously for up to ten minutes. There's no antivenom for their bites, but they tend to stay away from people, so don't worry. You're all safe up there on your horses. Besides, they're generally only active for three months a year. Outside that timeframe, they lay low. Fun fact," I add, "The Gila monster binge eats and can consume up to a third of its body weight in one session, but three or four meals give them enough calories to get through a year."

"What about the desert tortoise?" a man asks. "Do you ever see them?"

"I spot them regularly, but only because I know where to look. I'll take you around the canyon, and hopefully, we'll catch sight of one hiding between the rocks. They live up to eighty years and grow huge because they can fully retract into their shell, protecting them from predators. They blend into the scenery, so it takes some practice to identify them."

The sun lowers, creating a halo behind the rocks, and my group stares at the scene in awe. Some reach into their pockets for their phones, while others simply sit there, hypnotized by the view.

"You can get off your horses and go into the canyon to take some pictures if you like," I say. "Take your time, there's no rush." When my guests are heading to the canyon, I call the horses, and they gather around me while I wait. I like this part of the tour. It's a moment of peace in my busy day. Surrounded by seven horses and the soothing evening breeze that is a welcome break from the heat of the day, I always take a moment to reflect and analyze my group. It's important to me that they have a good time. Not just because I want good reviews, but because I genuinely love the desert and it makes me happy when others appreciate its beauty too, when they get excited about such simple things as a sunset, blooming cacti, the stars, or a rock formation. There's beauty in the little things, and being able to see them is a blessing.

Today, though, my mind keeps drifting back to Dakota. It's been two days since she left and I hope she got to Vegas safely, but there's no way of checking. Should I look her up? Keep in contact? There was definitely chemistry between us, and if I hadn't been called away for an emergency, I'm sure we would have ended up in bed together. And that kiss... I shiver as I relive it, then shake my head and roll my eyes. Women don't tend to stay on my mind, and I'm not the relationship type. At least, not anymore. My life is here, with my horses, and very few people are able to adjust to desert life. I've tried relationships, but too affected by the heat and the lack of nearby amenities, my girlfriends never stuck around. Tourists come and go, and sometimes, I meet someone I click with, and we have a fun night. That's the extent of my love life.

A woman comes rushing back and gets on her horse.

"Are you okay?" I pause and try to remember her name. "It's Sarah, right?"

"Yes, I'm okay, and it's beautiful," she says. "But I'm really scared of spiders. Mind if I keep you company instead?"

"Of course not." I smile. "The tarantulas are harmless, but I get it. They're pretty big and can be frightening if you're not used to them."

Sarah nods. "I just saw one the size of my hand and decided I'm better off up here." She strokes her horse. "She's adorable. What's her name again?"

"Silver," I say. "She's super sweet and playful, and the youngest of the bunch, apart from Dakota, who was born Friday night. I'll take you all to see the foal back at the ranch."

"Aww..." The woman places a hand on her heart and smiles. "I would love that. I live in New York, so I never get to do anything like this. It's so peaceful out here." She studies me. "Don't you get lonely, though?"

"Not really. I have a few friends who live nearby, and I have staff. And the group tours keep me busy," I add. "I talk to people most of the day, so when I have a moment to myself, I embrace the silence. I grew up here. It's what I'm used to."

"Have you ever left the state?" she asks.

I chuckle because I get this question a lot. People tend to think I'm an uneducated cowgirl who's never ventured beyond the ranch fence. They assume I'm some isolated desert dweller with no knowledge of the outside world. "Yes. I studied veterinary medicine at Washington State University, and I traveled through Europe for a year after I graduated. It was fun and interesting, but it also felt good to be back, and my parents weren't getting any younger, so they needed my help. I guess you could say I'm a little stuck here because I can't just pack up and leave for longer than a few days, but I don't mind that."

"Hmm... And what about your husband? Is he from around here?"

"My husband?"

Sarah frowns. "Oh, sorry, I just assumed the man who helped us saddle up—"

"Jose? That's not my husband," I interrupt her with an amused smile. "He works for me. I have a team of four, and he's been with me for five years. Great rider, but not very social, so he doesn't do tours."

The woman laughs. "I apologize. But he's handsome, right?"

"I suppose so." I shrug. "I'm gay, so men don't interest me in that way."

"Oh?" Her eyes widen. "That's great. I love gay people. My niece is gay, and she's single."

I also get that a lot, and I try not to laugh. Whenever I tell people I'm gay, they always have a family member, friend, or neighbor who swings my way, and they're always the most amazing people ever. It's sweet, though, and she means well, so I shoot her a smile. "I'm sure your niece is lovely."

Sarah's husband returns, stalling our conversation.

"You're missing out, sweetheart," he says. "Are you sure you don't want to come back for a picture?"

Sensing Sarah is uncomfortable, I hold out my hand to take his phone. "Why don't you get on your horse, and I'll take some pictures of you two here, together? It's a lovely backdrop."

7

DAKOTA

*S*ipping my coffee on my balcony, I'm slowly waking up. I was exhausted when I got here yesterday morning but singlehandedly carried everything upstairs, then made my bed and slept for ten hours straight. After that, I unpacked a few boxes, as I needed my towels, toiletries, and kitchen utensils. In the evening, I went for a walk to get groceries and explore my new neighborhood.

Committing to a six-month rental contract in the Art District was a bit of a risk as I wasn't sure if I'd like it here, but so far, it seems lively and safe. It's a short drive to the strip, but it's not jammed with traffic or crowded. There are privately run coffee shops here and restaurants with outdoor seating. Coming from California where being outdoors was a huge part of my life, it seemed sensible to move somewhere with a balcony so I wouldn't feel claustrophobic. It's a three-story building and I'm on the first floor, above a Mexican restaurant.

I've never lived outside California before, so it's all very surreal. My apartment is modest, but the view from my balcony makes up for the size. This side of Las Vegas Boulevard is lined with wedding chapels; I can see three from here alone. There's the Little White Chapel, The Little Vegas Chapel, Chapel of the Flowers, and farther down the road more heart-shaped neon signs fight for attention among others that promote hotels, motels, restaurants, and a strip club. In the distance, the sun beats down on the glass and steel of the towering casinos. It's already warm and it's only the beginning of June.

The door to the restaurant below opens and a man comes out. He sits on the terrace with a coffee, lights a cigar, and props his feet up on another chair. The top of his head is bald, and whatever gray hair he has left is pulled into a small ponytail.

He looks up as I shift in my chair. "Good morning," he says.

"Good morning." I smile at him and raise my coffee cup. "Are you the owner?"

"Yeah. I'm Gabriel." He narrows his eyes at me. "Are you the new tenant?"

"Yes. I'm Dakota. I just moved here from California."

"Welcome to Vegas, Dakota." He takes a long draw from his cigar, then expertly blows out a perfect ring of smoke. "What brings you here?"

"A new job," I say. "I'll be managing the spa in the Quantum."

"A manager, huh? Most newcomers don't want to live around here. They think the Art District unsafe, with all the strip clubs and graffiti and such."

"Oh..." I frown. "Is it?"

"No." He shakes his head. "It's totally fine as long as you avoid the area behind The Strat. And there's great food on your doorstep," he adds. "We serve the best tacos in town. Not the Tex-Mex nonsense. Real ones."

"Yum. I'll definitely come and sample them." I realize I'm lucky to have a friendly local downstairs, as I feel a little lost with the long list of things I need to do. "Do you happen to know anyone who buys used cars? I need to sell my old pickup. It's not practical here."

"As a matter of fact, I do." Gabriel gets up from his chair and points to the right. "There's a gas station over there. The owner's brother deals in used cars, so ask him. I sold my previous car to him a few years back, and he was friendly and gave me a good price."

"That's great. Thank you." Conscious I'm still in my robe, I give him a wave. "Well, I'd better get dressed. It was nice meeting you, Gabriel. I'll be sure to sample your tacos very soon."

I head inside and into the bathroom where laundry is piled on top of the already full laundry basket. As I start sorting it so I can put a wash on—I haven't had time to do my laundry since I arrived—I spot Frankie's clothes. I threw them in when I got here and forgot all about them. They're dusty and smell of the stables, but I still inhale against the fabric in hope to detect a hint of her scent. I wonder if she's thinking of me. It's unlikely; I was probably just a passing opportunity for a bit of fun; a likeminded woman who happened to be single. Still...she'd want her clothes back, right? I could send them by post? Or...I could drop them off? It's only a short drive and it's not like my days off are fully booked with social engagements.

The circus that is Las Vegas plays out before me. It's not even midday and I'm already overwhelmed by the sheer energy this city holds. Strolling down the strip, I take in the crowd. Some people are laughing and talking, others are looking tired and lost. I wonder what their stories are, and where they're heading. There's a sense of excitement in the air, like anything can happen here, and I'm with them all the way.

Still in two minds about my move as I know I'll miss California, their enthusiasm makes me hopeful. *I can do this. I can start over, and I can be happy here.*

My move wasn't entirely career focused. Deep down, I wanted to get away from Newport Beach, and from my ex in particular, whose nearness was haunting me. Moving in the same circles as the woman I used to love was toxic and painful, at least for me. I regularly saw her walking past with other women, and as we used to hang out in the same bars and still have mutual friends, it was hard to avoid her. Clearly, Lina had less trouble moving on than me.

She thought I was unadventurous, and I thought she was too impulsive. We weren't the best combination. With clashing personalities, we never stood a chance, but we still stayed together for four years.

Being far away from Lina seemed like the best solution, and perhaps I wanted to prove to myself as much as to her that I *was* adventurous. Still, I miss her in those fleeting moments when I'm confronted with memories of her. A song, a picture, a smell...it can be anything that takes me back.

When my employer offered me this opportunity, I embraced it. It's a chance to rebuild my life and progress in my career. Lina is now a ghost of the past, I tell myself, and I push her to the back of my mind. If only I'd slept with that cowgirl. Compared to my other rebound attempts, Frankie would have been a spectacular one—I rarely have such fiery chemistry with women. It was fascinating to watch her with her mare, comforting and whispering sweet words to calm her down. She really has a way with horses, and I admire that.

I've thought of that kiss since we said goodbye and keep reliving the flirtations, the looks, and the way she caressed the hair at the back of my neck and made me melt into a puddle... Of course, she's a player and does this with tourists all the time. How else is she going to have fun in the middle of nowhere? It's clearly the only way, and I get that.

A group of rowdy men walk past me, ripping me out of my thoughts. They're already intoxicated, or maybe they pulled an all-nighter. Two women are sitting on the stoop with a takeout cocktail in hand and an older couple is arguing over money. I've never been a gambler and I certainly won't fall down that trap now that I live here.

Passing several famous casinos, I'm surprised how few bars are directly on the strip. They're all out of sight, hidden away in the huge hotels or on the top floors of skyscrapers. Finally, I reach the Quantum and feel a hint of excitement.

The taxi rank at the entrance is a smooth, reflective surface that seems to hover just above the ground, creating an illusion of floating vehicles. It's embedded with interactive LED panels that respond to the movement of the cars, tracing dynamic patterns of light as they pass through, and I imagine this looks amazing at night. A holographic concierge system hovers near the entrance, providing real-time information and assistance to guests. It's exactly what I expected after researching the hotel casino online; the Quantum invites guests to experience the thrill of the future with a nod to the past. It's seventies' space age meets 2040s, if that's a thing.

Heading inside, I find a blend of sleek, modern design with a retro-futuristic twist. The gaming floor is a vibrant mix of neon lights and cutting-edge technology. Vintage arcade games are seamlessly integrated with the latest slot machines, creating an atmosphere that pays homage to the golden age of gaming while embracing the innovations of tomorrow. The interior is adorned with metallic accents and holographic displays, and VR corners with comfortable chairs and meditative music and visuals provide a temporary escape from the madness.

There'll be plenty of time to explore in the coming weeks, so I take the elevator up to the top floor, where the pool and spa area are situated. Thirty floors up is my new salon, and I can't wait to see it.

8

FRANKIE

"**G**ood girl, Dakota." I smile at the foal's first attempt to run. She's getting her long legs tangled and isn't quite coordinated yet, but she'll get there. Seeing her thrive as she explores her new world makes me a little emotional. She's outside for the first time, and all the intriguing smells and sights are distracting her from basic coordination. It's adorable how her mother encourages her to follow within the pasture next to the farm.

Our horses have a good life. They love to take my guests for rides, and they have plenty of space to roam when they're not on duty. Some haven't had an easy start in life; I've rescued a few from meat farms, and one of them was found abandoned along the road. A few horses were very nervous initially, but all in all, even the emotionally damaged ones have learned to trust again.

"She's getting there," Jose says with a chuckle. "She's definitely not the smartest one of the bunch—she doesn't show any signs of life skills or sense of danger awareness—but she's cute."

I laugh. "Don't insult her, she'll be the top horse in no

time." Although I'm defending Dakota, he's got a point because the foal seems to struggle with simple things like walking, running, and staying in her mom's presence. Frankly, I've never seen this kind of behavior in horses first-hand, and even checked if she might be semi-blind, but she's not. On the upside, Dakota's not scared of anything and she's incredibly friendly. "She'll be great with kids," I say.

"What kids?" Jose shrugs. "We don't allow kids on the rides."

"Not yet. But maybe it's something we should consider." I focus my attention back on Dakota and laugh when she decides to roll around in a pool of mud close to the water station. "Have you heard of any ponies that might need a home?"

"Because we're not busy enough as it is?" Jose jokes. He grabs his phone from his pocket and scrolls. "I saw there was one at the rescue center in Henderson. He's four years old."

I sigh and realize I shouldn't have asked. Jose is more clued in than I am when it comes to rescue horses. I try not to look at the websites because I'm a sucker and will adopt them all if I get too involved. "Just the one?"

"Yes. His name is Marty. But I wouldn't go getting a pony in a hurry. It won't be beneficial for the business..." He chuckles. "Although he might make a nice friend for Professor Dakota."

"Professor Dakota? I take it there's a hint of sarcasm in that nickname?"

"None whatsoever," Jose says with a grin. "Anyway, I've got to go. I need to drive my kid to the dentist. I'll send you the link to the pony."

I wave him goodbye, then grab a beer from the fridge

and head to the porch. We don't do p.m. tours on Sundays, so I have the rest of the day to myself. I prop my feet up on a stool and settle back to enjoy the view of Dakota's first day outside. With Lawrence clearing, cleaning, and grooming the horses, Jose and two other riders helping me with the tours and day-to-day activities, and two cleaners—Jose's wife and her friend—who also prepare breakfast for the guests, I'm not buried in work anymore, which has been a welcome change from last year when I only had two staff members on my team. Fully booked now, I can easily afford to take a few days off from time to time, and that's given me some much-needed breathing space.

A car pulls up my drive, and moments later, my friend Rennie appears.

"Hello, my friend. I come with gifts." She puts a six-pack on my porch table and plonks down in the chair beside me. Her hands are slightly stained with motor oil, a testament to her day job as a mechanic. "Leslie dropped me off. She's going to the garden center, but she'll be back in a few hours. You know I hate that place." She opens a beer and grins. "Mind if I keep you company?"

"Do I have a choice?" I joke when I hear her partner honking the horn before she drives off.

"Not really." Rennie lets out a long sigh. "Leslie's getting aloe vera plants for the front yard, but you know what she's like. She'll spend ages talking to the shop assistants while deciding which plants to get, and an hour later they'll be discussing their family relationships, period cycles, and everything in between. And then, they'll exchange numbers and she'll add another friend to her long list." She sighs. "The love of my life is super social and I don't like people."

"I'm people," I say.

"That's different. You're calm, like me. You don't get

overexcited about TV programs and politics and shopping. That's why I like coming here. You're my sanctuary."

"I'll take that as a compliment." I clink my beer with Rennie's. "Let's hope you get a few hours of peace, but don't forget that Leslie's a saint for putting up with you too."

"Hey, aren't you supposed to be on my side?"

I laugh, raising a hand. "Says who? I'm Switzerland, I don't pick sides."

"But you're *my* friend."

"Exactly. That's why I'm being honest with you. Leslie has her quirks, but so do you. You're completely OCD when it comes to cleaning—even something as simple as a dirty plate in the sink upsets you."

"Hmm..." Rennie takes a moment to think about that, then decides to change the subject. "The new foal is so cute," she says, turning her attention to Dakota. "Is she running in a funny way or is it just me?"

"Yeah, she's a little uncoordinated but no less adorable," I say. "So, what's happening with you?"

"Nothing much. But I saw Lawrence at the grocery store, and he told me you had a stranded woman over. Someone from California?"

"Yes. She got a flat tire in the desert. She was lucky I was doing my night tour and spotted her."

"A damsel in distress?" Rennie arches a brow. "Was she attractive?"

"Very." I smile. "But we had the birth, so I was up all night, and nothing happened...well, apart from a kiss goodbye the next morning after we changed her tire and filled up on oil."

"A kiss, huh?" Rennie nudges me. "You're so bad. Taking advantage of a lady in need."

"I wasn't. I swear, she was totally gay and so up for it. I

couldn't believe my luck when I realized she liked me back. We had serious chemistry."

Rennie stares at me in disbelief. "An attractive lesbian was stranded, and you had chemistry? Holy fuck! Where is she now?"

"In Vegas. I mean, I hope she got there with that old pickup. She was moving for a job." I shake my head when Rennie gawks at me. "That's it, there's nothing more to it. I don't even have her number, and I'll probably never see her again."

"But why didn't you ask for her number?"

"What's the point?" I raise a brow. "You think she's going to come here and hang out in the desert with me?"

"I like hanging out in the desert with you."

I chuckle at Rennie's comment. "Yeah, but you're antisocial."

Rennie shrugs, taking a swig of her beer. "What's not to like? Fresh air and silence. It's paradise."

I nod, a smile tugging at my lips. "True. But most people need their creature comforts and entertainment options."

"Well, that's their problem," Rennie says, leaning back in her chair. "Still a shame you didn't get her number."

I absently pick at the label on my beer bottle. "Yeah. I can't seem to stop thinking about her. She's stuck in my head."

Rennie studies me for a moment, her expression thoughtful. "Sounds like she made quite an impression."

"Yeah."

"Have you tried looking her up?" Rennie asks. "I mean, you said she was moving to Vegas for a job, right? Can you find her contact details?"

"Easily. She's the new general manager of the spa at the Quantum, but I don't want to be that person. If she wanted to stay in touch, she would have given me her number or asked for mine. Anyway, she knows where to find me."

"I suppose so," Rennie says. "It sucks, but sometimes these things just aren't meant to be."

We lapse into a comfortable silence, sipping our beers and enjoying the warm breeze. In the distance, I can hear the nickering of the horses, a sound that never fails to soothe my soul.

"Hey," Rennie says eventually. "I hope you meet someone. I want that for you."

"I'm fine, Rennie. I'm not looking."

"Sure. But you know what?" She nudges me with a mischievous smirk, and I know she's about to fire off one of her terrible jokes.

"What?"

"You never know who might come riding into your life next. Your happily ever after is out there, waiting for you to lasso it."

9

DAKOTA

"*A*re you going to miss working here?" I ask Andy, the outgoing general manager of The Vegas White Salon. It's been a lot to take in this week, but he's been very helpful with my transition. He's tall, immaculately groomed, and he looks permanently surprised from a little too much Botox. From what I've seen, the team loves him, so it will be hard to fill his shoes.

"Yes," he admits. "But new adventures call, and I've been working hard since we opened four years ago. It's time to enjoy my new life as a kept man."

"What does your husband do?"

"He's an investor, but he's retiring next week and we're going to travel the world for a while, starting with Paris." Andy claps his hands in glee. "I've never been there. Have you?"

"Once. It's beautiful." I smile. "You're going to have such a great time."

"And so will you, dear." He pats my shoulder. "I was nervous to let go, but now that I've spent the week with you, I'm confident you'll do an amazing job."

"Thank you. I'll do my best, and I appreciate all your help getting me up to speed."

"No problem." Andy opens the door to his office. Unlike the rest of the hotel, the top floor where the spa is situated is flooded with natural light, and there's even a skylight in here. Everything is white, and apart from a few beautiful big plants, there's only a desk, two chairs, a desktop computer, and an iPad. All White Spas are paperless, and I love working without clutter around me. "Well, this is yours now," he says. "I might leave early if you don't mind. I've already said my goodbyes and there's no point hanging around, right?"

"No, you go, and don't worry. I won't bug you." I walk him to the exit and wave him out, then take a deep breath and turn to face my new salon. It's a blank canvas, ready for me to make my mark.

Dressed in white lab coats with their hair slicked back, my team members look like doctors. Our LA branch didn't have a dress code, but here we have to embrace the theme of the hotel, and I must admit, it's effective. As it's a franchise, the Vegas White Salon is run similarly to the LA branch, but this one is much bigger and offers additional treatments and hydrotherapy. We have seven treatment rooms, three hair-dressing stations, three saunas, three small pools for private bookings, and adjacent to the salon, there's a spectacular pool on the rooftop, complimentary to hotel guests.

I walk out to soak up some sun and I'm greeted by the panoramic views of the cityscape beyond the main pool. It's always busy but never crowded, as all pool visits have to be booked in advance. In line with the Quantum's theme, the poolside is sleek and white, providing a stark contrast to the vivid colors of the city below. An LED-lit bar serves freshly squeezed juices and eclectic cocktails, and cabanas with sheer, automated curtains offer privacy while still maintaining a view. Each cabana is equipped with smart controls that allow guests to adjust lighting to create their desired ambience. At night, the poolside area is transformed into a dynamic entertainment space with holographic projections showcasing futuristic performances.

What draws most guests here, though, is the immersive T-shaped pool that spans the entire south side of the building and cuts through the middle of the pool area. The underwater projectors and spotlights create the surreal experience of swimming in a dreamscape with otherworldly creatures that follow the swimmers.

"It's cool, isn't it?" Serenity, one of the beauty therapists, joins me with an iced coffee in hand.

"Spectacular."

"You can order coffee at the bar, free of charge, and we can book the poolside on our days off. Did Andy tell you that?"

"Yes, he did. It's a nice perk." I see she's taken off her lab coat and she's wearing a short, white onesie. "Are you done for today?"

"Yeah. I'm heading home in a bit," she says. "Just wanted to check in with you. How are you finding it so far?"

"Personally, I'm a little overwhelmed," I say with a chuckle. "But that's normal, right? New city, new job. I haven't had much time to settle in yet, so I'll use the weekend to sort out my apartment, but I love the team and I'm excited to work with all of you."

"We're excited too." I'm not sure if Serenity means it; in my experience, people don't like change, but she seems very sweet. "We have regular cocktail meetups with the team," she continues. "It's in a bar downtown and you're always welcome to join us. Andy did sometimes. I just wanted to let you know so you won't feel left out."

"That's very kind. I might take you up on that."

"Great. Andy told me you moved here by yourself. Vegas isn't the easiest city to meet new people, so if you ever want to go for a coffee or need help with anything, you have my number." Serenity heads to the bar before I have the chance to reply, and I frown as I stare after her. I must admit, I didn't expect my team to be so welcoming and it's a pleasant surprise.

I take another moment to savor the view from the rooftop, the sparkling city stretching out before me like a glittering jewel. The warm breeze carries a faint scent of chlorine and sunscreen, mingling with the distant sounds of laughter and clinking glasses from the bar. It's a world away from Frankie's peaceful ranch, but there's a certain allure to the energy and vibrancy of Vegas. Maybe, just maybe, this will be my forever home.

Lost in thought, I almost don't notice when Serenity reappears at my side with a second iced coffee. "Here," she says, pressing the cool drink into my palm. "I thought you might need a little pick-me-up after your first week. No sugar, right?"

I blink in surprise, a grateful smile spreading across my face. "Thank you, that's so thoughtful."

She shrugs. "Hey, we girls have to stick together. Plus, I figured you could use a friend. Starting over can be tough."

I nod, taking a sip. "You can say that again. I don't think I've ever felt so out of my depth. I've already noticed the clients here are a lot more demanding than in my old branch."

Serenity laughs, a bright, infectious sound. "Oh, honey, we've all been there. My first week on the job? I think I cried myself to sleep every night, wondering what the hell I'd gotten myself into."

"Really? You seem so calm."

She snorts, shaking her head. "Please, I'm just a better actress than most. Trust me, behind this flawless facade, I'm a hot mess like everyone else."

"Well, here's to being hot messes together, then." I grin, clinking my cup against hers.

"So, tell me," Serenity says. "Any lucky man in your life somewhere? Or are you single and ready to mingle in Sin City?"

"Um, no. No lucky man. I'm actually gay and very much single."

"Yay! One of us!" Serenity claps her hands in delight, practically bouncing on her toes. "My girlfriend has a ton of single friends. Stick with me and we'll have you paired off with the hottest bachelorette in town faster than you can say 'I do.'"

10

FRANKIE

*I*t's been a week since Jose sent me the link to Marty the pony, and as I can't get the poor thing out of my head, I've decided to take him on. If he stays anxious and no one adopts him, the shelter might have to put him down, and he deserves to be loved after a difficult start in life. Besides, I already have twelve horses and a foal, so what's an extra pony? It will not only make Marty's life better, but guests will undoubtedly enjoy his company too, once I get him used to people.

It's normally a forty-minute drive to Henderson, but with the horse trailer behind my Range Rover, it takes me much longer. It's not easy to navigate with a long vehicle, and as I drive slowly and carefully, a queue forms behind me.

Once again, I think of Dakota and wonder how she's doing. I could drive through Vegas and make a stop at the Quantum. She might be there, and she might want to see me. But then again, she might have forgotten all about me already, or maybe she's busy and not in a position to talk. Nearing one of the junctions that lead to the city, I decide it's a bad idea. I don't want to come across as pushy, and with the horse trailer behind me, it will be close to impossible to find a parking space. If Dakota wanted to stay in contact, she could have looked up my number on the ranch's website, but she hasn't, and that tells me enough.

To take my mind off her, I turn on the radio and hum along with a country tune I vaguely recognize. I pass several farms and working ranches. Very few provide a similar experience to Red Rock Ranch, which is why we're always fully booked. I know most of the owners; my parents knew their parents, and I went to school with some of their kids. Apart from small talk at the grocery store, we don't really socialize anymore, and that's the way I like it. Far from open-minded, they were never my kind of people, but being fellow ranch owners, we occasionally help each other out.

The equestrian rescue center is just off Highway II, and Rosie, the manager, greets me as I pull up in front of the main building.

"Good morning, Frankie. It's been a while."

"Not that long," I say, arching a brow. "Last time was when I picked up a mare that turned out to be pregnant."

"Oh, yes. You told me about that, and it was as much a surprise to us as it was to you. How is she doing?"

"She's good. She gave birth a week early, and her little girl is very cute." I'm still not convinced Rosie didn't know Sahara was pregnant, but I let it slide. "Anyway, I'm here to see Marty."

"Yes, you said so on the phone, and I was so, so happy you were interested in him. He's an anxious little boy, but I know you'll be able to domesticate him and make him feel welcome in your beautiful family." Rosie smiles widely. "Follow me." She glances at me over her shoulder. "By the way, Marty has a special friend. It would be amazing if you could take them both as they're kind of inseparable."

"No, Rosie." I stop and stare at her. "I know exactly what you're doing, and emotional blackmail won't get you anywhere. You know I'd take them all if I could, but I can't. I have a business to run, and the only way I can afford to save your horses is if they can be trained to do tours or entertain my guests."

Rosie nods. "I know, but just take a look. That's all I'm asking."

"I'm not looking," I insist. "I'm here for Marty, and that's it. I know the others are in good hands with you, and I don't want to see them."

"Because you're a softy," Rosie says with a mischievous twinkle in her eyes. "Well, you're going to have to face him anyway, because Marty and Dobby are in a stable together."

I take a deep breath and blow out my cheeks. "You did that on purpose."

"I swear, I didn't. We tried to separate them, but it upsets them to be apart." Rosie opens the barn doors, and I keep my eyes fixed straight ahead as she leads me to Marty. If I met all her horses, I'd be bankrupt in no time. They're expensive to keep, which is why, sadly, so many are abandoned.

"Here he is," Rosie says, leaning over the partition to ruffle a hand through Marty's mane. "He trusts me, but he's not great with strangers. I know you can change that, though." She points to the back of the stable, where a donkey is sniffing Marty's behind. "And that's his bestie, Dobby."

"You've got to be kidding me." I glance at the cute little pony, then at the donkey that is slightly bigger. "They're both adorable, but what am I going to do with a donkey?"

"I don't know... You've never had ponies before either, so why not give it a go? Besides, kids can ride donkeys. They'll hardly notice the difference." Rosie opens the door to let me in. "They seem okay with you. Want to go in and say hello?"

"Don't tell me you didn't plan this," I mutter, but I go in anyway. Marty retreats to the back of the stall. He's cautious but not terrified. "Will you come in with me?" I ask Rosie. If Marty sees that Rosie trusts me, perhaps he will warm to me too.

"Sure," she says, following me. We both stay still so Marty can get used to our presence, but it's Dobby who comes first.

I crouch down, holding out my hand for him to sniff. He approaches cautiously, his long ears twitching with curiosity. After a moment, he nuzzles my palm, his velvety muzzle tickling my skin.

"Well, hello there, handsome," I murmur, gently scratching Dobby behind his ears. "Aren't you a friendly one?"

Dobby brays softly, as if in agreement, and I can't help but chuckle. There's something endearing about his awkward, gangly charm.

Marty, on the other hand, is still hanging back, eyeing me warily from the corner of the stall. I can see the tension in his small body, the way his muscles quiver beneath his shaggy coat.

"It's okay, little guy," I say softly, keeping my voice low and soothing. "I'm not going to hurt you. I just want to be your friend."

Rosie makes a small clicking sound with her tongue, and Marty's ears perk up. Slowly, hesitantly, he takes a step forward, then another.

"That's it," I encourage, holding my breath as he inches closer. "You're doing great, Marty. Just a little bit farther."

Finally, after what feels like an eternity, Marty is close enough to sniff my outstretched hand. His nostrils flare as he takes in my scent, and I hold perfectly still, letting him make the first move. And then, wonder of wonders, he butts his head against my palm, seeking attention. I laugh in delight, gently stroking his forelock.

"There you go, buddy. See? I'm not so scary after all."

Rosie beams, her eyes crinkling at the corners. "I knew he'd like you."

I nod, my heart swelling with affection for these two misfits. They may be a little rough around the edges, a little wary of the world, but there's a sweetness to them that's impossible to resist.

"You have to admit, they make quite the pair," Rosie continues.

I study Marty and Dobby, who are now nuzzling each other affectionately. Dobby is nibbling on Marty's ear, and Marty is leaning into the touch, his eyes half-closed in contentment.

"Yes, they're adorable," I say, shaking my head in amusement. "Though I have no idea what I'm going to do with a donkey. My guests come for horseback rides, not to experience the thrill of the open range at a leisurely two miles per hour."

We both burst out laughing, startling Marty and Dobby out of their cuddle session. They blink at us, looking mildly offended by the interruption.

"Sorry, boys," I say, struggling to keep a straight face. "We didn't mean to disturb your moment. I promise to be more respectful of your bromance in the future."

Rosie pats Marty on the rump when they both start prodding and sniffing me again. "I think that's your cue to load 'em up, Frankie. So you'll take them both?"

"Yeah, I'll take them." I sigh, already picturing the chaos and extra work that Dobby will bring to the ranch. But somehow, I can't bring myself to mind.

11

DAKOTA

*A*lthough I'm grateful to Serenity for extending an impromptu Saturday night invite, I'm also a little nervous as I enter the bar in one of the bigger casinos in town.

The space is dimly lit, with neon signs casting a pinkish glow over the sleek, modern decor. The walls are adorned with abstract art, and the furniture looks like it belongs in a high-end nightclub rather than a casual after-work hangout. I feel a little out of place in my simple sundress and sandals as I scan the room for my colleagues.

I spot them in a corner booth, huddled together and laughing. Serenity sees me and waves me over with a perfectly manicured hand. "Dakota, over here!" she calls out, her voice carrying over the thumping beat of the music. I make my way over to the booth, weaving through the crowd of well-dressed patrons. As I get closer, I can see that my colleagues have already started on their drinks—beautiful cocktails served in fancy glasses with outrageous garnishes.

"Hey, everyone," I say, sliding into the booth beside

Serenity. "Sorry I'm a little late. Traffic was a nightmare. It's a birthday celebration, right?"

"No worries, darling," drawls a tall, slender man with impeccably styled hair. "We've only just gotten started. I'm Luca, by the way, the birthday boy. I took some time off, so I haven't been at work, and I've been dying to meet you."

He holds out his hand, and I shake it, feeling slightly intimidated by his air of sophistication. "Nice to meet you, Luca. I'm Dakota."

"Oh, we know who you are," says a woman with red hair and a mischievous glint in her eye. "Serenity's told us all about the new boss from California. Only good things, though. I'm Scarlett, by the way. A friend of Serenity and Luca's."

"It's nice to meet you," I reply, admiring Scarlett's chic ensemble—a fitted black jumpsuit with an asymmetrical neckline. "I love your outfit. You look amazing."

Scarlett preens and smooths a hand over the fabric. "Thank you. It's actually a Zaifa Afali. I know Zaifa personally, which has its perks."

"Zaifa is the best," Luca chimes in. "She's so beautiful, and I love her so, so much. Why didn't you invite her?"

"She's got a celeb fitting tonight," Scarlett says. "Bella d'Angelo."

Luca stares at Scarlett, wide-eyed. "Bella? Well, ask her to bring Bella along later. I want to meet her."

I've seen many movies with Bella d'Angelo. It seems unlikely that a superstar like her would have drinks with us, but I keep that to myself and turn to the petite woman with a pixie cut I haven't had the chance to greet yet. "Hey, Zoe. Good to see you." I've worked with her on a few shifts, and she seems friendly.

"Hey there. Glad you could join us," she says. "What are you drinking?"

"Hmm... I haven't decided yet." As the server approaches our table, I quickly scan the menu and decide on a vodka, lime, and soda. It's my go-to drink—refreshing and always a safe choice—but when I place my order, Scarlett reaches out and touches my arm.

"Oh, honey, no. You can't order a boring vodka and soda on your first night out in Vegas!" she exclaims, then turns to the waiter. "Give us another minute, please."

I feel my cheeks flush, suddenly self-conscious. "Oh, I don't know. I guess I'm just used to keeping it simple."

Luca leans in, shaking his head. "Darling, simple is not the Vegas way. You need a drink that's as fabulous and eye-catching as you are!"

Zoe nods enthusiastically, already pointing out colorful concoctions on the menu. "Here. Look at this one! The Mermaid's Kiss—it's bright blue with edible glitter and a candy cane mermaid tail garnish. So cute for pics."

"And this Unicorn Dreamtini," Scarlett chimes in. "It's pink and shimmery, topped with rainbow cotton candy. Imagine how amazing that would look on your Insta feed."

I blink, a bit taken aback when I realize they're being serious. "I'm not really big on social media. I usually just go for what tastes good."

They all exchange puzzled glances, as if I've said something utterly bizarre.

"Babe, it's not just about the taste," Luca explains patiently. "You can't *see* taste. It's about the aesthetic, the vibe, the whole experience."

"Exactly," Zoe agrees. "A stunning cocktail is like the perfect accessory. Think of it as a designer handbag. It pulls your whole look together and makes for a killer photo op."

I still don't get it but decide to give in. "Okay, okay," I say, holding up a hand with a chuckle. "You guys choose."

They all jump in at once, pointing out their favorites and debating the merits of each one. Finally, they settle on a neon pink creation called the Flaming Flamingo—complete with a sugared rim and an actual flaming flamingo garnish.

It almost singes my eyebrows when the waiter lights it, and I sit back until the flame has died down, then take a sip. It's utterly sweet and not my thing, but apparently, flavor is of no importance.

"So, tell us about yourself," Luca says, leaning forward. "What brought you to Vegas? Besides the job, of course."

"Oh, you know, just looking for a change of pace. Newport Beach was getting a little stale, and I thought Vegas would be an exciting new adventure."

Scarlett nods, sipping her drink. "I can totally relate. I moved here from New York a few years ago, and it was the best decision I ever made. The energy in this city is like nowhere else."

"Totally," Zoe agrees. "And the people are on another level. Celebs, high rollers, influencers... Speaking of..." She whips out her phone and extends her arm, angling for the perfect selfie. "Okay, guys, squeeze in! Let's capture this moment."

We all lean in, smiling brightly as Zoe snaps a series of photos. I can't help but feel a bit awkward—I've never been one for excessive selfie-taking, preferring to live in the moment rather than documenting every second for social media.

But Zoe seems thrilled with the results, immediately posting the best shot to her Instagram. "Tagging you, Luca!" she sings as her fingers fly over the screen. "This lighting is amazing for your bone structure."

Luca grins and pulls out his own phone, eagerly checking the post. "Ugh, I love it. Thanks for the tag, babe!"

They're both engrossed in their screens, monitoring the likes and comments rolling in. I glance around the bar and realize they're not the only ones—everywhere I look, people are snapping photos of their artfully arranged cocktails, posing for selfies, or capturing their outfits in the flattering neon light.

It's a far cry from the cozy beach bars I frequented back home, where the focus was on good conversation and connecting with the people around you. Here, it seems like everyone is more concerned with curating their online image, presenting an alternative version of their lives for public consumption.

"Did you guys hear about the woman who came into the salon yesterday?" Zoe asks, never taking her eyes off the screen. "She dropped ten grand on a treatment package."

"Yes, that seemed outrageous," I agree. "Does that happen a lot?"

"From time to time," Serenity says. "Who was it?"

"A local." Zoe says. "Her husband is in real estate. He owns a few casinos around here too. She has a ton of celebrity friends, so who knows? She might recommend us."

I listen to the conversation, feeling a little out of my depth. These people seem to thrive on name-dropping, and I find it hard to relate.

"What about you, Dakota?" Luca asks. "What celebrities have you met?"

"Ehm...not many, really," I admit. "And honestly, I rarely recognize celebrities. If they've been in my salon, I probably didn't even know it."

Scarlett gasps. "What? That's crazy! Well, you'll have to

learn how to play the game here. It's all about who you know."

I shrug. "I just want to do my job, make a few friends, and rebuild my life. I'm not interested in climbing the social ladder."

At that, they burst into laughter. "We'll talk in six months," Luca says. "See how you feel about it then." He spreads his arms and gestures to the table. "How else do you think I got this booth? I know the bar owner. We hook up from time to time."

"Good for you." I grin. "I bet you're not short of male attention."

"They love me." Luca flexes his biceps. "All this goodness is here to be enjoyed. What about you? I heard you're into the ladies." He winces when Serenity nudges him, then turns back to me. "Sorry, she told me. Hope you don't mind."

"That's fine, it's no secret." I smile. "But I'm single, and I'm not ready to date yet. It's only been a year since my previous relationship ended."

"A year? Girl, that's like an eternity. Everyone knows what the best way is of getting over someone."

"Oh yeah? Let me guess...getting under someone?" I shake my head. "To each their own, but that's not my thing."

"What happened?" Serenity asks. "Did she hurt you?"

"We weren't right for each other," I say. "But I won't lie, it hurt how quickly she moved on. It tells me maybe there was someone else all along."

"Probably. You should trust your intuition."

"Honestly, I don't care anymore whether she did or didn't cheat on me. It's in the past, and I want to look forward now." I square my shoulders and put on a brave face. Although the thought still stings, I'm adamant about moving on. The torture of seeing my ex with someone else did me no favors.

As the evening wears on, Luca and Scarlett argue over which influencer has the best skincare routine, while Zoe regales us with tales of her weekend partying with a group of high rollers. Serenity keeps trying to draw me into the conversation, but I find myself zoning out. I want to know about their lives, but no one seems interested in personal conversations.

Finally, after what feels like an eternity, I make my excuses and slip out of the booth. "This was fun, everyone, but I should probably head home. Early start tomorrow and all that."

Serenity pouts. "Aw, really? But we're heading to a club."

I force a smile. "Maybe next time. I'm still getting settled in, and I don't want to be too tired for work tomorrow."

As I hail a taxi, I think of my last night back home, when my friends threw me a going-away party. We sat on the beach, drinking wine and talking about everything and nothing, laughing until our sides ached. There was no pretense, no posturing—just genuine connection and affection. I'll find it, I tell myself. I'll find here what I had there. It just takes time.

12

FRANKIE

A sleek, silver Audi A3 makes its way up the drive, kicking up a cloud of dust in its wake. It looks out of place among the rustic surroundings of the ranch, way too clean to belong to anyone around here. As the car comes to a stop, the driver's side door opens and a familiar figure steps out. It's Dakota.

I put down the saddle I'm holding and wipe my hands on my jeans, suddenly conscious of the horsehair clinging to my clothes. I take off my hat and run a hand through my short hair, trying to tame any stray locks before putting it back on. *Why am I so nervous?*

She looks different from the last time I saw her—more put together, more polished. Her long, blond hair is styled in loose waves that cascade down her back, and she's wearing a white sundress, cinched at the waist with a thin, braided belt. The skirt flutters around her knees in the desert breeze. On her feet are a pair of strappy sandals, and as she walks toward me, I notice little details: the delicate gold necklace that glints in the sun, her pale-pink nails, the subtle hint of makeup that enhances her natural beauty. It's clear that she has put effort into her appearance today, and I can't help but feel a little flattered.

In her hands, she holds a bundle of clothes—my clothes, the ones I'd lent her. She smiles as she approaches, and my heart skips a beat.

"Look what the cat dragged in. Nice wheels," I say, sauntering over to her with a grin on my face.

Dakota laughs. "Thanks. I sold Henry. I won't lie. I'm a little sad about it, but he's not practical in Vegas, and not the kind of vehicle I can pull into the Quantum with either."

I shoot her an amused grin. "It would certainly feel out of place there. This is quite the step up."

Dakota shrugs, a hint of sadness flickering across her face. "I did love that pickup. But it was time for a change. New city, new job, new car…it just seemed fitting."

"You look great," I say. "I didn't expect to see you back here so soon. Couldn't get enough of the ranch life, huh?"

"Well, I couldn't keep your clothes forever, could I?" she says, holding out the bundle to me. "I figured I should return them in person, seeing as you're my knight in shining armor and all."

I chuckle as I take the clothes from her, our fingers brushing in the process. It causes a flutter in my belly. "I prefer 'cowgirl in jeans,' but I'll take it," I quip, trying to play it cool. "Join me for a drink?"

"Only if you have time."

"For you, always," I say as I lead her toward the porch. "So, how's life in Vegas treating you?"

"Oh, you know, it's an adjustment," she says. "But I'm getting there. The job keeps me busy, and it's only been three weeks since I moved. All I can say is, it's a huge change from home."

As she speaks, I notice her gaze drift from my eyes to my

lips, then back again. The air between us feels charged, and I clear my throat, trying to focus on her words rather than the way her sundress hugs her curves.

"I can imagine," I say, my voice a little huskier than I intended. "But you look like you're settling in nicely. I almost didn't recognize you."

Dakota laughs and reaches out, her fingers lightly brushing my arm. "Well, I figured I should clean up a bit before coming to see you. After the state you found me in last time..."

Her touch lingers, and my pulse quickens. "You look beautiful now and you looked beautiful then," I say, holding her gaze.

We stand there on the porch for a moment, neither of us moving, the tension palpable. Dakota bites her lower lip, and I find myself following the movement, fighting the urge to close the distance between us.

"I'm sorry," I say, snapping out of it. "Where are my manners? What are we drinking?"

"I'd love a coffee."

"Great idea. I could do with one myself," I say, and as I slip inside, Dakota follows me.

She leans against the counter while she watches me make coffee. The low sun is streaming in through the kitchen window, making her hair shine like spun gold. I almost forgot how gorgeous she was, and her presence is making me a little self-conscious.

"You know, I've been thinking about that night," I say, glancing over at her. "And the morning you left."

Dakota nods and meets my gaze, her blue eyes curiously taking me in. "What's happened in your life since?" she asks. "Are you dating anyone?"

"No, I'm not dating. What about you? Have you met

someone special in Vegas?" I hand her a coffee, and she smiles over the rim of her cup.

"No. Dating's been the last thing on my mind."

There's another loaded silence between us. My fingers itch to touch her face, to tangle in her hair, and the urge to kiss her is overwhelming. I notice a flicker of something in her eyes—expectation? Desire? Or is it just my own wishful thinking reflected back at me? I didn't think twice about kissing her last time we said goodbye, but now I'm hesitant, unsure if I'm reading the situation correctly.

"Come on," I finally say. "Bring your coffee. Let's go visit Dakota. I'm sure she'll be thrilled to see you again."

As we walk toward the stables, I can't shake the feeling that something has shifted between us. It was simple when we met. We flirted, we kissed. But now I'm not sure how to act around her. Should I make a move? Should I ask for her number?

When we reach the paddock, I let out a whistle and call out, "Dakota! Come here, girl!"

The little foal's ears perk up at the sound of her name, and she comes galloping over, her gangly legs eating up the distance. Dakota laughs in delight as the foal nuzzles her hand, seeking attention.

"Oh, look at you!" she says, running her fingers through the foal's silky mane. "You've gotten so big!"

I lean against the fence and watch them. "She's actually a lot smaller than she's supposed to be and her coordination is off. I suspect she's a little mentally challenged too, but she's adorable and sweet."

"Aww..." Dakota kisses the foal. "You're perfect," she whispers. "And don't let anyone tell you otherwise."

"Hey, I've got a couple more critters I think you'll like to meet," I say, opening the gate to let her through. "They usually hang out behind the barn together."

Dakota raises an eyebrow, intrigued. "More new horses?"

I shake my head, an amused smile tugging at my lips. "Not exactly. These two are a little...unconventional."

We cut through the paddock with sweet Dakota on our heels and walk around the barn. As soon as Marty and Dobby catch sight of us, they come trotting over, their ears pricked forward in curiosity.

"Dakota, meet Marty and Dobby," I say, gesturing to the odd couple. "Marty's the handsome pony, and Dobby's the long-eared charmer."

Dakota's eyes widen in surprise and delight as she takes in the sight of the mismatched pair. "Oh my goodness, they're so cute." She extends a hand for them to sniff and chuckles when Dobby nuzzles her neck as she bends down. "Where on earth did you find them?"

"Funny story, actually. I went to the rescue center to adopt Marty for kids to ride on, but apparently, he and Dobby are a package deal, so here we are."

As if to illustrate my point, Dobby starts nibbling on Marty's ear, eliciting a contented snort from the pony.

Dakota laughs, shaking her head in amazement. "And they just...hang out?"

"Yeah. For now. I'm training them so hopefully they'll be okay with kids. I haven't tested my theory yet. I let them roam freely outside the paddock sometimes, as they haven't shown any interest in exploring the area. They're obsessed with food, so they come up to the porch for a snack from time to time."

"That's so funny." Dakota meets my eyes. "You have a nice life going on here." Her phone buzzes and she sighs as she glances at the screen. "Damn," she mutters, her brow furrowing. "It's work. I've got a VIP client coming in for a last-minute appointment. I've been told it's a difficult woman, so I should probably be there in case she starts making impossible demands."

"Duty calls, huh?"

Dakota nods, looking genuinely regretful. "I wish I could stay longer."

"Hey, no worries. I get it. The life of a high-powered salon manager waits for no one."

"It's really not as glamorous as you think," she says with a chuckle, then hesitates. "But maybe we could meet up again?"

"I'd like that." Stopping myself from making a move, I cradle my mug with both hands as we walk back to her car.

Dakota pulls a business card out of her pocket and hands it to me. "Here's my number. Message me so I have yours."

"I will." We linger by her car, and I think she's going to kiss me, but her phone pings again, and she rolls her eyes in frustration.

"I'm sorry. I have to hurry, apparently."

And then, before I can respond, she's sliding into the driver's seat. "Call me," she says, her voice carrying over the purr of the engine.

13

DAKOTA

I've barely set foot in the White Spa when a man glances at my badge and grabs my arm in passing. "So you're the manager," he barks, not bothering with a greeting.

"That's right." I shake myself out of his grip. "Is there a problem?" I ask, stepping back to create some space between us. I don't like his attitude; it disgusts me.

"We need a couples massage and a treatment for her." He gestures to the scantily clad woman beside him. Their monogrammed designer clothing and air of entitlement announce their status as hotel VIPs. The man, tall and broad-shouldered with slicked-back dark hair and a watch that probably costs more than my entire wardrobe, puts his arm around the tall, blond woman whose ample bust is so enhanced it's given her stretch marks. "What's your most expensive treatment? I saw you have diamond facials."

"We certainly do."

"Good. She wants one," he says, seemingly deciding for her. I know his type; he's the kind of guy who will tell her what to wear, what to eat, and when to speak.

"Our reception team can help you with that," I say, forcing a smile. "Although I believe we're fully booked for today. How about you make an appointment for tomorrow?"

"That's not an option. We're leaving tomorrow, and she wants it now." He points to my badge. "You're the general manager, so make it happen."

"That's not my job, I'm afraid. But if you speak to our reception—"

"I don't queue," he barks, cutting me off.

Glancing behind me at the two people discussing treatments at the reception desk, my patience is faltering. Rude behavior makes me furious, but I've never raised my voice at a customer and I won't start now. "How about you leave me your number?" I suggest. "I'll ask someone to get back to you with available time slots."

To my surprise, the man laughs as if that's the most ridiculous thing he's ever heard. "Do you know who I am?"

"I—"

"I don't think you understand," he interrupts me again, his voice taking on a harder edge. "I'm not asking. I'm telling you. She wants a diamond facial. Now."

"I can ask Zoe to come back from her break," Serenity, who has overheard the conversation, chips in. "I think she had a cancellation."

"See?" The man glares at me. "She can make it happen. It seems like they appointed the wrong manager."

Taking a deep breath, I count to three. Although I'm grateful for Serenity's quick solution, I don't want to set the wrong precedent. It wouldn't be fair to Zoe to take her off her break. "If you wait in the lobby, one of our team members will bring you a glass of champagne to enjoy while I check if our beautician is available."

The man growls something about "not waiting for

anyone," but he still heads to the couch with his woman in tow. Our junior receptionist immediately springs into action and brings them their drinks along with a small plate of finger food. Everyone is always in such a hurry here. The entitled folks who come to Vegas for fleeting visits think they can storm in anytime, anywhere, and make impossible demands just because they're carrying around a stack of dollar bills.

"Zoe says she's good to go in five minutes. I'll book them in now before the slot's gone," Serenity whispers, then heads to the reception desk. I'm still shaking and barely recovered from the incident when Luca approaches me.

"Dakota, I'm sorry to bother you, but we have a situation in room two with a VIP client," he says, his usually calm demeanor slightly ruffled.

I frown as I follow him. "What's going on?"

Luca sighs. "It's Mrs. Rosenberg. She's a regular here, the one I messaged you about. She can be a bit...demanding. She's booked in for a full makeover package, but she wants it done in half the usual time."

"Half the time? That's not possible."

"I know," he agrees. "She's insisting. She says she has an event to get to and can't be late, but we don't have anyone to do her hair until seven."

I pinch the bridge of my nose, feeling a headache coming on. "Okay, let me talk to her. I'm sure we can come to a reasonable compromise."

Following Luca to treatment room two, I find a woman in her late fifties who is impatiently tapping her fingers on the edge of the reclining treatment chair. She's dressed head to toe in shocking pink, her hair perfectly coiffed and her makeup flawless. She looks like she's already had a full makeover and I wonder why she even bothered with an appointment.

"Mrs. Rosenberg?" I ask, approaching her with a professional smile. "I'm Dakota, the new general manager. I hear you're in a bit of a rush today."

The woman looks me up and down, her gaze sharp and appraising. "I don't have time for chitchat," she snaps. "I need a diamond facial, a mani-pedi, highlights, and a blowout, and I need it done in an hour. Can you handle that, or do I need to take my business elsewhere?"

I blink, taken aback by her abrupt tone. When I first started, I assumed the dramas here were incidental, but it seems to be the norm. "Mrs. Rosenberg, I apologize, but an hour simply isn't enough time to provide all of those services at the level of quality we pride ourselves on. Perhaps we could prioritize the services that are most important to you and schedule the others for another time?"

Mrs. Rosenberg scoffs. "Unacceptable. I'm in the penthouse suite and I expect VIP treatment. I don't care how you do it, just make it happen."

My patience wearing thin once again, I force myself to keep my tone even. "Mrs. Rosenberg, I understand your frustration, but it's simply not possible."

The woman's eyes narrow, and she points at me as she straightens herself in her chair. "Listen, missy," she hisses, her voice low and threatening. "I don't think you understand how things work around here. When I say 'jump,' you say, 'how high?' I've been coming to this salon for years, and I've never had a problem getting what I want. Don't make me take this up with your superiors."

My heart's pounding, but I refuse to back down. "Mrs. Rosenberg, I am the highest authority in this salon. And while I deeply appreciate your business, I simply cannot make this happen for you today. I apologize, but my decision is final."

Mrs. Rosenberg gets up from the chair, and for a moment, I think she might actually strike me. Her face is flushed with anger, and her hands are clenched into fists.

"Fine," she spits. "I'll take my business elsewhere. And I'll be sure to let everyone know about the terrible service I received here." With that, she turns on her heel and stalks out of the treatment room.

As soon as she's gone, I let out a shaky breath, my knees feeling weak. Luca is at my side in an instant, his hand on my shoulder.

"It's the first time someone's said no to her," he mumbles, looking utterly shocked.

"What? But there's no way we could have done that. And why is everyone so rude today?"

He shrugs. "Welcome to Vegas, honey. Some people are not used to being told 'no.'"

I shake my head in disbelief. "But surely, we can't just give in to their every demand? What would Andy have done?" I'm aware the question doesn't make me sound like a confident leader, but I'm genuinely curious how he dealt with people like Mrs. Rosenberg.

"Andy would have probably tended to her personally to get the job done. He used to work over sixty hours a week to keep everyone happy."

"Andy did treatments?"

"Most days," Luca says. "But honestly, I also think it's the reason he left. It was getting too much for him. We're limited in our space and treatment rooms, so he couldn't justify hiring extra staff and it was the only way to get people like Mrs. Rosenburg off his back."

I take a deep breath and blow out my cheeks. "Well, I

won't be doing that. I was hired to run this place, not to fill in the gaps night and day. If I did, I wouldn't be able to focus on the bigger picture."

"I know." Luca squeezes my shoulder. "It's a delicate balance. We have to keep the VIPs happy, but we also have to maintain our standards. It's not always easy." He taps the pocket of his white lab coat. "But when I'm having a bad day, I remember the generous tips I'm given, and I'll jump if they want me to jump. It's as simple as that."

14

FRANKIE

*T*he sun hangs high in the sky, beating down on the ranch with a relentless heat that shimmers off the ground. It's the kind of day that makes you want to find a shady spot and cool off with a tall glass of lemonade, but there's no rest for the wicked, as they say. It's only late June, but I can already feel this summer is going to be a tough one.

I'm leaning against the fence of the paddock, watching our latest batch of guests enjoy some downtime with the animals. It's a private family booking: a couple with two kids who are six and ten. They wanted privacy, so they've paid a hefty sum to have the ranch to themselves, and I'll take them riding anytime they want.

The parents are sitting on a nearby bench, chatting and sipping iced tea, while the kids are absolutely entranced by Marty and Dobby. The little girl, who introduced herself as Sadie with a gap-toothed grin, is giggling with delight as Marty nuzzles her hand, prodding her for the treats I gave her to feed them. Her older brother, a serious-looking boy named Ethan, is more reserved, but I can see the wonder in his eyes as he strokes Dobby's velvety nose.

It's a heartwarming sight. There's just something about the pure, unbridled joy that animals can bring out in kids. They've begged me to let Marty and Dobby sleep in the guesthouse, and although I'm letting them roam freely during their visit, I can't allow them to go inside. Not only would they be uncomfortable, but they'd eat the furniture, shit everywhere, and I'm not insured to keep animals with my guests overnight.

"Would you look at that," Jose says, coming to stand beside me, his ever-present cowboy hat tipped low over his brow. "Those two are regular Dr. Dolittles."

I chuckle, nodding in agreement. "Yeah. Marty and Dobby seem to be eating up the attention, too. They both like kids. That's very promising."

Dobby lets out a loud bray, causing Ethan to jump back in surprise before dissolving into laughter. Sadie joins in, her high-pitched giggles mixing with the donkey's honks in a joyful cacophony.

It's hard to believe that just a few short weeks ago, these two were the most timid creatures on the ranch. But slowly, surely, they came out of their shells. It started with short walks around the paddock and the farmhouse. Each day, they grew a little braver, a little more curious about the world around them.

As I watch them interact with the kids, I can see the transformation that's taken place. Marty trots around with his head held high, his coat gleaming in the sun. He's found confidence, a sense of belonging that warms my heart. And Dobby, sweet Dobby, is right there by his side. The donkey is kicking up his heels, braying with joy as he chases after

Marty in a game of tag. His ears are perked up, his eyes bright with mischief and delight. The bond between these two really is something special.

"You know," I muse, an idea beginning to take shape in my mind, "I bet we could make a go of a little petting zoo, maybe with a café attached. Give folks a chance to interact with the animals up close and personal instead of just riding them."

Jose turns to look at me, one eyebrow raised skeptically. "A petting zoo? Frankie, we've got our hands full with the ranch as it is. You really want to add more critters to the mix?"

I shrug, surprised I even voiced the idea out loud. It's something I've thought about but never seriously considered until now. "Why not? We've got the space for it, and it could be a real draw for families. Imagine kids coming out here to feed the goats and the chickens, pet the bunnies, maybe even take a pony or donkey ride."

Jose snorts, shaking his head. "Right, because what we really need is a bunch of city slickers running around, trying to put saddles on the chickens."

I laugh, punching him lightly on the arm. "Come on, it wouldn't be that bad. We could set it up in the old shed by the north pasture, fix it up real nice. And we could start small, just a few animals to begin with."

"Like what, exactly?" Jose asks. "Potbellied pigs? Fancy chickens with pom-pom butts?"

I roll my eyes. "Sure. We've already got Marty and Dobby, who are clearly naturals with the kids."

Jose makes a noncommittal noise, but I can see the gears turning in his head. "I suppose it could work," he admits grudgingly. "But it'd be a hell of a lot of extra work, Frankie."

"I know." I take a moment to consider that, my eyes drifting back to Sadie, who is now attempting to braid Marty's mane with clumsy, determined fingers. The pony stands patiently, his eyes half-closed in contentment as the little girl chatters away to him. "You and Maria could bring your kids to work on weekends. They'd have other kids to play with, and they'd love hanging out with the animals."

My comment seems to resonate with Jose as he nods and chuckles. "They'd love that. I suppose you'd have to hire more staff, but it might pay for itself."

"Damn straight. Parents are always looking for ways to entertain their kids, and there's nothing like this for miles around."

"And it would be a good way to diversify the business, make sure we're not putting all our eggs in one basket, so to speak," Jose says. "Birthday parties, school field trips, that sort of thing." He turns to me and laughs. "I ain't changing no diapers, though."

I hold up my hands in mock surrender. "Fair enough. You can stick to the heavy lifting and the charm offensive."

"Oh, is that what we're calling it now? And here I thought I was just a pretty face."

"Please. You're about as charming as a cactus," I say. "But luckily for you, the animals don't seem to mind."

The easy camaraderie between us is a balm to my soul. Jose has been by my side through thick and thin, a constant presence in the ever-changing landscape of my life. He started working for my father at the tender age of sixteen, and thirty-five years later, he's still here. I don't know what I'd do without him. "What do you think of the café idea? Nothing fancy, just a place for folks to grab a bite and relax while hanging out with the animals."

"That could be interesting," he says, lowering the rim of

his hat to shade his face from the sun. "As long as we keep it simple, I suppose."

"Exactly. And we could even sell some of our own produce—you know, fresh eggs from the chickens, maybe some cactus chutney. Give people a taste of the ranch life. Plus, it could be a real gathering place for the locals," I add, warming to the theme. "I mean, think about it—there's only one diner around, and it's not exactly the most welcoming spot. But a little café on a ranch? That could be a real draw."

"Why now?" he asks. "This farm has been the same for so long."

"I don't know..." I shrug. "I've always run it the way my parents did, and it's never occurred to me I can do with it what I want until now. Maybe it's time for a change."

"What will your parents think of it?" Jose wiggles his eyebrows and I laugh. He knows how stubborn my father is. It took years to get him off my back. When I first took over, he came by every day, convinced it would all fall apart if he wasn't here. "When did you last see them?" he asks.

"They were here last week. And to answer your first question, you know my dad. He's not going to be comfortable with anything. Remember when I had the solar panels installed?"

Jose chuckles, shaking his head. "How could I forget? He went on about it for weeks, saying it was a waste of money and that we'd never see a return on the investment."

"Exactly. But you know what? Those panels have already paid for themselves, and we're saving a bundle on electricity."

"And now you're thinking about a petting zoo and a café... Your old man is going to struggle getting his head around that."

"Sure," I say. "But maybe it's time to stop worrying about

what my parents will think and start focusing on what I think is best for the ranch. This place has so much potential, and I want to see it thrive."

15

DAKOTA

I let out a long sigh as I merge onto the highway, the glittering lights of the Strip fading in my rearview mirror. I feel like I can breathe again, the suffocating weight of the city's expectations and demands lifting from my shoulders with every mile that passes.

I don't even realize where I'm going until I'm halfway there, the endless stretch of desert highway giving way to the familiar red rocks and scrubby vegetation on the outer reaches of Las Vegas. Before I know it, I'm turning down the road that leads to Frankie's ranch, my heart pounding as I approach.

I park my car and sit for a moment, trying to gather my thoughts. I know I should have called first, should have given Frankie some warning that I was coming. But the truth is, I didn't plan this. I just got in my car and started driving, letting my instincts guide me to the one place where I knew I could find some peace after a stressful week.

Stepping out of the car, I take a deep breath and let the dry desert air fill my lungs. It's blissfully quiet here, and it's where I want to be right now. If she's not home, I'll just sit in my car for a while and listen to the horses whinnying.

I make my way up the porch and raise my hand to knock on the door, but before I can, it swings open, revealing a surprised-looking Frankie.

"Dakota?" she says, her brow furrowed in confusion. "What are you doing here? Is everything okay?"

The concern in her voice is enough to break me, and the tears I've been holding back all day start to spill down my cheeks. I never thought I'd burst into tears in front of her, but here I am, sobbing. I've been so tense, holding in so much, I guess my emotional dam burst when I least expected it.

"I'm fine," I lie, my voice cracking. "I'm sorry, I know I should have called, but I just... I needed to get out of the city."

Frankie's expression softens, and she reaches out to pull me into a hug. I bury my face against her shoulder, inhaling the familiar scent of hay and horses and something uniquely Frankie.

"Hey, it's okay," she murmurs, rubbing soothing circles on my back. "You're always welcome here, you know that."

I nod against her shoulder, taking a shuddering breath. We stay like that for a long moment, just holding each other, until finally I pull back, wiping at my eyes.

"I'm sorry," I say again, feeling embarrassed. "I didn't mean to just show up like this."

Frankie shakes her head, a small smile tugging at the corner of her mouth. "Don't apologize. I'm glad you're here. Come on inside, I'll make us some tea and we can talk."

I follow her into the cozy living room and take a seat on the worn leather couch while Frankie busies herself in the kitchen. She returns a few minutes later with two steaming mugs, pressing one into my hands before settling down beside me.

"So, what's going on?" she asks gently, her knee brushing against mine. "Talk to me."

I take a sip of the tea, letting the warmth soothe my raw throat. "It's...everything," I say, staring down into the mug. "Vegas, the people, the job. It's not what I thought it would be. "

Frankie nods, her expression understanding. "It must be a big adjustment," she says. "Especially coming from the coast."

"It's not just that," I say. "It's the entitlement, the attitude, the way everything revolves around money, status and image. I've had more run-ins this week than I have in my entire life. So many of my customers are rude, and..." I trail off, thinking of the way Luca and Scarlett had shrugged off Mrs. Rosenberg's behavior like it was no big deal. "They're not like the people I'm used to," I finish weakly, feeling tears prick at the back of my eyes again. "I'm constantly having to prove myself and it's draining."

Frankie sets her mug down on the coffee table and takes my hand, her callused fingers intertwining with mine. "I'm sorry," she says softly. "That sounds really tough."

I nod, swallowing hard. "I just don't know if I can do it anymore. I've only been there a month and a half, but I already feel like I'm losing myself. The environment is so toxic."

Frankie squeezes my hand, her eyes searching mine. "Then leave," she says simply, reaching up to tuck a strand of hair behind my ear. "Don't lose yourself. If it's not for you, it's not for you. I mean it. If Vegas isn't working for you, then don't force yourself to stay. You deserve to be happy."

"I know," I say softly. "But I worked so hard for this and I'm not a quitter."

Frankie is quiet, her thumb rubbing over the back of my hand. "Well," she says finally, "are you working tomorrow?"

"No, I have two days off. I couldn't get out of there fast enough," I add with a sarcastic chuckle.

"Then why don't you stay here until you have to go back to work? Just to clear your head, figure things out."

My heart leaps at the suggestion, but I shake my head. "I know you're busy with the ranch, and I don't want to be in the way."

"You could never be in the way," Frankie says firmly. "But I am fully booked so you'll have to stay on the sofa or in my room."

I feel my cheeks flush at the implication, but I can't deny the thrill that runs through me at the thought of finally sharing a bed with her. "You know I prefer your bed. I think we established that weeks ago." I pause. "Are you sure that's okay? I swear, I didn't plan this."

"I know you didn't." Frankie's eyes never leave mine. "And I don't want anything from you. I'm not trying to trick you into sleeping with me, if that's what you think."

"You're not?" Despite my distress, my lips pull into a small smile. "That's a shame."

"Fine. I take it back." Frankie shoots me a mischievous grin. Her hand comes up to cup my cheek and she brushes my tears away. "I'd love it if you kept me warm tonight."

"Because it's so cold here in the desert," I joke in a dramatic tone. Already, I feel my mood shift, arousal replacing my anxiety. It's so easy with Frankie; she can take my mind off my worries in a heartbeat just by looking at me. "I didn't plan this," I say again, inching closer. "But I like where it's heading."

"Me too." Her gaze lowers to my lips and the air between us is electric. "But you're upset and I don't want you to..." Her voice trails away and slowly, giving me every chance to pull away, she leans in too, her breath ghosting over my skin.

"You don't want me to what? Kiss you?" I tease. My pulse kicks into overdrive, desire and anticipation warring. I press my lips to hers and then there's no more talking, no more hesitation. Frankie pulls me tightly against her and claims my mouth in a searing kiss. I open for her eagerly, surrendering to the drugging slide of her lips and tongue. It's like being consumed, set ablaze from the inside out. No one's kissed me like her before, and I feel like I'm falling apart and being put back together, all at once.

Dimly, I register the bunching of Frankie's shirt in my hands, the firm press of her body against mine as she lowers me back onto the couch. She covers me like a living flame, the heat of her seeping into my skin, my bones.

I nip at Frankie's bottom lip and she groans, a sound that shoots straight to my core. Emboldened, I slide my hands under her shirt, mapping the flexing muscles of her back, the ridges of her spine. She's stronger than she looks, all coiled power and leashed intensity, and it only makes me want her more.

Frankie makes a sound low in her throat, almost a growl, and then she's all over me, one hand slipping under my dress, caressing my thigh, while the other splays across my neck. I gasp against her mouth, my hips rolling as I lose myself in the taste and feel of her, and when we finally break apart at the sound of voices outside, we're both breathing hard, our faces flushed with arousal.

"Are you expecting company?" I ask in a breathless whisper.

Frankie rests her forehead against mine and sighs. "No.

They're my guests. Lawrence is on duty tonight, but I'd better go and check if everything's okay. Just so he won't disturb us." She reluctantly gets up and stares down at me, a flirty smile playing around her mouth. "Don't go anywhere. I won't be long."

16

FRANKIE

"I'm dirty," I say when I return, still riled up from our passionate make-out session.

"Oh, I know you are," Dakota teases, licking her lips as she looks me up and down. She's still splayed on the couch, her chest heaving fast like she can't wait to continue what we started.

I laugh as I walk up to her, fighting the urge to lower myself on top of her again. "Seriously. I'm covered in dust and horsehair, and I'm sweaty. I really need a shower." I hesitate. "But you could join me?"

"Now there's an idea." Dakota gets up, wraps her arms around my waist, and brushes her lips against mine. "I'm feeling a little dirty too." The way she rubs herself against me sets me on fire, and in a reflex, I reach for the hem of her dress and pull it over her head. I should probably offer to at least cook her dinner first, but I don't think either of us is interested in that right now. I've never felt so impatient, such an urge to be all over a woman.

The heat between us soars as we make our way to the

bathroom, clumsily undressing each other in the process. I nearly trip as I slide down my jeans and try to step out of them while walking, and Dakota's bra hook gets stuck in her hair. I chuckle as I remove it and toss it on the bathroom floor.

I'm about to step back and drink her in with my eyes, but my vision is obstructed when she pulls my shirt over my head, followed by my sports bra. And then we're near-naked, Dakota standing before me in a tiny, white thong and me in my black briefs. She locks her eyes with mine as she slides the thin straps down her thighs and steps into the shower. Her gaze is intense as she waits for me to do the same.

When I join her and turn on the shower, we simply stare at each other for long moments, taking each other in, and I shiver despite the steam beginning to fill the room. She's breathtakingly beautiful, her tanned skin glistening with droplets of water that trail down the elegant lines of her body. As she steps fully under the spray of the shower, her blond hair turns darker, slicked back from her face, and her blue eyes seem even more vivid in the soft light.

She has the kind of figure that belongs on the pages of a magazine—all long, lean limbs and gentle curves. But it's more than her physical beauty that makes my breath hitch. It's the way she's looking at me, with a scorching heat that makes my knees go weak, and how she runs her hands over her wet hair, seducing me.

"Come here. Are you shy, cowgirl?" she whispers, although she knows very well I'm far from shy. When she pumps some shower gel into her palm and starts rubbing it over her breasts, I close the distance between us and lose all control. Grabbing her behind and pulling her against me, I claim her mouth and moan at the slick slide of skin against skin.

Dakota responds eagerly, her tongue tangling with mine as she wraps her arms around my neck, pressing the full length of her body against me. I tighten my grip on her, my fingers digging into her firm ass as I turn us around and push her against the wall. She winces at the cold tiles against her back, but the smile playing around her lips tells me she likes it when I take charge.

Grinding into her, my hands begin to wander, gliding over the sleek expanse of her back, the flare of her hips, the taut plane of her stomach. I want to touch her everywhere at once, feel every dip and curve. I want to learn what she likes and make her scream in pleasure. I press open-mouthed kisses to the column of her throat, tasting the clean, slightly floral scent of her skin.

Dakota's head falls to the side, giving me better access, and I take full advantage, kissing, sucking, and biting while my hands explore her breasts, squeezing her nipples until she's a moaning mess in my arms. Her fingers trail over my skin in return, exploring my breasts, my behind, my inner thighs. She takes her time, her touch alternately feather-light and firmly purposeful, driving me mad with want.

Bringing my mouth to her ear, I whisper, "What do you want? Tell me."

She responds by taking my hand and sliding it down between us until my fingers are on her sensitive flesh. "Fuck me, Frankie. I need you."

Her plea almost sends me insane with arousal. As I skim her lips and explore her wet heat, she lets out a strangled moan, her hips jerking forward, and I swallow the sound with a kiss. I pull away for a moment to take her hands and bring them above her head against the wall, holding them with one hand while my other slips back between her legs. She moans louder and her eyes flutter closed as I slowly enter her with two fingers and push into her.

The curves of her body respond to my touch, rolling against me. As my fingers slide through her wet heat, I marvel at the way she feels, soft and so incredibly ready for me.

Dakota's breath hitches, her moans becoming louder, more urgent. My thumb traces teasing circles around her clit, and I revel in the way her body shudders in response. For a moment, she wriggles in my grip, but the smile around her mouth tells me she likes being held.

"God, Frankie," she breathes, her voice husky with need. "I've wanted you since we met." Her hips buck against my hand, and I start fucking her, matching the rhythm of her movements with my own. Her breaths come in ragged bursts as I thrust deeper, harder.

My lips find hers again, and we kiss hungrily, tongues tangling, teeth grazing. It's a raw and desperate kiss and I can't get enough of her. I want to consume her, possess her, own her.

I know she's close. I can feel it in the way her body tenses, the way her breath catches in her throat. I curl my fingers inside her, and it's all she needs. With a shuddering cry, she comes undone, her body trembling against me.

I hold her through it, my fingers still moving, coaxing every last bit of ecstasy from her. When I finally let go of her wrists, she wraps her arms around my neck and collapses against me, her breathing heavy and ragged on my shoulder.

For a moment, we just stand there, the water washing

over us, our bodies pressed together. I can feel her heartbeat against my chest, rapid and hard.

"Somehow I just knew that would be amazing," she whispers, her voice still shaky from her climax. Lifting her head to look at me, her hand slides between my thighs, and I gasp at her touch. Her other hand squeezes my behind while she kisses her way down my neck, her lips and tongue leaving goose bumps on my flesh.

Turning us around and gently nudging me against the wall, she presses all of her into all of me, making me throb and ache for her. When her mouth reaches my breasts, she takes her time, worshiping every inch of them. My nipples are hard and sensitive, and the way she teases them with her tongue makes me moan loudly while my hands tangle in her wet hair. I can feel the need building inside me, an almost unbearable pressure.

Dakota's mouth travels lower, her hands spreading my thighs while she gets down on her knees. The anticipation is almost too much, and when she finally presses her lips to my center, I cry out, my entire body arching off the wall. She takes her time, finding all the right spots and applying just the right amount of pressure while she squeezes my behind and pulls me against her.

My fingers lace tighter into her hair as she brings me closer to the edge. The world narrows down to her and me alone, and I feel like I'm going to explode.

"Please," I beg, my voice breaking. "Don't stop."

She doesn't. Her tongue moves faster, and it's too much, too intense. When she sucks my clit into her mouth, my climax hits me like a tidal wave, my body shaking uncontrollably as I throw my head back and moan, the pleasure almost blinding in its intensity. Dakota holds me through it, kissing me until I'm completely spent, my legs barely able to hold me up.

As the water cascades over us, she straightens herself and shoots me a smug smile before she cups my face and kisses me softly. "You know," she murmurs against my lips, "I think we're both a lot cleaner now."

17

DAKOTA

*T*he gentle sway of the horse beneath me is soothing, a rhythmic motion that quiets my racing thoughts. I'm getting used to the feel of it, the way my body moves in sync with the animal, the subtle shifts in balance and pressure that keep me steady in the saddle.

Ahead of me, Frankie rides Texas with an easy grace, her posture relaxed. She looks like she was born to be on a horse, like it's as natural to her as breathing. I admire the way she moves, the fluid strength in her muscles, the confident set of her shoulders.

We've been riding for a while now, picking our way through the rugged desert terrain. The heat is dry and bearable, tempered by a breeze that whispers through the scrubby vegetation.

My body feels deliciously sore as memories of our passionate night together flood my mind. I shiver each time I recall the way Frankie's hands felt on my skin, the taste of her lips, the sound of our gasps and moans. Waking up in her arms this morning, I felt a sense of contentment and ease that I haven't experienced in ages. The stress and frustration of my job, the loneliness and isolation I've felt since moving to Vegas—it all melts away in her presence.

There's something about Frankie that just feels right, like we've somehow skipped the awkward "getting to know you" phase and jumped straight into a deep, instinctual connection. Being with her is effortless, and I can't bring myself to overthink it. For once, I just want to live in the moment without worrying about what comes next.

Frankie casts me a glance over her shoulder, a knowing smile playing at the corners of her mouth. She looks unfairly gorgeous out here in her element, and I feel a flutter low in my belly as our eyes meet.

I flush, turning my attention back to the trail ahead, trying to focus on the rhythm of the horse's steps instead of the pulsing ache between my thighs, but it's a losing battle.

She slows her horse to a walk, falling back to ride beside me. "You're getting pretty good at this," she says, nodding at my improved posture. "A natural, I'd say."

"I have a good teacher," I reply. "She's not bad to look at either."

Frankie chuckles, shaking her head. "Flattery will get you everywhere, Miss Vegas. The hat suits you, by the way."

"Thanks." I tap the front of the cowboy hat I borrowed from Frankie. Her tan leather hat with braided band is almost identical, but it looks softer, molded to the shape of her head over time, and the brim, originally flat and wide, now curves slightly upward at the sides from years of being tugged on. I can't imagine her on a horse without it. She's wearing jeans and a white shirt, and I'm in yesterday's dress and a pair of borrowed cowboy boots.

I've noticed how she glances at me when a gust of wind blows the hem of my dress around, revealing more of my thighs than appropriate for public viewing. Not that there's anyone around here—we haven't passed another soul since leaving the ranch. Out here, it feels like we're the only two people in the world, a thought that's both exhilarating and a little unnerving.

Frankie's eyes run appreciatively up and down my bare legs. "Careful there," she teases. "You keep flashing me like that and we might have to take a little detour off the trail."

Heat floods my cheeks, and a thrill of anticipation zips down my spine. The idea of Frankie pulling me off my horse out here in the open desert is tempting.

"Behave, cowgirl. You were the one who insisted on giving me a proper desert experience."

"Oh, I'll give you an experience all right," she practically purrs, and I nearly swallow my tongue at the blatant innuendo. "But I suppose you're right. Plenty of time for other... activities later."

"I'll hold you to that." I'm so turned on I have trouble focusing on riding, but Frankie just smirks, clearly pleased with herself for getting me so flustered. She's good at that, I'm learning—pushing my buttons in the most delicious ways, keeping me constantly on my toes. It's new for me, this kind of playful, flirtatious dynamic, and I'm all for it.

We ride in silence for a while, the only sound the crunch of hooves and the occasional birdcall. I take in the stark beauty of the landscape around us, the red rocks and the stubborn vegetation that clings to life in this harsh environment.

"I can see why you love it out here," I say, breaking the silence. "It's so peaceful, so...untouched."

Frankie nods. "It's special. There's a raw power to the desert, a kind of brutal honesty. It doesn't try to be anything other than what it is. A place with the sheer will to survive against all odds."

She points to a cluster of spiky plants with vibrant yellow flowers, their petals almost luminescent against the red sand. "Those are desert marigolds," she explains, her voice taking on a lecturing tone I imagine she uses in her tours. "There aren't many around at the moment; they usually bloom in the spring, after the winter rains." She then gestures to a gnarled tree in the distance, its twisted branches reaching toward the sky. "And that's a Joshua tree. There are a lot of them in the area where I found you stranded. Some of them are over a thousand years old, can you imagine?"

"Wow...if these trees could talk..." I turn to her. "They freaked me out that night. They looked like figures."

"Yeah, they can be a little unnerving in the dark. You looked so helpless and out of place next to your truck. It was kind of adorable."

"I've never been so happy to see anyone in my life." I laugh and shoot her a wink. "I'm still happy to see you, but for different reasons now." I can't seem to tear my gaze away from her face, from the animated expression and the lively gleam in her eyes. It hits me that I have a crush on Frankie. A serious full-on crush.

"You're staring," she says teasingly. "See something you like, Miss Vegas?"

"Maybe," I reply coyly, biting my lip to hide my smile. "But I think you already knew that."

"Well, the feeling is mutual." She opens her mouth to continue, then shakes her head with a grin. "I want to show you something."

We urge our horses forward and Frankie leads the way, guiding us toward a narrow canyon that cuts through the red rock like a jagged wound.

As we enter the canyon, the temperature drops slightly,

the air feeling cooler against my skin. The walls rise up on either side of us, towering cliffs of striated stone that glow in the slanting light. And then, as we round a bend, I see it—a hidden valley, a secluded haven nestled between the stark red rocks. Unique rock formations rise from the desert floor, their shapes sculpted by wind and time. Sparse vegetation dots the landscape where hardy shrubs and cacti that have adapted to the harsh conditions.

Spanning the distance between two rock formations is a graceful stone arch, its curve so smooth it almost looks man-made, its slender form stretching across the void like a bridge.

"That arch is incredible."

"Yeah. It's my secret spot," Frankie says. "I always stop here for a break in the shade when I'm out riding alone." She brings Texas to a stop, swinging down from the saddle before she helps me off Savannah, my horse. "What do you think?"

"It's otherworldly."

Frankie takes my hand, and we climb onto the flat surface underneath the arch while the horses stay below in the shade. We sit beside each other, and I run my hand over the weathered stone.

"That's millions of years of erosion right there. Wind, rain, and the relentless march of time, all working together to create something so beautiful."

"I love your secret spot," I say, my voice echoing off the walls surrounding us. I study Frankie's profile, tracing the lines of her face with my eyes, the way her dark lashes fan out against her cheeks, the curve of her full lips, the cute little crease that appears between her brows when she's deep in thought or looks into the sun. She's beautiful in a way that goes beyond physical attractiveness—there's a fascinating strength and a rawness to her.

Frankie turns to face me, our noses almost brushing with the proximity. Her eyes flick down to my mouth, then back up to meet my own, a silent question in their depths. "What are you thinking?" she murmurs. "No, wait. Let me guess... I think you want me to kiss you."

"Busted." I smirk as I lean in closer, pressing my lips to hers. Frankie responds immediately, her free hand coming up to tangle in my hair, pulling me closer as she deepens the kiss.

Kissing Frankie is intense, all-consuming, and utterly addictive. She maneuvers me so I'm sitting on her lap, chest to chest, one leg on either side of her. Grasping my behind, she squeezes, urging my pelvis into her as we start to rock in a slow, undulating rhythm that causes me to gasp into her mouth.

My hands are in her hair, tugging gently as I change the angle of the kiss, taking control. Frankie seems happy to let me lead, her lips parting in a soft moan as I trail kisses along her jaw. Her scent surrounds me, an intoxicating blend that makes my head spin.

Minutes pass, or maybe hours—time seems to lose all meaning when I'm wrapped up in Frankie like this. We spend long moments simply exploring each other, hands roaming and mouths tasting, lost in a bubble of mutual desire and discovery.

Finally, the need for oxygen forces us to part, our foreheads resting together as we pant softly, sharing breath in the charged space between us. Frankie's lips are kiss-swollen and glistening, her eyes dark and hazy with want, and I know I must look much the same.

"That was…" she starts, then shakes her head with a rueful chuckle. "Wow."

"Definitely wow," I agree, grinning like a fool. "If I'd known desert rides with you ended like this, I would have let myself get stranded in the wilderness a lot sooner."

Frankie laughs. "And here I thought you came for the scenery."

"Oh, I came for the scenery," I quip. "I'm just more interested in the view from right here." I punctuate my words with a roll of my hips, grinding down against her.

Frankie's breath hitches, her fingers flexing on my waist. "Careful, Miss Vegas," she warns. "Keep that up and we might not make it back to the ranch."

I lean in close, my lips brushing the shell of her ear as I whisper, "Is that a promise or a threat?"

Frankie turns her head, capturing my mouth in a kiss that steals the air from my lungs and all thought from my mind. When we break apart, both of us breathing hard, her eyes are molten with desire.

"Both," she whispers, already working at the buttons of my dress. "Definitely both."

18

FRANKIE

*S*itting in a booth at the Starlight Diner with Rennie, I'm nursing a cup of coffee and picking at a slice of apple pie. The diner is quiet for a Sunday, with only a few regulars scattered about, their murmured conversations blending with the soft clatter of dishes from the kitchen.

Rennie, always the curious one, has been pestering me for details about Dakota ever since I mentioned her in passing. "Come on, Frankie," she begs. "You can't just drop a bomb like that and not give me the juicy details. Did you two, you know...get it on?" She waggles her eyebrows suggestively.

I roll my eyes and chuckle. "Jesus, Ren, keep your voice down."

"Sorry." Rennie snorts, taking a sip of her coffee. "Please, I know you. You've got that look in your eyes. You slept with her, didn't you?"

I sigh, running a hand through my hair. "Fine, yes, we were all over each other all night and the next day. It was great. Amazing."

"Wow." Rennie gawks at me, speechless for a beat. "Okay. And now what? When are you seeing each other again?"

"We didn't plan anything. We were naked in bed after a horse ride when my next guests arrived two hours early, so I had to rush and get dressed. I told her she could stay another night, but she didn't want to distract me from work, so she left."

"But it was good?"

"Yeah."

"And she clearly likes you back, or she wouldn't have returned to the ranch and stayed over."

"I think she likes me, but keeping it casual is probably the best thing for us. Our lives are just different, so it's never going to be more than it is now."

Rennie leans forward, her eyes narrowed. "How can you be so sure?" She points to my phone. "Come on, let me see a picture of this mystery woman."

I hesitate for a moment, then scroll through my phone with a sigh. "Here." I show her a picture of us, the only one we took together. We were sitting on the horses and were about to head into the desert. Dakota asked me to take a selfie of us and send it to her. She looks stunning, her blond hair falling around her shoulders from underneath the cowboy hat, her blue eyes sparkling with excitement as she smiled for the picture.

Rennie whistles, raising her brows. "Damn, Frankie. She's a knockout. No wonder you're all twisted up over her." She zooms in, studying Dakota closer. "And she looks right at home on the ranch."

"Everyone feels at home at Red Rock for a visit, but that doesn't mean it's for her," I say, typing her name into my search engine. I might as well admit I've looked her up since we first met, and I know exactly where to find pictures of her. In this particular photo, she's wearing a slinky red dress and sky-high heels. She's laughing at something off-camera, her head thrown back while she raises a hand. The picture was taken at a Christmas party at her previous salon, and her colleagues are just as glamorous as her.

"Oh...Jesus, that's a whole other level of hot and dreamy." Rennie continues to scroll and clicks on a link to the Vegas White Salon. There's a picture of Dakota sitting in her office, looking pristine and in charge. "Her office looks like something out of a sci-fi movie," she says.

"Yeah. See what I mean? Our worlds are so far apart, it makes no sense."

"Yup," Rennie admits. "That's some fancy stuff, and you're right. You're probably a terrible match."

"Exactly. Hence the casual comment." It's not what I wanted to hear, but at least Rennie's being honest.

"But as long as no one gets hurt, casual is cool, right?"

"Of course. I'm not complaining. Anyway, there's zero pressure, we'll see how it goes." I grin and decide to change the subject because I don't want to overthink it. Part of me is pretty sure I'll see Dakota again, and that's enough for me. "You know," I say, "I've been thinking about maybe opening up a café on the ranch, along with a little petting zoo for kids."

"Oh?" Rennie frowns. "Tell me more."

"Well, think about it. The Starlight Diner is pretty much the only place around here. You and I like coming here, but it's not exactly the most charming spot."

Rennie chuckles and nods toward a trucker who's sleeping with his head resting on the bar. "That's putting it mildly. I'm pretty sure I saw a cockroach the size of my fist in the bathroom last week."

"I saw it too. Let's not even go there." I pause. "But what if there was another option? A place where people could come and relax, grab a bite to eat, and hang out with some cute animals? It could be a real gathering spot for the community."

"That's not a bad idea. Not a bad idea at all," she says. "It could bring in some new business for the ranch. Get people interested in horseback riding." Rennie leans back in her seat with an amused grin. "Look at you, Frankie. Entrepreneur extraordinaire."

"Hey, a girl's gotta dream, right?" Glancing around, I scan the diner. "By the way, where's Leslie? I thought she was joining us?"

Rennie points at the car park through the window, and I laugh when I see Leslie talking to one of the waitresses. She's clearly on her break, having a cigarette and eating a doughnut at the same time. "Ah. That explains it. She never made it inside…"

"Nope. She doesn't even know this waitress. She went straight up to her and asked if she was new here—she's so nosy—and she's been outside talking to her ever since." Rennie rolls her eyes. "It's a good thing I'm not jealous. Leslie will literally strike up a conversation with anyone who's willing to respond."

"She's definitely a social butterfly," I agree as I observe Leslie expressively waving her hands around before bursting into laughter. "Should we order her something?"

"No, leave her," Rennie says. "I'm quite happy sitting here talking to you. If she joins, I won't be able to get a word in edgewise."

"Fair enough. More pie for us, then." I flag down the waitress and order another slice, along with a refill on our coffees.

As we wait for our order, Rennie leans in. "So, back to this café idea. Can you please get some micro pigs? I fucking love them, but they're so messy to keep as pets."

I nearly choke on my coffee. "God, imagine... You and a pig with your cleaning OCD. You wouldn't survive a day."

"I know, but they're so adorable. Will you get one? Please? Pretty please?"

Just then, the bell over the diner door jingles and Leslie breezes in. She spots us and makes a beeline for our booth, sliding in next to Rennie with a bright smile.

"Sorry, ladies. Got caught up in the most fascinating conversation with Marlene, the new waitress. Did you know she's a professional taxidermist? She specializes in creating these incredibly lifelike dioramas of desert animals. She just finished a piece with a coyote and a jackrabbit locked in an eternal game of chase. Can you imagine?"

Rennie and I exchange a slightly horrified glance.

"That's...certainly unique," I manage.

Leslie nods eagerly. "Right? I was so intrigued, I invited her over for dinner on Friday. She's going to bring her portfolio to show us."

Rennie shoots me a panicked look before she turns back to her girlfriend. "Oh, um, that's great, honey. I can't wait." Her smile is a little too bright, her tone a tad strained.

"I knew you'd be excited," Leslie continues. "It's not every day you meet someone with such an unusual talent. Would you like to join us, Frankie?"

Rennie is kicking my leg under the table. I know she desperately wants me to accept the invite. She's not that comfortable around strangers, but I've been there before and I've learned my lesson.

"Sorry. I have plans," I lie.

Rennie kicks me again, harder this time, and I have to bite back a yelp. I'll be paying for this later, I'm sure, but for now, I'm just glad to have dodged that particular bullet.

19

DAKOTA

*S*tepping out onto the terrace of the restaurant below my apartment, I'm immediately enveloped by the warm, dry air of the Nevada afternoon. The sun beats down from a cloudless sky, casting sharp shadows across the terra-cotta tiles and the wrought-iron tables and chairs scattered about.

I've been a regular here since I moved, and the small table overlooking the street has become my usual spot. I take a seat, grateful for the umbrella providing a welcome respite from the sun, and feel the tension of the day starting to melt away as I settle into the cushioned chair. It's only four p.m. and I don't have to be back in my torture tower tomorrow either. I've done so much overtime lately that I decided I deserved to leave early.

Gabriel, the owner of the restaurant, spots me from inside and makes his way over, a warm smile on his weathered face. "Dakota, mi amiga!" he calls out. "How are you on this beautiful day?"

"I'm good, Gabe. Just happy to be off work and spending some time outside."

He nods, wiping his hands on his apron. "I hear you. But it's been a scorcher today, huh? Can I get you something to drink? Your usual?"

"That would be great, thanks. A margarita sounds perfect right about now."

Gabriel chuckles as he points a finger at me. "One super-zesty margarita, coming right up. You sit tight and relax, okay? You work too hard, mi amiga."

I laugh, shaking my head. "Hey, you're one to talk. I don't think I've ever seen you take a day off."

He shrugs and waves a hand. "What can I say? I love what I do. And besides, someone's gotta keep this place running smoothly."

With that, he disappears back inside, leaving me to my thoughts. I let my gaze wander over the terrace, taking in the colorful potted plants. It's a cozy, inviting space, one that feels like a little oasis in my crazy new life.

A few minutes later, he returns with my drink, setting it down on the table with a flourish. "One margarita, extra lime, just the way you like it."

I take a sip, savoring the tart, refreshing flavor. "Mmm, perfect."

"I know." He grins, pulling out the chair across from me and taking a seat. "How are things with you? How's work going?"

I shrug, tracing my finger along the rim of my glass. "It's going okay."

"You don't sound too enthusiastic."

"No, it's fine, really. Busy, as always." I'm not going to bug him with my doubts about the move and my job. About how I struggle to make genuine connections and burst into tears in my office at least twice a week. How I feel like I'm drowning, like I'm losing a part of myself with each passing day. The clients are demanding and often rude, their entitlement grating on my nerves. I'm constantly biting my tongue, forcing a smile when all I want to do is scream.

It's not just the clients. It's the whole atmosphere of the salon, the pressure to be perfect, to maintain this image of glamour and sophistication. I feel like an impostor, playing a role that doesn't quite fit. It's exhausting, this constant facade. But what choice do I have? I can't just quit; I worked too hard for this.

My team is friendly, but I doubt I'll ever be close to any of them. They're a different species, thriving on Instagram likes rather than small pleasures. Driven by social status, they don't get joy from simple things like a good conversation or a perfect margarita, especially when it doesn't come with theater and outrageous presentation or an interesting location to tag.

Truthfully, Gabriel is one of the few real people I've met here, and I cherish our daily small talk, even if it's just a "good morning." I like the way he sits with me without asking when he feels I need company, and he also senses when I prefer to be left alone.

"I like my team," I continue, not wanting to sound like a downer.

"That's good. It's important to like the people you work with. Makes the long hours a little more bearable, no?"

"Definitely," I agree. "So what's new with you? How's business?"

"Oh, you know. Same old, same old. Although I'll be taking all the furniture inside later tonight. I don't know if you heard, but there's a big storm coming our way, so I'm closing the terrace in a few hours."

"Yeah, I heard something about that." Looking up at the

cloudless sky, it's hard to believe the weather will shift. "But it's just a little rain and heavy winds, right?"

Gabriel shakes his head, a serious expression settling over his features. "I wouldn't be so sure about that. Storms and heavy rainfall are rare here in Nevada, but when it does come, it can be quite severe."

"What do you mean? Like, flash floods and stuff?"

He nods, leaning forward and resting his elbows on the table. "Exactly. The thing about the desert is the soil is so dry and hard-packed that it doesn't absorb water very well. So when we do get a lot of rain all at once, it just runs right off the surface and can cause some pretty serious flooding."

I frown, my mind immediately going to Frankie and her ranch. "What about ranches? Are they in danger?"

"They can be, yes. Especially if they're not prepared for it. It's not something most people think about, living in the city like we do. We just make sure nothing blows away and those who live in basement apartments tend to evacuate for the night. But for folks out there in the desert...it can cause a lot of destruction."

"I...I have a friend who lives on a ranch. Do you think she'll be okay?" I ask.

"I'm sure she will be. If she's been living out there for a while, she probably knows how to prepare for these kinds of things." Gabriel shoots me a reassuring smile. "But it never hurts to check in, you know? Make sure she's got everything she needs, just in case."

I nod. "Yeah, you're right. I'll do that."

"Good. And hey, if she needs anything, you let me know, okay? I've got plenty of supplies here at the restaurant. Water, canned goods, flashlights...whatever she needs."

His kindness takes me aback and I meet his eyes with a

grateful smile. "Thank you, Gabe. That's...that's really kind of you."

He waves a hand, shaking his head. "It's nothing. That's what friends are for, right? We have to look out for one another in Sin City."

"Right. Friends," I say with a smile. Is that what we are? Friends? I didn't think we'd reached that point yet, but this is the one place I come to when the day has gotten to me and I need my daily dose of "normal."

"You know," Gabriel continues, "I've been through my share of storms in this life. Both the literal and the figurative kind. And if there's one thing I've learned, it's that the most important thing is to have people you can count on."

"You're right," I say. "That's what really matters, in the end. The people we love and the connections we make." I hesitate for a moment, wondering how honest I should be. "It's not easy to find that here."

"I know." He huffs. "You won't find it in the casinos, that's for sure."

Gabriel's words strike a chord. "Yeah. The casinos, the clubs, the constant hustle...it's all so surface level."

He shrugs. "I used to be a part of that world. But with age, I've learned that the most meaningful relationships come from the most unexpected places."

"Yeah..." I think of Frankie and the ranch while I take another sip and note a feeling of unease creeping up on me. I care about her and I want her to be okay. "I'm with you on the unexpected," I say. "My friend with the ranch...she rescued me when I was stranded in the desert. We only met by chance and we have nothing in common, but she means a lot to me. She's a real person. No pretense, no front. She's just herself."

Gabriel shoots me a smile and a wink as he gets up. "Well, then you'd better go check on her. Again, I'm sure she'll be prepared, but there's nothing like a helping hand."

20

FRANKIE

*T*he sky is an ominous shade of gray as I step out of the house, the air heavy with the promise of rain. I can feel it in my bones—the way the pressure drops and the wind picks up, whipping past me with a mournful howl.

I've been keeping a close eye on the weather reports, tracking the storm as it moves closer. They're predicting serious rainfall, the kind that can cause flash floods and landslides, turning the parched desert into a muddy quagmire. But there's another problem weighing on my mind— the tours. I've had to cancel all the rides scheduled for the next few days, knowing it won't be safe to take the horses out in these conditions. It's a blow to the business, especially during peak season, but I don't have a choice.

Making sure the animals are safe is my priority as I head toward the stables, my mind racing with the list of tasks that still need to be done. I need to move the hay bales to higher ground to make sure they don't get soaked and ruined, check the hinges on the stable doors to ensure they're sturdy enough to withstand the force of the wind, and make sure the horses are safe, especially the young foal.

Jose is already hard at work moving hay bales. He looks up as I approach, wiping the sweat from his brow with the back of his hand. "Boss," he greets me, his voice gravelly with fatigue. "I asked Lawrence to move the horses inside. They're restless—I think they know it's coming."

I nod, my jaw tight with tension as Lawrence enters with the last of the horses. "Great work," I say, noting their troughs are full and that they have plenty of food and water too. "You already beat me to it."

"Yeah, I think we're good," Jose says. "What about Dakota? Should we leave her here?"

I walk over to Dakota and hesitate when I see she's nervous. She can feel the tension in the other horses and she's shuffling on the spot. "I'll take her inside. It will be less noisy there."

"Inside the house, you mean?"

I shrug. "She's fragile. I don't want her to panic and hurt herself." I glance from Jose to Lawrence and back. "You two go home to your families. The storm is closing in and I don't want you to be stuck here."

Jose nods. "Do you have enough supplies? Food? Water? Flashlights and batteries? Just in case the roads get washed out and you're cut off from town for a few days."

"Yeah. Don't worry about me," I assure him, frowning as I hear a clap of thunder in the distance. "Go. Get your asses home. I'll finish up."

"Are you sure?" Lawrence asks. "I can—"

"No, absolutely not." I open the stable door and wait for them to leave. They're so sweet and loyal; I'm sure they'd even go as far as to stay here if I asked them to. But I've been through this many times and I can handle it. "Thank you so much," I say, and as I wave them out, I'm shocked to see Dakota getting out of her car in the driveway.

"Hey!" I call out, my voice carried away by the gusts as I approach her. "What are you doing here?"

She looks up at me, her eyes wide with worry. "I heard about the storm. I wanted to help, to make sure you and the animals were okay."

"You didn't have to do that." I pull her into a long hug. "It's not safe driving in this weather."

"Well, I'm here and I'm safe," she says matter-of-factly. "So tell me, what can I do? I brought supplies, by the way."

I shake my head and chuckle. "You're a lot more stubborn than I thought. You know you might be stuck here for a while, right?"

"I know. Hence the supplies. And being stuck with you isn't such a bad thought." She smiles. "Anyway, I have the day off tomorrow."

I have a feeling the roads might be flooded for more than one day, but I keep that to myself. It's too late; she's already here and she can't drive back now. The wind is picking up and the first raindrops are starting to fall.

"Okay, if you insist..." I hand her my key ring. "Can you please close all the shutters on the guesthouse and the main house? I have a few things to finish up here."

I make quick work of securing all the stable doors and bring a hay bale into the house before I head back to pick up the foal. She protests as I lead her out of the stables, and I know I've made the right decision. As soon as we enter the house, she calms. The living room is much quieter; there's less heavy creaking and howling.

"It's going to be okay," I whisper while I tie her to a beam in my living room. For a creature with very little fear, she's exceptionally nervous about the storm. I move the couch, so she has more space, and put the hay in front of her along with a bucket of water. It's the first time I've had a horse in the house and it feels bizarre, but special treats and our company should keep her happy.

Dakota bursts into giggles when she walks in and sees us. "Are we three girls having a pajama party?" she jokes, putting down the large crate she's holding.

"Most people would stock up on canned goods and bottled water, but leave it to you to prioritize the finer things in life," I say, raising a brow as I take in the contents. "Are you trying to get me drunk and take advantage of me, Miss Vegas?"

Dakota feigns a look of wide-eyed innocence, placing a hand over her heart. "Why, Frankie, I would never! I'm just here to provide essential supplies and moral support during this trying time." She walks up to Dakota and strokes her lovingly. "Hey, there. Sweetheart. Are you scared?"

"She was nervous," I say. "So I decided it was best to take her in. I don't want her to get hurt or traumatized. It gets really noisy in the stables."

Dakota nods. "What about the other horses? And Marty and Dobby?"

"Marty and Dobby are fine as long as they have each other, and the horses have been through storms before. Anyway, I can't have a house full of horses."

"No. Of course not." She grins. "The shutters are closed. I've double-checked them all, and I put the supplies from the car in the kitchen, if that's okay. This was the last batch."

"There's more?" I ask.

"Yeah. There's a lot more." She winces. "Costco was on my way and I guess I got a little carried away."

"Thank you, that's so sweet. But again, you shouldn't have—"

Dakota hushes me and presses a finger to my lips. "Hey, it's a pleasure. I didn't know what you liked so I brought a bit of everything. Cheese, crackers, olives, bread, pickles, cured cuts..." She winks. "And a few bottles of good wine. As you said. Priorities."

I chuckle and close the distance between us. Outside, the wind howls and heavy raindrops start tapping against the shutters. Despite my slight unease about the night ahead, Dakota showing up is a pleasant surprise and I can't say I mind being locked up with her.

"You're amazing, you know that?" I murmur, running my hands down her arms.

"I know," she jokes, shivering at my touch. "So, what else can I do? Tell me what you need." There's a mischievous glimmer in her eyes as she wraps her arms around my waist.

"You can kiss me," I say, brushing my lips against hers. "That's what I need."

Dakota's mouth finds mine, and we lose ourselves in each other as the storm picks up outside. When we break apart, both a little breathless and flushed, Dakota grins as she looks up at me. "I'm glad to be of assistance."

21

DAKOTA

I've never experienced a storm like this, the kind that makes the walls shake and the windows rattle in their frames. Even Frankie couldn't predict the intensity, the way it slams into the ranch with a fury that seems almost personal. Now, huddled together on the couch, we hold our breath as it unleashes its full power. The shutters are closed tight against the onslaught, but I can still hear the wind whistling through the cracks.

Frankie notices my discomfort and pulls me closer, her arm a reassuring weight around my shoulders. "It's okay," she murmurs. "We're safe here. I promise the ranch has weathered worse storms than this."

"And the stables?" I ask.

"The stables are sturdy too. The horses will be fine."

A sudden crash from outside makes me jump, my hand clutching at Frankie's arm. She just chuckles.

"That'll be the old mesquite tree," she says calmly. "It loses a few branches every time we get a storm like this. Nothing to worry about."

The lights flicker and then go out, plunging the room

into darkness. I let out a yelp of surprise, my heart hammering. I feel mildly embarrassed about my reaction. I was supposed to help her out, not be another burden to bear.

"It's okay," Frankie says again, then turns on the flashlight she had ready on the coffee table. "I've got plenty of candles, just give me a second."

She disentangles herself from me and starts lighting the candles we've placed around the house, anticipating a power cut. I get up and help her, checking on Dakota to make sure the candles don't scare her. The foal seems fine though; she's standing in the corner, sleeping with her head lowered and her ears relaxed.

"There." Frankie lights the last candle and opens one of the bottles of red wine I've brought. "How about a glass to calm your nerves?"

"Can you tell I'm a little jumpy?" I shoot her a goofy grin as I open the crackers.

"You look like a deer in headlights." Frankie hands me a big, wooden chopping board, and I start plating the snacks I've brought while she pours the wine. "Would it help if I told you this farm has withstood storms for over fifty years?"

"That long?"

"Yeah. My father built Red Rock Ranch when he was twenty-one. Well, not all by himself," Frankie adds. "He had help, of course. My grandfather left him some money and he used it to build a home and a business for him and my mother. Back then, it was a cattle ranch. It wasn't until the nineties that they built the guesthouse and started focusing on horses. By the time I took over, the ranch was purely aimed at tourism." She pours wine into two glasses and hands me one. "The first thing I did was modernize the ranch. My father hated that, but I think part of him understands I had to."

"Do you see them often?" I ask.

"They visit a few times a month and sometimes I go and see them in Vegas. My father prefers to come here, though. He loves to sit on the porch with a cold beer and criticize everything I do." Frankie laughs. "The man doesn't like change. I can tell you that."

"But he changed the business model from cattle to tourism, right?"

"Only because Mom threatened to leave. They worked so hard, and she felt lonely on the ranch. Mom's a very social woman. She thrives when she's around people. So, it seemed like a logical solution. She played the host and Dad did the tours," Frankie says. "He called me earlier and threatened to come over to help me out with the storm. I'm glad I told him to stay away now."

"Because I'm here?"

"Yes. Needless to say, I prefer having you to myself." Frankie clinks her glass against mine and takes a sip. "You'd like my parents, though. They're sweet people."

"I'd love to meet them." I'm not sure if it's too soon for such a comment; after all, we're not in a relationship, but Frankie doesn't seem to mind. "Did you like growing up on the ranch?"

"I did." Frankie picks up the glasses, and I follow her back into the living room with the grazing board. "It was just life as I knew it. I never questioned it. Most of my friends from school lived on ranches, and I've always loved animals, especially horses." She sits and drapes her arm over the couch's back, an invitation for me to slide against her. Our easy conversation has taken my mind off the storm, and sipping my wine, I feel more at ease.

"I can tell you love horses. It's beautiful to see you with them."

"What can I say? I'm a sucker for animals." Frankie smiles as she glances over at the foal, then sets her glass down and turns to me. "So tell me about your parents. What do they do?" She points a finger at me. "Let me guess. I bet your father was in banking or something."

I widen my eyes at her. "Seriously? Why do you think that?"

"I don't know. You seem like you come from a wealthy, stable background—a city background. Working father, housewife mother perhaps?" Frankie winces. "Actually, I shouldn't make assumptions. Not everyone is so lucky to have had a good childhood with both parents around."

"Don't worry, it's not a sore subject." I laugh because she couldn't be farther from the truth. "I think you'll be surprised."

"Oh?" Frankie arches a brow. "Do tell."

"My parents were actually farmers," I say with a smirk. "Not cattle farmers, but fruit farmers. I grew up on a farm too."

"You didn't..."

"I'm not kidding. Dad was a third-generation farmer just outside Newport Beach. Mom wasn't so keen on farm life, so she sold everything after Dad passed away and she's currently cruising the world with her best friend."

Frankie stares at me for a beat and squeezes my hand. "I'm so sorry about your dad. When did he pass away?"

"It's been ten years now," I say, lowering my gaze to my feet. "He died of a heart attack. He was twenty-three years older than Mom, so there was a huge age gap there." Although I've processed my father's death and I'm able to talk about him just fine now, I still feel a stab of loss each time I mention him.

"That's a significant age gap."

"Yeah. They always seemed happy to me, though, but I didn't realize how badly Mom wanted to get out of there until she was suddenly stuck with the responsibility of five hundred fruit trees." I shake my head with an amused smile. "As soon as the farm was sold, she packed up and boarded the first available cruise liner. It was some distant dream she'd always had, and now she was able to do as she pleased, so she went for it. She bought a small apartment in Newport Beach, and has been back and forth since then but she lives for adventure."

"Where is she now?" Frankie asks.

"Somewhere in the Caribbean. She left just before I moved here, and she'll visit me once she returns."

"Good for her." Frankie looks at me curiously. "Are you close to her?"

"Yes, I'd say we're close, even though we don't see each other that often anymore. I definitely take after her rather than Dad."

Frankie nods and studies me like she's trying to imagine what my mother might look like, then asks, "In what way?"

I take a moment to think about that. "Well, growing up, I didn't like living on a farm at all, and with Mom being a little bored, we'd jump at any opportunity to venture into the city. We'd dress up for the day and go window shopping and eat ice cream on the promenade as we both loved people watching. We didn't get to do it very often, Mom was always busy with the farm, but I loved those days with her. When I was a teenager, I couldn't wait to get out of there. The farm was quite remote, so while friends could wander into town to meet up at the mall, I had to beg my parents to drive me."

"You must have loved starting college," Frankie says.

"Oh, yes. Moving to campus was like Christmas. My dad

gave me his old truck—it's the truck I arrived in. I packed up and never moved back home."

"You've had that truck since then?" Frankie winces. "It must have stung to let go of it."

"Yeah…" I think of Henry, all alone in a plot somewhere, surrounded by other forgotten cars, gathering dust. It feels like I've abandoned a loyal friend. The thought of no one talking to him or patting his dashboard for good luck makes my heart ache. I realize now that every time I spoke to Henry, I was really speaking to my father, keeping his memory alive through our shared connection to that old truck.

"I get it," Frankie says, her fingers lacing with mine. "Letting go of something that's been a part of your life for so long…it's never easy." She pauses, her thumb rubbing circles on the back of my hand. "But sometimes, it's good to make room for new adventures, and who knows? Maybe your old truck will be the start of someone else's story now, just like it was for you."

"Whatever their plans are, it's not going to get them very far," I joke. "It was—" Before I can finish my sentence, a loud crack of thunder shakes the house, making me jump. Dakota lets out a frightened whinny, her hooves scrabbling against the wooden floor.

Frankie is on her feet in an instant, moving to soothe the frightened foal. She murmurs to her, stroking her nose until the animal calms under her touch.

"It's okay, sweet girl," she coos. "You're safe here, I promise."

I smile as I watch the tender exchange, moved by the depth of Frankie's compassion. She has such a way with animals, a natural empathy that goes beyond mere skill or training.

Frankie looks up and catches my eye. "She'll be fine," she says. "Are you?"

"Yes," I say honestly. The storm is raging on outside, but here with Frankie, I've never felt more comfortable. "It's quite romantic, don't you think? The storm, the candles, the wine..."

"Don't forget the horse in the living room," Frankie adds with a grin as she comes and sits next to me again. She pulls my legs over her lap and strokes my calves. "So you always hated living on a farm and now you're stuck on one."

"That's different. I like it here," I whisper, leaning in to kiss her. "Your ranch is the one place I long for when I'm having a bad day, and I'm not a teenager anymore. Nowadays, I prefer to avoid all the action."

"Then you're in the right place because there won't be much happening here tonight."

I smile against Frankie's lips and curl my hand around her neck. "Are you sure about that?"

"Well, I suppose that depends on your definition of 'action,'" she whispers.

I grin, trailing my fingers along the collar of her shirt. "Why don't you show me what kind of 'action' a cowgirl can rustle up on a stormy night?"

22

FRANKIE

The first thing I notice as I drift into consciousness is the warm weight pressed against my side. I'm on the couch, and for a moment, I'm disoriented, my mind still hazy with sleep. But then the events of the previous night come rushing back, and a smile spreads across my face. Dakota is nestled against me, her head resting on my shoulder and her arm draped across my waist. She looks peaceful in sleep, her features soft and relaxed, and I feel a surge of tenderness well up inside me.

I'm so lost in the sight of her that I don't hear the front door open or the sound of footsteps approaching. It's only when a familiar voice breaks the silence that I realize we're not alone.

"Sorry, boss," Jose says, his eyes widening as he raises his hands. "I didn't mean to interrupt. This looks like quite the sleepover."

I'm suddenly wide awake and sit up quickly, dislodging Dakota in the process. At least we had the sense to put some clothes back on before we fell asleep.

"Jose," I say, trying my hardest to sound casual. "I didn't hear you come in."

He chuckles, shaking his head. "I didn't expect anyone but the foal in the living room. I just came to pick her up, but I should have knocked."

I glance at Dakota, who is waking up. "We were just...the storm ..."

"Hey, no need to explain to me," he says. "I'm just glad to see you're all safe and sound." He moves over to the foal and wraps his arms around her neck. "Come on, little lady," he whispers, nuzzling her nose. "Let's get you back out to your mama. I'm sure she's missing you."

"How did you even get here?" I ask. "Is the road clear?"

He points to his rubber boots. "No. My wife dropped me off at the crossing, and I walked from there. I'll call her when I need a pick-up later. The water came up to my calves in some areas. It definitely won't be clear to drive today."

"That bad, huh?" Dakota mumbles next to me. She sits up and runs a hand through her hair. "Good morning, by the way. I'm Dakota. I think I saw you yesterday in passing when I arrived."

"That's right. Good morning, I'm Jose. I'm sorry I woke you."

"No, please don't worry," she says. "I'm here to help, so just tell me what I can do."

"That's very kind of you. I'm sure there's plenty to be done around here today." Jose glances between the two of us. "I imagine you both could use a good, strong cup of coffee first, though."

"I certainly wouldn't mind one." Dakota breaks away from me and yawns as she rises to her feet. I miss her already and part of me is glad we'll be stuck with each other for another night. "I'll make coffee," she says. "Jose? Milk? Sugar?"

"Just black, please." Jose starts untying the foal from the beam, and I can tell he's fascinated by the circumstances. I'm very private and he's rarely seen me with a woman like this; if they're guests, they usually go back to their own room, or stay in bed while Jose and I have our morning meeting in the kitchen.

"You shouldn't have come in with the flood. You're soaked," I say, pointing to his jeans.

He waves it off. "I have a spare pair of boots and some clothes in the stables. You know me—I couldn't just hang around at home, not knowing what state the ranch was in. This is practically my second home."

"I appreciate it," I say, meeting his eyes with a grateful smile. "So, what's the damage?"

"Not much. A broken branch, some flooding, of course, and I found one of the rocking chairs on the drive. One armrest is missing, but I think we can fix it."

"Good." I get up and pat his shoulder before I stroke Dakota. "You're a good friend, and I'm glad the damage isn't too bad." I scan the living room for my boots and find them under the hay. The space smells of stables. "I'd better go check on the horses."

"Already done," Jose says, gently tugging Dakota toward the door. "They're all fine, but I left them inside as even the higher pastures are still very muddy. I'm sure they could all use some TLC, though, after a night like that." He taps his cowboy hat and leads Dakota outside.

"I'll be right there." I'm still half asleep and wrestling with my boots.

"I'll bring over the coffee and join you when it's ready," Dakota says. She looks rumpled and adorable, her hair tousled and her eyes heavy-lidded, and I feel a rush of affection for her as I tug on the second boot and close the distance between us to kiss her.

"Sorry about the intrusion. I forgot he lets himself in sometimes. Take your time. Have a shower if you want."

"It's fine, I'll wait. We'll get muddy out there anyway."

"You're probably right about the mud," I murmur, pressing another kiss to her lips. "But I promise I'll make it up to you later with a nice, long soak in the tub."

With a final squeeze of Dakota's hand, I step out into the morning light. The storm may have passed, but its presence lingers in the damp earth and glistening surfaces. Rainwater pools in every dip and hollow, from shallow puddles that barely cover the toe of my boot to deeper, murky expanses that could easily soak me to the knee. The ground squelches beneath my feet, saturated and soft, as I carefully navigate the waterlogged terrain.

As I approach the stables, I hear the nickering of the horses, and feel a rush of relief. They sound calm, content even, and I say a silent prayer of thanks for the sturdy walls and strong roof that kept them safe through the night.

I find Jose inside, the foal already reunited with her mother. Sahara is nuzzling her daughter and checking her over.

"See? All good here," he says. "We got lucky, boss."

"We did." I climb up to the hayloft to check for leaks. "It's dry!" I call out before peering out of the small window to catch a glimpse of the road in the distance. Or at least, what used to be the road. Now, it's more like a river, the floodwaters rushing over the asphalt in a churning, muddy torrent. I can see debris caught in the current—branches, leaves, even a fence post or two, all swept away by the force of the water. It's a sobering sight, and I realize we really have been lucky.

Climbing back down from the hayloft, I hear footsteps approaching and turn to see Dakota walking in with three mugs of coffee. She hands one to Jose and one to me.

"Thanks," I say, stealing a flirty glance. "This is exactly what I needed."

Dakota smiles. "So, what's the plan? How can I help?"

I look around, taking stock of the situation. "Well, first things first, we need to clear any debris that might have blown onto the ranch. Broken branches, loose boards, anything that could be a hazard to the horses."

Jose nods in agreement. "I'll start on that. You two want to check the fence line? Make sure there aren't any gaps where the horses could get out?"

"Sounds good," I say, already mentally mapping out the perimeter of the pastures. "We should also check the water troughs, make sure they're not contaminated with any floodwater."

Dakota sips her coffee, her expression determined. "Lead the way, boss," she says with a playful salute.

I chuckle, shaking my head at her antics, but I can't deny the warmth that blossoms in my chest at her eagerness to help. "All right then, let's get to work."

23

DAKOTA

*T*he roads are still flooded, making it impossible for me to return to the city, so Frankie and I are stuck at the ranch for another day. Jose has gone home to his family, leaving just the two of us, which I don't mind at all. Now that we're alone, the tension between us is searing again. We're stealing glances, exchanging smiles and flirty comments like two teenagers, jumping at any opportunity for physical contact.

We're in the stables, tending to the horses, and I'm practically swooning as I watch Frankie move from stall to stall, checking on each horse with a practiced eye. She runs her hands over their flanks, murmuring softly while she strokes their noses.

"Can you hand me that brush?" she asks, pointing to a soft-bristled grooming brush hanging on a nearby hook.

I grab the brush and pass it to her, stealing a kiss in the process. I can't help myself; being around Frankie does something to me. It's like every nerve ending in my body is hyper-aware of her presence and constantly yearning for her.

Frankie starts brushing down the mare in front of her, Chestnut in name and color, using long, smooth strokes that make the horse's coat gleam. I pick up another brush and move to the next stall, trying to mimic what she's doing. It's peaceful, almost meditative, and I find myself relaxing into the rhythm of the task.

"You're giving off a good vibe," she says, glancing over at me with a smile. "The horses can sense when someone is comfortable around them. It puts them at ease."

I grin back at her, feeling a flush of pride. "I've always loved animals," I admit. "I used to beg my parents for a pony when I was a kid, but they drew the line at dogs. They said it was hard enough taking care of the fruit trees, let alone additional animals."

"I guess it's a good thing you're stuck here with a whole stable full of them then," Frankie teases.

"Not just the horses," I shoot back at her. "I like being stuck with you."

"I can't say I mind either." Frankie's lazy smile widens, and the way she looks me up and down gives me butterflies.

"Have you ever been stuck on the farm with a woman before?" I ask.

"Once," she admits, and I feel a little pang of what might be jealousy. She told me she wasn't one for relationships, and although I have no doubt she's popular with the ladies, it still takes me by surprise.

"Care to share?" I ask, trying my best to sound casual.

Frankie hesitates and looks like she'd rather avoid the subject.

"It's okay. We don't have to talk about it," I quickly say. It's strange how close I feel to her already, yet we're not in a relationship. I wouldn't mind knowing where I stand as I don't like the idea of her seeing other women while we're...well...I'm not sure what to call whatever this is between us.

"No, I don't mind." Frankie keeps her gaze fixed on the horse. "The last time I had someone here with me after a flood...well, it was my ex."

"Oh?" I pause in my brushing.

"Yeah. Her name was Melanie. She lived here with me for about six months, a couple of years back."

"So you were in a serious relationship?"

"More of a whirlwind romance," she says. "As I said, it only lasted six months."

I wait, sensing there's more to the story.

"She was a marketing executive in Vegas," Frankie continues. "We met at a bar downtown and hit it off right away. I brought her out here for a weekend, and she never really left."

My eyebrows shoot up. "She moved in?"

"Yeah. It all happened really fast. She stayed here most nights when we first met, so when her lease ran out in Vegas, it made sense for her to move in."

"Oh... Where did it go wrong?" I ask softly.

Frankie shrugs. "She got bored. Decided this life wasn't for her after all. Melanie was very social, always flitting off to this party or that event. I'm just not wired that way." She glances at me, something unreadable in her expression. "I guess the novelty wore off after a few months because she started spending more and more time away from the ranch. She often stayed with friends in the city so she wouldn't have to make the drive back in the middle of the night, and then one day..." Frankie swallows hard. "She packed her bags, said she couldn't do it anymore. That was it."

"I'm sorry," I murmur, feeling a pang of sympathy. "That must have been really hard."

"It was." Frankie's voice is quiet, tinged with an old hurt. "Feeling like my life, my home, wasn't enough for her...it stung, I won't lie. But I don't blame her either, and there are no hard feelings. Besides, being on my own suits me better. It's easier that way."

There's a finality to her words that makes my stomach twist. Hearing her talk about relationships like they're inevitably doomed to fail bothers me more than it should.

"Well, for what it's worth," I say, trying to lighten the mood, "I really like it here. The ranch, the horses...you."

Frankie chuckles, but there's a hint of melancholy in it. "I've heard that before," she says softly. "And I appreciate the sentiment, I really do. But I've also learned not to put too much stock in it. People say a lot of things in the moment."

An awkward silence descends, both of us unsure where to go from here. I don't want to push, to overstep whatever tentative boundaries we've established. But I also can't stand seeing Frankie look so resigned, so alone even with me standing right here.

While I'm scrambling for something to say, Frankie seems to shake herself out of her reverie. A familiar, playful glint enters her eyes, and she drops the brush and saunters over to me, backing me up against a nearby hay bale.

"But enough about my uninspiring romantic history," she teases, her hands settling on my hips. "I believe I promised to make up for this morning's interruption, didn't I?"

"Hmm, did you?" I breathe, my pulse already quickening at her proximity. "I'm not sure I recall... Please remind me."

Frankie grins and leans in to capture my lips in a kiss. I melt into her, my arms winding around her neck as I give myself over to the rush of sensation. She's doing that in-charge possessive thing again that sets my libido on fire, holding me, pulling me in, and taking what she wants. Her hands slip under the hem of my shirt, tracing patterns on my lower back, and I arch into her touch, craving more.

We sink down onto the hay bale, lost in a tangle of roaming hands and heated kisses. The horses, the storm, the outside world—all of it fades away until there is only this, only us, wrapped up in each other as the afternoon sun slants through the stable windows. In the back of my mind, I know we're treading dangerous ground. I want her way too much to give up, even if it will never go further than casual for her. But with Frankie's lips on my skin and her hands in my hair, I can't bring myself to care. For now, in this stolen moment out of time, I let myself get lost in the thrill of her touch, consequences be damned.

24

FRANKIE

*D*akota and I sit on the porch, the desert stretching out before us like an endless sea of shadows. The storm has left behind a world washed clean, with the scent of damp earth and creosote heavy in the air. The moon is full and bright overhead, casting a silvery glow over the landscape. It's a different kind of beauty than you see during the day—softer, more mysterious. The cacti and scrub brush shimmer in the pale light, their edges blurred and dreamlike.

I take a deep breath, savoring the stillness and the sense of peace that always comes in the aftermath of a storm. Sipping her wine, Dakota keeps giving me sideways glances that make me think she's got the same thoughts, but we're in a weird space. I'm not sure if I should bring up our "situation," if we should talk about what we're doing. It might be necessary to establish some ground rules for our casual sleepovers, but then again, I don't want to ruin this beautiful thing we have by overanalyzing it.

Dakota's shoulder brushes against mine as she leans back in her recliner chair that is right next to mine. She's wearing nothing but one of my old T-shirts and boxers, her long legs and perky behind on display. It's turning me on more than she knows.

"This is nice," she murmurs. "I can't remember the last time I felt so relaxed."

I smile, glancing over at her. She looks ravishingly beautiful in the moonlight, her blond hair gleaming and her eyes bright. "You needed a break."

"Yeah." Dakota nods, her gaze drifting out over the horizon. "Vegas is exhausting, even when I'm not working. Although I've met some nice people, I wouldn't class hanging out with them as relaxing."

I meet her eyes. "And why is that?"

Dakota chews her lip as she ponders the question. "I guess... I guess we're just very different," she finally says. "With my friends back home, I talked about everything and nothing. Sometimes we had deep, meaningful conversations, and sometimes we simply goofed around and gossiped. But I never felt like I had to be someone I wasn't around them. It was natural." She pauses. "With the people I've met here, I'm always worried if I'm wearing the right outfit or if I look good in their pictures, as I'll no doubt end up on some social account for their thousands of followers to see." She rolls her eyes. "It's all about the latest hotspot, who you know, the most Instagrammable cocktail, the hippest brands... I find it hard to engage when everyone's so focused on image."

"Do you miss your friends?" I ask. "Do you regret moving to Vegas?"

Dakota tilts her head from side to side. "I miss them, but that wouldn't be a reason for me to move back. I can always visit them, and I'm sure they will visit me." She shrugs. "But maybe Vegas is not for me. I feel lonely there and that's crazy because I'm constantly surrounded by people and rarely get a moment to myself apart from when I'm home."

"Crowds can be lonely too," I say.

"Yes," she agrees as she takes my hand and gives it a squeeze. "I don't think a break was what I needed. What I really needed was connection, so thank you."

"Anytime. You know where to find me." A warmth blooms in my chest, a sense of affection that catches me off guard. "I think you'd like my friends, Rennie and Leslie. You should come over sometime when they're here. I promise you, neither of them has more than twenty followers," I joke. "My best friend Rennie is totally antisocial, and her partner, Leslie, is the complete opposite, but both in the best ways. They're real people."

"Real is good, and if they're your friends, they must be amazing people." Dakota's smile widens, and something that looks like intrigue flashes over her features. "Thank you, that's really sweet. Do they know we've been..."

"Yes," I interrupt her, sparing her from trying to phrase something we haven't defined yet. "I told them I found a beautiful, stranded woman in the desert and they've been asking about you ever since." I wince as I feel a blush creep to my cheeks. "I mean, I haven't shared details, of course. Just that we've seen each other a few times and that I, well... they know I like you."

Dakota chuckles at my sudden inability to form a sentence. "I don't mind who you tell," she says with a grin. "So you like me, huh?" Her teasing tone makes me blush even more.

"I won't lie," I say with an awkward shrug. "I really do."

"Well, I like you too." Dakota glances down at her feet, equally flushed now. "So you wouldn't mind if I stopped by more often?" she whispers, leaning in. Her breath is warm against my skin.

"I wouldn't mind at all. I love having you in my bed."

Dakota's eyes narrow. She sets her wine glass down, and the corners of her mouth turn up in a seductive smile.

"Oh, really?" she murmurs, leaning closer. "Are you sure about that?"

"Positive," I reply, a little breathless. Her proximity is making my heart race. "I want you here." Before I can process what's happening, Dakota gets up to straddle my lap. She's close enough that I can feel the heat radiating from her body, and the light scent of her shampoo fills my senses. Her hands come up to rest on my shoulders, and she gazes down at me, her eyes dark with intent. "You want me here?" she asks, her voice dropping to a whisper. "Like this?"

I swallow hard, my hands moving to rest on her hips. "Yes. Fuck, yes."

Dakota leans in, her lips grazing my ear as she whispers, "Good. Because I've been thinking about this all day."

Her words send a shiver through me, and I tighten my grip on her hips, pulling her closer. "Is that so?" I murmur, my voice trembling with anticipation.

"Uh-huh." Dakota pulls back just enough to look into my eyes. Her gaze is intense, filled with a desire that makes my pulse quicken. "I've had dirty thoughts," she whispers with a smile. "Very, very dirty thoughts."

"Tell me."

She shakes her head, licking her lips. "Tell me what you want first, cowgirl."

Hesitating for a moment, I shift my hands to her behind. I've had many fantasies I haven't voiced, but by the way she calls me "cowgirl," I have a feeling we're on the same page and she wants me to take charge.

"Hmm...I think I'd like to tie you up and spank you with my riding crop," I say, squeezing her. I'm not sure if I've taken it too far, but Dakota's breath hitches as she shifts in my lap and grinds into me, clearly loving that idea.

"Fuck," she whispers. "And then what?"

Squeezing my thighs together, I feel myself getting wet. She has no idea what she does to me. "I like to leave some room for surprises. Are you up for that?"

Dakota nods slowly, then leans in to kiss me. Her hands tangle in my hair as she moans against my mouth, pressing her body firmly against mine. I can feel every curve, every inch of her warmth, and the friction alone is almost too much to bear. The kiss deepens, becoming more frantic, and the tension builds between us, a coiled spring ready to snap.

Dakota's hands roam over my back, my arms, and I can't get enough of her, can't pull her close enough.

I stand up and she wraps her legs around my hips as I lift her and carry her inside to the bedroom.

"Mmm...you're strong. I like that," she murmurs when I lay her down on the bed and crawl over her. Wedging my thigh between her legs, I feel her wetness through her panties, and it takes all my restraint not to fuck her right there and then.

Meeting her eyes, I trail a finger over her lips, her chin, and her neck, down to the dip between her breasts. "Now tell me what you want."

"I already told you I'm up for surprises. Do with me as you please." She shivers when I cup her breast and squeeze her nipple through her T-shirt, her abdomen tightening against me. She's so responsive.

"Do you trust me?" I ask.

Dakota nods and swallows hard. "Yes, I trust you."

25

DAKOTA

*M*y heart pounds hard as Frankie's fingers trail over me. Her intense gaze makes me nervous and aroused. I need more—the pressure of her knee between my thighs, her mouth on mine. I need all of her, now.

I've never done this before. The idea of being tied up is new, thrilling, and a little scary, but I want to be at her mercy more than anything.

Frankie lifts the hem of my T-shirt slowly, her eyes never leaving mine as she pulls it over my head, exposing my bare skin. "God, you're beautiful," she murmurs, her voice low and husky. She reaches for the silk ties she has ready. "Are you sure you want this?"

I nod, my breath coming in short gasps. "Yes...I'm all yours."

Her eyes darken, and she gives me a reassuring smile. "Tell me to stop at any moment. Just say it, and I'll untie you immediately."

Frankie moves with confidence, deftly securing my wrists to the bedposts. She's done this before, I realize. How many women has she done this to? Were they special to her? Was she in love with them?

The restraints make me feel vulnerable, and I tug, testing them. Knowing I can't break free is daunting, but it equally excites me.

Frankie's demeanor shifts as she gives the ties one last tug. She becomes more assertive, her eyes glinting with a teasing challenge. She leans in, her mouth brushing against mine before tracing her tongue over my upper lip. Her knee presses firmer against my pussy, and I know she can feel how wet I am. I wish she'd take off her robe; I long for her skin against mine and love to see her naked.

"How's that?" she asks. "Not too tight?"

"No," I reply, my voice trembling. "It feels fine. I've never..."

"That's okay." Frankie shoots me a wicked smile. "Just relax. This is for your pleasure. I'd never do anything to hurt you."

She kisses me again, her lips trailing from my mouth down to my neck, sending waves of pleasure through me.

I arch my back, trying to get closer to her, but each time I do, she pulls back. The sensation of being unable to move, of surrendering to her, is both frustrating and sexy as hell. I want to touch her, but I can't. I want to kiss her, but she won't let me. I have no idea what she's planning on doing to me, and that's a sweet torture.

Frankie's hands move to my breasts, her fingers splayed wide as she massages them. She's watching me closely, and I know she loves seeing me like this. "Let's see how sensitive you are," she says in a low purr, suddenly pinching my left nipple.

I bite back a yelp and wince, but it's a delicious kind of pain that spreads through my body and pools between my legs. I'm already throbbing, and she hasn't even touched me there.

"Did you like that?"

"Yes," I breathe, my body trembling with need. "Please, Frankie. Don't stop."

She smiles, a slow, seductive smile that makes my heart race. "Oh, I'm not stopping. We're just getting started."

Frankie moves back onto her knees, her hands trailing lower, down to my stomach. Shivering with anticipation, I've never felt so vulnerable, so exposed, yet so alive. Her touch is electric, and the way she looks at me makes me feel like I'm the only person in the world she desires.

I lift my hips, and she chuckles softly, her eyes glinting with amusement and desire. "Patience, Dakota. I want to savor every moment."

She's both gentle and demanding, her fingers teasing and exploring. She finds my sensitive spots with such intuition, it's hard to believe we don't know each other that well. Her fingertips slip into my panties, skimming the thin strip of hair between my thighs, and just as she's about to go lower, she pulls back and straightens herself.

"Frankie," I whisper. "Please..."

But Frankie gets off the bed, leaving me flustered and confused. She heads over to her wardrobe, pulls something out, and my breath catches at the sight of a black, leather riding crop. The next thing she pulls out is a black cowboy hat, which she puts on with a mischievous grin. The sight of her with the hat and crop evokes a surprising physical reaction in me.

She walks back to the bed with the riding crop in hand, her eyes locking on to mine with a predatory gleam. The way she looks at me, as if deciding exactly how she's going to devour me, makes my pulse race and my body throb with need. The air is thick with tension, and I'm caught between wanting to beg for her to use it and reveling in the exquisite waiting game.

She stands by the bed, dragging the crop over her palm, her eyes never leaving mine. I'm breathing hard, my body trembling with desire. Then, slowly, she brings the crop down, letting it graze over my skin in the lightest of touches. She starts at my ankle, dragging it up over my calf, teasingly slow, causing a tingling sensation in its trail. My whole body is tuned to her, every nerve ending alive.

"Are you sure you want this?" she asks. The crop continues its slow journey, now moving over my knee and up my thigh.

"Yes." I glance at the crop, drawn to it. "I'm sure."

A wicked smile curves her lips. "Good girl." The crop moves higher over my hip, grazing the sensitive skin just above my panties, and I can't help the whimper that escapes me. She brings it up to my stomach, pressing down just enough to send a jolt through my body, then, suddenly, she strikes me.

The sharp, sweet pain spreads through me, mixing with intense arousal, and I gasp, my hips lifting off the bed involuntarily. More than anything, I'm shocked that the sensation leaves me craving more.

"Are you okay?" she asks again, something curious in her gaze—perhaps fascination, but I'm too flustered to think straight.

"Yes."

"Would you like me to do it again?"

Taking a deep breath, I ball my hands into fists and nod.

"Speak up. I need to hear you say it."

"Yes," I repeat, loving the authority in her voice. "Please do it again."

Frankie moves the crop higher, trailing it between my breasts. The anticipation builds to a fever pitch, and then she brings it down with a sharp, stinging strike across my left breast. The sudden pain makes me cry out, but it's a good kind of pain. I'm panting, my wrists tugging at the restraints as I crave more of that intense sensation.

Frankie watches me with a hungry stare, clearly enjoying my reaction. "Again?"

"Yes."

She bites her bottom lip as she brings the crop down again, this time striking directly across my nipple. The pain is sharper, more intense, and it makes me cry out louder. But the pleasure that follows is even more powerful, spreading through me in pulsating waves.

"Do you like that?" Frankie asks.

"That feels so...good..." Still catching my breath, I can barely speak.

She brings the crop down again, hitting my other nipple with precision. Pain and pleasure blend together in a dizzying mix, making my head spin. I'm lost in the sensation, throwing my head back as she alternates between my breasts in softer strikes before she stops, trailing the crop down to my hip.

"Can I take these off?" she taps the fabric of my panties, then wedges the crop under the lace edge.

"Uh-huh." I'm a heaving mess, trembling and writhing.

Frankie pulls them down and tosses them on the floor. Even though she's seen me naked before, I feel so much more exposed now that I'm at her mercy. Her eyes roam over me and settle on my throbbing pussy.

"Spread your legs," she commands, and her words make me squirm.

I move my thighs apart slightly, but she shakes her head. "More."

Swallowing hard, I do as she says, then brace myself for the crop again. This is beyond anything I've ever felt, and I wonder why I've never had such desires before. Maybe it just didn't cross my mind. My previous partners were not as adventurous as Frankie and we certainly didn't have the fiery chemistry we share.

I'm torn out of my vague thoughts as the crop hits my inner thigh, and something between a groan and a moan escapes me. I'm so sensitive, and even though I know the pain will be worse higher up, I want her to go there.

"Do you want me to stop?" As Frankie asks the question, she drags the crop up, resting it dangerously close to where I need it most.

"No. Don't stop." I wiggle, searching for contact, but she ignores my plea and takes another moment to study me.

"You're incredible," she murmurs. "I love seeing you like this, and you have no idea how much I want to fuck you right now."

"Then do it." I'm panting, my body trembling. "I need you."

She finally gives in and moves the crop to my pussy, dragging it up and down. The moment it touches my clit, I gasp and almost levitate off the bed. I'm about to climax when she lifts it and strikes me right there, violently pulling me away from the blissful edge I'm balancing on.

"Fuck!" I squeeze my eyes shut tight and moan. I'm burning and aching and still I want more—anything to feed this agonizing yearning.

Frankie drops the crop and smiles. "Wait there and don't go anywhere," she teases, then returns to her wardrobe. I can't see what she's grabbing, as she's wearing her robe and has her back turned to me, but I have an idea when she steps into something. I want to touch myself so badly I don't even realize I'm tugging at my restraints until my wrists are getting sore, so I stop trying to free myself.

Frankie turns around. Her robe is hanging open now and she's wearing a black strap-on. "Are you okay with this?" she asks, approaching me.

"God, yes." I can't tear my eyes away from her, my heart racing with nerves and excitement.

Frankie takes off her hat and climbs back onto the bed, positioning herself between my legs. Her hands are gentle as they caress my thighs, moving upward slowly. She's taking her time, savoring every moment, and it's driving me wild.

She leans down, kissing me deeply, her tongue exploring my mouth with a deliberate slowness that makes me whimper. Her moans tell me she's struggling to hold back as her hands move to my hips, and she adjusts herself so the tip of the strap-on brushes against my clit. I gasp at the contact, my body arching toward her, and she begins to push inside me.

The sensation is overwhelming, a perfect blend of pleasure and tension as my body adjusts to the intrusion. I cry out, my head falling back against the pillows, and Frankie pauses, giving me a moment to catch my breath.

"Does that feel good?" she whispers, reaching up to take my hands.

"Fuck," I pant, my body trembling. "It feels amazing."

She smiles and starts to move again, her thrusts slow and controlled. Each movement sends waves of pleasure through me, building steadily until I'm a trembling mess beneath her. The restraints around my wrists keep me grounded, adding to the intensity of the experience. I'm completely at her mercy, and it's exhilarating.

Frankie's eyes never leave mine, her gaze intense as her breaths quicken. She picks up the pace, her thrusts becoming more rhythmic, more insistent. I know she's close from the friction of the harness; I can feel it in her movements and hear it in her ragged breaths and hoarse moans.

I'm so close too, the tension in my body coiling tighter with each movement. The friction, the pressure, the look in her eyes—it's all too much, and I can't hold back any longer.

"Frankie," I gasp, my voice breaking.

"I've got you," she murmurs. "Let go with me."

Her words push me over the edge, and I come undone beneath her. The orgasm crashes over me, powerful and all-consuming, as my body convulses.

Frankie lets out a loud moan as her hands tighten around mine. She doesn't stop, riding out my climax with steady, measured thrusts, prolonging the blissful sensation until we're both left trembling and breathless.

Then she presses soft kisses to my lips, my cheeks, my forehead. I'm still tied up, but in this moment, I've never felt safer or more cherished.

"I think you liked that," she whispers with a grin, pulling at the ties that come undone easily.

"Mm..." I wrap my arms around her and pull her in to kiss her. "I feel so...I don't know..." My mind churns, searching for the right word. "Liberated. Can I say that?"

"Of course. If that's how you feel." Frankie settles beside me, her body warm and comforting against mine, and we lie there in silence for a while, our breathing slowly returning to normal. "I think you needed it," she says. "You're overwhelmed with responsibility and pressure. Sometimes it's nice to have all of that taken away."

26

FRANKIE

The sound of gravel crunching under tires wakes me from my slumber. Dakota stirs beside me, her arm draped casually across my waist. My heart leaps into my throat. I know that sound. It's the old Buick, a relic from the eighties that my parents refuse to let go of. Panic sets in as I hear the familiar hum of my father's favorite tune, "Sweet Caroline," and Mom mumbles something about the fancy car in the driveway. *Oh God, they're here.*

"Dakota," I whisper, shaking her gently. "Wake up."

"Mmm, what's going on?" she murmurs, barely opening her eyes.

"My parents," I hiss. "They're here. Right now. Outside."

Dakota's eyes snap open, the sleepiness vanishing instantly. She sits up, her hair a beautiful mess, and I can see the questions forming in her mind.

"I'm so sorry," I say, scrambling out of bed. "They must have driven over as soon as it was light to check on the ranch after the storm. I suppose the roads are open again."

Dakota nods, already getting out of bed and reaching for her clothes. I throw on a pair of jeans and a T-shirt while I try to work out what to say to them. The last time I introduced a woman to my parents, she left two months later. They were devastated for me, and I don't want to go through that again. It's way too soon to introduce Dakota, but what choice do I have? I can't hide her in my bed. She'll have to leave for work eventually, and her car is in the driveway so they'll ask questions.

I can hear my father's voice getting closer to the door. "Mary, I'm telling you, it's fine. Everything is still standing."

"I know, Frank," my mother replies. "I just want to make sure she's okay. She didn't reply to the message I sent her last night."

"Okay, here goes nothing," I mutter as Dakota follows me out of the bedroom.

I open the front door just as my father's about to knock. He's a tall man, broad-shouldered, with a shock of silver hair and kind blue eyes that crinkle at the corners when he smiles. My mother, shorter and rounder, with darker hair streaked with gray, stands beside him.

"Morning!" I say, trying to sound cheerful and casual, as if this is a normal occurrence and I don't have a beautiful woman standing half-hidden behind me.

"Frankie!" my father exclaims, pulling me into a bear hug. "We were worried about you. How did you fare in the storm? How are the horses? It doesn't look too bad out here."

"Everything's fine, Dad," I reply, stepping back to let him and Mom into the house. "Just a few branches down, nothing major."

"Thank goodness," my mother says, hugging me tightly. Then her eyes drift past me, landing on Dakota. "Oh... We didn't realize you had company."

Dakota offers a polite smile. "Hi, I'm Dakota."

My father raises a brow but quickly recovers, extending his hand. "Nice to meet you, Dakota. I'm Frank, and this is my wife, Mary."

Mom gives Dakota a once-over, then smiles warmly. "Nice to meet you, dear. Sorry for barging in like this. I did see the car, but I assumed Jose had bought himself a new one."

"It's no problem," Dakota replies, shaking both their hands. "I was just visiting and got stuck here during the storm."

The four of us stand there for a moment, an awkward silence hanging in the air. My mind is racing, trying to figure out what to say next.

"Well, sit down," I finally manage. "Can I get you a coffee?"

"That would be lovely, sweetheart." My mother's eyes flick curiously between Dakota and me again.

As I move to the kitchen, I can hear my father humming again while he does a round through the house to check for cracks or leaks. He's never found one; I'm good with the upkeep, but that won't stop him from his usual inspection. I glance over my shoulder and see Dakota sitting beside my mother on the couch, both of them making polite conversation about the weather and the storm.

Making coffee, I attempt to calm myself. My parents have always been supportive, but they're also protective. The last thing I want is for them to start interrogating Dakota or making things awkward.

"So, Dakota," my father's voice breaks into my thoughts. "What do you do?"

"I'm the general manager of the White Spa at the Quantum Hotel in Vegas," Dakota says. "I moved here from Newport Beach, where I worked for the same company."

"Well, that's impressive." Mom sounds genuinely amazed. "We've heard wonderful things about that spa. Very high-end, isn't it?"

"It is." Dakota shoots me a smile as I head into the living room. "Our clients can be tough, though."

My father nods. "You must be very good at what you do."

"I try," she replies modestly.

"So, how do you know Frankie?" Mom asks.

Dakota meets my eyes again. There's a hint of uncertainty in hers, as if she's not quite sure what to share. "Frankie and I are friends," she says after a moment's hesitation. "I came over to see if she needed help before the storm, and then it was too late to return to the city."

Dad chuckles. "I take it you're not used to these storms. They always cause a few days of trouble, and that's if you're lucky."

"Yeah, I underestimated it," Dakota admits. "I never made it to work yesterday, so I should probably get going."

"Well, we're glad you're safe," Mom says. "And it's been wonderful to meet you. Perhaps we'll see each other again?"

"That would be lovely, Mary." Dakota stands up, and it's only then that I notice she already has her bag packed and ready.

As Dakota says goodbye and heads to the door, I follow her. My parents remain in the living room, watching us. At the door, Dakota turns to me, and for a moment, we just stand there, unsure of what to do. It feels weird not to kiss her goodbye, but I can't. Not with my parents watching.

Dakota seems to sense this too, so she gives me an awkward brush on the shoulder. Her fingers linger just a bit longer than necessary as she meets my eyes. "I'll call you."

"I can't wait to see you again," I whisper. "And sorry about this. I was going to make you breakfast and..."

"It's okay. I really do have to get to work." Dakota shrugs as she shoots me a mischievous smile. "Bye, cowgirl."

Clearly referring to last night, her comment makes me chuckle as I close the door and join my parents again. They're both looking up at me, and I feel like I'm facing a jury.

"So," Mom begins, her tone light but probing. "Tell us more about Dakota."

I take a seat, trying to recoup. "She's great. As she said, we're friends. We have been for a while, and I like her."

"Is that all?" Mom tilts her head as she regards me. "Because you're glowing, sweetheart, and the way you act around her..."

"What way? What are you talking about?" Aware I'm sounding more defensive than I meant, I lower my voice. "We're just friends. I mean..." There's no point denying it. Mom and Dad are always on to me. "It's early days," I finally say.

Dad grins. "Early days or not, you're blushing like a teenager."

Mom laughs, her eyes twinkling. "And that blush tells us everything we need to know."

27

DAKOTA

*A*s I drive back into the city, the peace and tranquility of the desert quickly fades away, replaced by the familiar chaos of Vegas. The noise hits me first—the constant hum of traffic, the blaring of car horns, and the distant thrum of music and laughter spilling out of the casinos.

A sense of dread settles in the pit of my stomach as I navigate the busy streets. It's a stark contrast to the easy, relaxed way I felt at Frankie's ranch.

Pulling into the car park of the Quantum, the feeling of unease only grows. The hotel looms above me, its shimmering facade and flashing lights a garish reminder of where I am and what I'm supposed to be doing.

I take a deep breath, trying to steady myself as I make my way inside. The casino floor is already bustling with activity, the ringing of slot machines, the music, and the shouts of excited players so loud it makes me wince. I weave my way through the crowd, my eyes fixed on the elevator that will take me up to the salon.

As the doors slide shut behind me, I lean against the

wall and close my eyes for a brief moment. The silence is a welcome respite, but it's short-lived. As soon as I step out onto the top floor, I'm greeted by the sound of raised voices.

"Dakota, thank goodness you're here!" Serenity rushes over to me, her face etched with worry. "Mrs. O'Hare is here, and she's throwing a fit because we don't have anyone available to give her a signature massage right at this moment."

I feel a flare of irritation at the mention of the demanding client who's caused me grief before, but I force myself to take a calming breath. "Okay," I say. "Let me talk to her."

I make my way over to where Mrs. O'Hare is sitting, her arms crossed and her face pinched with displeasure. "Mrs. O'Hare," I greet her, my smile strained but polite. "I apologize for the inconvenience. I was unexpectedly delayed by the storm, but I assure you we'll do everything we can to accommodate your needs today."

The woman sniffs, her gaze raking over me with disdain. "I certainly hope so," she says coldly. "I have a very important event to attend tonight, and my back is stuck. They told me there's no masseuse available. That's just absurd."

I nod, my jaw clenching with the effort to keep my expression neutral. "Don't worry, I'll tend to you personally," I say, gesturing for her to follow me. "Right this way, please."

I know I vowed not to do this, but today, it feels easier to give in than to argue with her. I wonder if that's how it started with Andy, if he figured that putting in the overtime and stretching his role was less stressful than dealing with complaints and negativity.

As I lead Mrs. O'Hare back to the treatment room, I catch sight of my reflection in the mirror. My hair is windblown, and my cheeks are flushed, a far cry from the polished, put-together image I usually present at work.

"Right, well, let's get started, shall we?" I say, trying to inject some cheer into my voice while I put on a white lab coat. I gesture to the massage table. "If you could just disrobe and lie face down, Mrs. O'Hare."

The older woman sniffs, eyeing the table with distaste. "Are you sure this is clean? It looks a bit...used."

I grit my teeth, counting to five in my head as I stare down at the immaculate massage table. The cover is crisp and clean, without so much as a tiny crease. "I assure you, Mrs. O'Hare, we adhere to the highest standards of hygiene here at the White Spa. The tables are thoroughly sanitized between each client."

"Hmm. Well, all right then." Mrs. O'Hare begins to undress, and I busy myself with setting up the room. I should have done this before I led her in, but I'm a little out of practice when it comes to hands-on treatments. I dim the lights, cue up some soothing music, and then turn to the shelves where the massage oils are kept. Except...I can't quite remember which one to use. I'm so used to my staff handling these details that I'm drawing a blank.

Aware of my impatient client, I quickly grab a bottle of essential oil at random. *Sandalwood. That will do.*

Turning back to the table where she is now lying, I drape a towel over her midsection. I pump some of the oil into my palms, rubbing them together to warm it before placing my hands on the woman's shoulders.

"Oh!" Mrs. O'Hare flinches at the contact. "What are you doing? Your hands are freezing!"

"Sorry about that," I mumble, rolling my eyes. My hands are perfectly warm, and I suspect she'll be doing this throughout the treatment. "They'll warm up quickly, don't worry."

I begin to work the oil into her skin, using long,

sweeping strokes to distribute it evenly. The scent of sandal-wood is rich and woody, and I breathe deeply, trying to let the aroma soothe my own frayed nerves.

"You know, when I was last here, my masseuse used a different oil," Mrs. O'Hare comments, her voice muffled against the face cradle. "It smelled like...like a summer garden. This just smells like my grandmother."

I bite back a sharp retort. The customer's always right, even when they're driving you up the wall. "My apologies, Mrs. O'Hare. We have a variety of oils, each with their own unique benefits. Sandalwood is known for its grounding properties, for promoting inner peace. I thought it might be just the thing to help you relax before your big event tonight."

It's a load of nonsense—I have no clue about the specific effects of sandalwood, but she seems content with the explanation.

"Hmm. Inner peace, you say? I suppose I could do with a dose of that."

I hum in agreement, focusing on kneading the knots from the woman's shoulders and upper back. I can feel the tension there, the tightness that comes from—in her case, as I doubt she has a desk job—holding on to too much anger.

My hands move on autopilot, following the patterns and techniques I learned a lifetime ago. It's muscle memory, my body remembering the motions even as my mind drifts.

Mrs. O'Hare, thankfully, keeps quiet, except for the occa-sional grunt or sigh as I work out a particularly stubborn knot. In my head, I run through my usual patter, the little speeches about pressure and problem areas that I used to give to all my clients.

"How's the pressure, Mrs. O'Hare?" I ask. "Is there any

area you'd like me to focus on? I feel a lot of tension in your lower back."

"Yes, that's right. My lower back," the woman responds after a moment. "It's been giving me grief for weeks but this morning it got unbearable. And you can go a bit harder—I'm not made of glass."

"Certainly." I move my hands lower, digging my thumbs into the small of Mrs. O'Hare's back. The woman lets out a low groan, and I take it as a sign to increase the pressure, leaning my weight into it.

By the time I'm finished with her, I feel like I need a massage myself, and the next few hours pass in a whirlwind of activity. I catch up on emails, juggle rotas, order oils, and sit through a long meeting with our accountant, all while keeping a smile on my face.

Frankie is on my mind and it's incredibly distracting. Every time I think of her strong arms holding me, her naked body draped over mine, I can barely hold it together. The thought of her does something intensely physical to me. My body still tingles from the sensation of the riding crop, and I'm sore in all the right places. I always needed to be in control, to have my hands on the reins. But when she tied me up, something inside me shifted. All I had to do was feel. And God, did I feel. Every touch, every stroke, every command—it was like my senses were on fire. I felt alive in a way I haven't in a long time.

Frankie was right. It does feel good to give away control, to put my power into someone else's hands. I never thought I'd enjoy it so much. The thought puzzles me, even now. Why have I never considered that before?

"Dakota, can I talk to you for a second?" Serenity's voice startles me as I'm sitting behind my desk, and I look up to see her hovering in the doorway of my office.

"Of course," I say, gesturing for her to come in. "What's up?"

She hesitates, shifting her weight from foot to foot. "It's just...you seem a little off today. Is everything okay? Did something happen while you were gone?"

I feel a flicker of panic at her words, a fear that she can see right through me, that she knows how much I'm struggling to keep it together.

"Everything's fine," I assure her, my voice light and breezy. "I'm just a little tired, that's all. It was a long couple of days." That's a lie. Physically, I feel more rested than I have in weeks, but I'm unable to come up with a different excuse.

Serenity nods, but I can see the skepticism in her eyes. "If you say so. But if you ever need to talk, you know I'm here for you, right?"

"I know," I say, keeping my smile stretched. "Thank you, that's very sweet."

When the door clicks shut behind her, I slump back in my chair, feeling the weight of the day pressing down on me. All I want is to crawl into bed and hide under the covers, but I can't do that. I have a business to run, clients to please, a reputation to uphold.

My gaze falls on the framed photo on my desk. It's a picture of me and my parents at my graduation, their faces beaming with pride as they pose on either side of me. I remember how it felt in that moment, the sense of accomplishment and excitement for the future, and I so badly want to feel that way again. And so I square my shoulders and tell myself to get a grip. *I can do this. I have to do this.*

28

FRANKIE

*T*he bell above the entrance tinkles, announcing my arrival as I push open the door to the diner. The place is nearly empty, just a few old-timers nursing cups of coffee at the counter and a couple of truckers hunched over plates of meat loaf in the corner booth.

I've been coming here for as long as I can remember, ever since I was a little girl riding shotgun in my daddy's pickup truck. Back then, the Starlight was a regular stop on our way to and from the cattle auctions. Now, it's a place of comfort, somewhere to come when I need a break from the ranch.

The diner itself is a study in classic Americana, all shiny chrome and neon lights. The exterior is a little weathered, the paint chipped and faded from years of exposure to the harsh desert sun. But inside, it's like stepping back in time, with its black-and-white checkered floor and red vinyl booths. Nothing ever changes here.

Rennie is sitting in our usual spot by the window, sipping her coffee, a shock of red hair and a wry, knowing smile.

"Well, well, well," she says. "Looks like we both survived the storm. Horses okay?"

"Yeah, everything's fine," I mutter, grabbing a menu from behind the napkin dispenser. "Texas was getting a bit restless after being in the stables for a few days, so I rode him here."

"That's so very cowgirl of you." Rennie glances at Texas, who's tied to a pole in the shade of the diner, resting from our ride.

I laugh. "He certainly enjoyed it. I could barely hang on the way he was galloping. So, how's everything on your end?"

"Also fine," Rennie says. "The house is still standing, and Leslie is happy because now she has an excuse to drive around and check on everyone."

I chuckle. "Any gossip?"

"Of course." Rennie snorts, leaning back in the booth and crossing her arms. "You know how she is—always getting involved. The Walters' cat was missing after the storm but apparently, he's returned now. The Lockers' farm got flooded pretty bad, so she helped them clear the debris." She narrows her eyes and leans in. "But Leslie wouldn't be Leslie if she didn't return with something a bit juicier than that, right?"

I grin. "Do tell!"

"Well, keep this to yourself, but she found out that old Mr. Turner has been growing plants in his basement." Rennie lowers her voice to a whisper. "Special plants, if you know what I mean."

"No way! The same Mr. Turner who has been campaigning against drugs for years?"

"The very same," Rennie says, her eyes twinkling with amusement. "He didn't have his hearing aid in, so he didn't hear Leslie coming. When she turned up, she found him surrounded by dozens of plants, rescued from his flooded basement. They were all out there, drying in the sun. She said she could smell them all the way from the driveway."

We both burst out laughing and I shake my head. "And then what? They exchanged gardening tips?"

"No, he begged her not to tell anyone. He said it was only for personal consumption, but she thinks there must have been sixty plants at least."

"So good old churchgoer Mr. Turner is running a shady business from his basement, huh?"

"It sure looks that way. Anyway, I'm glad things are getting back to normal. Life is so boring without TV or internet. There's only so many games of Scrabble I can take, and Leslie always wins." She takes a sip of her coffee. "At least we had each other, even though we've been driving each other crazy these past days. It must have been lonely out there for you. I was worried."

"I wasn't alone," I say, feeling a grin spread across my face. "Jose was there to help before the storm and..." I pause. "And Dakota showed up, just before it hit." Ducking my head, I'm suddenly fascinated by the list of daily specials. "So she was stuck with me."

"What?" Rennie gasps. "Miss Vegas?"

"Yeah."

"I bet you didn't play Scrabble," she says teasingly.

"No, there was no Scrabble involved." I'm aware of my goofy smile, but I can't help myself. "And then my parents showed up unannounced this morning. They were worried because I ignored my phone last night."

"Because you were busy with Miss Vegas," Rennie concludes. "And she was still there?" She laughs when I nod. "How was that?"

"Awkward," I admit. "Dakota had to go to work, though, so she didn't stick around. I told Mom and Dad she was a friend, but they didn't buy it. You know, it's strange. I haven't felt this way about someone in a long time. It's both exciting and terrifying." I take a deep breath, then meet Rennie's eyes. "I'd like you and Leslie to meet her sometime."

Rennie's eyes light up as she leans in. "Really? It's been years since you said anything like that. Is it serious?"

"I honestly don't know. I'm not sure if she'll even stay in Vegas, so I'm not getting too carried away. She's not a fan of Vegas, and I don't think she's built for desert life either."

"Well, then it's good to be cautious."

"Yeah." I've had similar thoughts myself because I don't know if I'm strong enough to watch Dakota walk away. I'm already halfway in love with her even though it's all so new.

"But we'd love to meet her," Rennie quickly adds, shifting in her seat. "I don't have anything fancy to wear, though, and I can't rock up in this..." She gestures to her ripped jeans and old college T-shirt.

"Of course you can. I don't get changed for her."

Rennie points a finger at me. "You dress like that around her?"

I shrug. "It's who I am. She's never seen me any other way."

"And she's still into you?" Rennie throws her head back and laughs. "She must really like you."

"Hey, I look fine!" I exclaim. "And she happens to like my faded jeans and cowboy hats." A flash of arousal shoots between my thighs, remembering last night, but before my mind can drift any farther, Mabel, one of the waitresses who has worked here for as long as I can remember, interrupts us.

"Sorry, honey. I got stuck with that trucker over there. He kept complaining about the coffee, said it was too strong."

"There's nothing wrong with your coffee, Mabel." I shoot her a wink. "It's delicious, just like your cake. Did you make any today?"

"I sure did." She smiles. The real draw of the Starlight, aside from the coffee, is their famous cactus cake, made by Mabel. It's a local specialty, a moist, spicy cake made with pureed prickly pear cactus and topped with a tangy lime frosting, only served when Mabel is working. It's the kind of thing that sounds strange at first, but one bite and you're hooked. "What can I get you?" she asks. "The usual?"

"Please."

"Okay, one black coffee and a slice of cake coming up." Mabel wobbles off. She's in her early seventies, and even though they've hired a few new waitresses, she still insists on working at least four shifts a week. She pauses by the trucker's table to give him a pointed look. "Darlin', they all say my coffee is fine, so if you can't handle it, maybe you should stick to warm milk." She gives him a wink and continues on her way, leaving the trucker with an embarrassed grin.

"She's such a charmer," Rennie says with a chuckle. "So, will you be bringing your new flame here for a date?"

I laugh. "Absolutely. Nothing says 'welcome to my world' like the Starlight Diner's charm and a side of Mabel's sass."

29

DAKOTA

I'm perched at a table on the terrace of El Rincon, nursing a margarita as I wait for Serenity. The restaurant is alive with the chatter of families gathered around tables, savoring Gabriel's famous street tacos.

I glance at my watch just as Serenity hops out of a taxi, waving as she approaches. I invited her here because I need to talk—really talk—about everything that's been weighing on my mind.

"Hey!" she calls out, giving me a quick hug before settling into her seat. "Thanks for the invite." Her eyes dart around, taking in the casual atmosphere with a mix of curiosity and slight confusion. In her polished outfit, she's a stark contrast to the homey feel of the restaurant.

Her heels click on the tiles as she shifts in her chair. "I just finished work. I got changed there and came straight here."

"Busy day?" I ask. "Any drama?"

"Always." Serenity chuckles. "But everything is sorted, so don't worry about it."

"We can move inside," I suggest. "If it's too warm for you out here."

"No..." Serenity hesitates as she takes in the restaurant once more and frowns. "No. It's nice. I never sit outside. I'm either at work, at home, or in a dark bar or nightclub. I could do with a bit of daylight, but I feel totally overdressed."

"Don't worry about it, you look great." I'm aware we make an odd pair—me dressed in leggings, sneakers, and a T-shirt, my hair pulled back into a messy topknot, and Serenity in a cocktail dress, heels, and full makeup. I should have probably mentioned El Rincon was low-key, but it didn't cross my mind.

"So, who recommended this restaurant?" she asks.

"I actually live up there," I say, gesturing to the balcony above us. "I come here at least twice a week. They have amazing tacos."

Serenity seems surprised to hear this. "You live here?"

"Yeah. I told you I lived in the Art District."

"You did, but I guess I thought it would be more..." She bites her lip and stops herself. "Sorry, it's very charming. I just meant—"

"Yeah, it's not exactly the Quantum, is it?" I interrupt her, sparing her from more embarrassment. "But I like it here. It's a nice escape from the Strip and I'm not into high-rises."

Just then, Gabriel arrives by car with a crateful of limes. His face lights up when he sees me, and he hurries over. "Dakota, mi amiga!" he says, setting down the crate to give me a hug.

I pat his shoulder and kiss his cheek before I step back. "Hey, Gabriel. It's good to see you. Have you been out shopping?"

"Yes, it's been busy. We were out of limes already, so I've

stocked up for tonight." Gabriel turns to Serenity. "And who is this lovely lady?"

"This is Serenity. She works with me at the Quantum."

Gabriel extends his hand. "Bienvenida, Serenity. I see you don't have a drink yet. How about I make you a delicious margarita?"

"You've got to try one, they're excellent," I assure her, then finish my own drink. "And I'll have another one too, please."

"He seems nice," Serenity says when he disappears inside. "And it's so interesting to meet you away from the team and work. It's not what I expected. But in a good way," she quickly adds.

"Oh yeah? So what does your life look like?"

"Truthfully, pretty simple," Serenity admits. "I live in a small one-bedroom apartment in a nice, serviced building, but the rent is extortionate and the Vegas nightlife is expensive, so I always struggle at the end of the month. When I have days off, I tend to spend them by the pool at the Quantum, and when I go out, it's usually with people from work, so my private life and work life are pretty intertwined." She smiles. "I don't mind, though. My plan is to work my way up and be where you are one day, so I'm all in."

"You're very good at what you do," I say, returning her smile. "You're great with people."

"Thank you." Serenity tilts her head and regards me. "Can I ask you a personal question?"

"Sure."

"Are you happy in your new role?"

Meeting her eyes, I hesitate for a beat, then shrug. I know I'm probably crossing a line here. As the general manager, I should be confident and in charge. But Serenity is the one person I feel closest to at work, and I need to talk to someone who will understand. Still, I'm not supposed to show vulnerability, especially not to my team. "I'm struggling a little," I admit. "It's not the calm spa environment I'm used to, and maybe I was naïve to assume it would be similar to my previous hub in Newport Beach."

"Same company, different city. Makes all the difference," Serenity says. "I'm so sorry you feel that way. Are you disappointed? Do you regret taking the job?"

"I don't think I'm cut out for it," I say. "The managerial part is not the issue. It's the customers I have trouble dealing with." I shake my head. "I'm sorry. I shouldn't be telling you this."

"No..." Serenity reaches over the table and takes my hand. "I'm glad you told me, and needless to say, this stays between us."

Gabriel returns with our margaritas and places them on the table with a flourish. "For the lovely ladies. Enjoy!"

"Gracias, Gabe," I say. "And could we have a plate of mixed tacos please?" I turn to Serenity. "Are you hungry?"

"Sure, I could eat." She sips her drink and moans. "Mmm...you weren't lying about the margaritas. Delicious."

"Right? There's something about drinking a margarita in the sun that just makes sense."

"So true." Serenity raises her glass and takes another sip. "So what did you love about your old job?"

"My customers," I say, and we both burst out laughing. "Seriously, I like helping people, making them feel good. I've always loved working with people."

"Until now," Serenity jokes with a wry smile. "Yeah, okay. I get it now." She rolls her eyes. "The Quantum attracts a certain type and that's not going to change. For what it's worth, though, I think you're doing an incredible job. But if it's making you unhappy, maybe it's time to rethink things."

"Maybe. How do you cope with the difficult customers?" I ask, pleasantly surprised at how easy it is to talk to Serenity. She's so open and relaxed, now that it's just the two of us.

"Two things," she says, lifting a finger. "Firstly, I visualize a clear, protective barrier between myself and the customer. This barrier represents my emotional boundaries. It allows me to see and hear the customer but shields me from absorbing their negative emotions."

"And that works for you?"

"It took some practice, but yes, it works, and I'm able to emotionally distance myself." Serenity holds up two fingers now. "Secondly, I picture the customer as a character in a story or a movie, not as a real person. I imagine them as a frustrated cartoon character who is temporarily out of sorts. It takes the human aspect out of it." She shrugs when I burst out laughing.

"But you're always so composed," I say. "I would never imagine all this goes on in your head while you stand there talking to them."

"Well, it's true and I swear, it works for me. I even give them nicknames and imagine myself calling them by those names."

"Oh yeah? Like what?"

Serenity hesitates. "I'm not sure I should tell you since you're my boss," she says humorously. "But if you insist...let's start with Mrs. Rosenberg. I call her Mrs. Quack-Quack, and I imagine her as a duck because she has this annoying loud, nasal voice and that beak of hers never stops opening and closing. She kind of walks like a duck too, don't you think? With a slight wobble..."

Serenity's revelation about Mrs. Rosenberg's nickname makes me laugh harder than I have in days. I had no idea she was so funny. "I can totally see that! You're right, she does have that walk."

"Exactly. Feed her some crumbs and she'll calm down a little." Serenity giggles along with me. "And then there's another regular, Mrs. Davenport. Her first name is Vicky, and I've nicknamed her Veiny Vicky."

"Because of that throbbing vein on her temple?"

"Yeah. It grows when she gets angry." Serenity is on a roll now, clearly enjoying sharing her absurd fantasies with me. "And little puffs of steam come out to show her rising blood pressure," she continues. "When Vicky calms down, her vein shrinks back, deflating like a used party balloon."

I'm still laughing and need a moment to compose myself. "I'll never be able to see them in any other way now," I say with a snort. "Do you do the same with the non-regulars?"

"If they're nasty, sure. And if it helps, I'll share them with you next time.

We fall into easy conversation, discussing the latest events at the Quantum, the clients who've made an impression, and the ever-changing dynamics of our team. It feels good to unwind, to let the conversation flow without the constraints of our professional roles.

Our tacos arrive, and as we eat, Serenity tells me about her girlfriend. In turn, I find myself opening up about Frankie. It feels natural, like I'm talking to an old friend rather than a coworker.

I realize how much I needed this—not just a break from work, but a genuine connection with someone who understands the unique challenges of our job.

"Thanks for coming today," I say. "I really appreciate it."

Serenity's eyes light up, and she reaches across the table to give my hand a squeeze. "Are you kidding? This has been great for me too," she says with a chuckle. "I never get to vent like this. You know what? We should make this a regular thing."

I find myself nodding enthusiastically. "I'd love that. Gossip Wednesdays?"

"Gossip Wednesdays it is," she agrees, raising her glass in a toast. "To new friendships and surviving the Quantum together."

30

FRANKIE

*T*he bonfire crackles and pops, sending sparks dancing into the night sky. I lean back in my chair, nursing a cold beer and enjoying a quiet moment of respite after a long day of riding lessons, tours, and tending to the horses.

My guests are gathered around the fire, happily discussing their adventures. I've spent the past few days getting to know them, learning their names and stories. They're a diverse group, ranging from a young couple on their honeymoon to a retired businessman looking for a bit of adventure. They all have one thing in common: they want to become comfortable around horses and learn how to ride.

It's not the first time we've organized a four-day mixed retreat like this, but the concept is fairly new, and Jose and I are still learning as we go along. Our guests are thoroughly enjoying themselves, though, and that's the most important thing.

"Living out here must be amazing. It's like something out of a movie," Hank, the retired businessman, says. "I'm envious of your life. The freedom you have here, the connection to nature. It's something most people only dream about."

I nod. "Yes, it's wonderful, and I feel very lucky. But don't underestimate the amount of work that goes into mucking out stables and tending to the horses, not to mention cleaning that damn grill every night," I joke, pointing at the outdoor cooking station. "It's non-stop."

"Well, the food was delicious," Hank says, patting his belly. "You're good with the grill."

"Thank you," I say with a chuckle. "We try to keep it as simple as possible since we're a small team. Our local diner delivers the salads and side dishes, and the communal drinks fridge makes it easier too. Our cleaners who take care of the rooms make breakfast in the mornings and also prepares the lunch packs. It's far from five-star service, but it works."

"Who needs five-star service on a ranch? This," Tom, one of the honeymooners, says, opening the fridge to help himself to another cold beer, "this is all part of the charm." He heads back to his spot on a log and puts his arm around his wife, Sarah.

"Tom and I have been talking about how we came here to learn to ride, but we've gotten so much more out of it. The peace and quiet, the beauty of the landscape...it's incredible," she says.

Tom nods in agreement. "It's been a real escape for us. We're from the city, so this is like another world. We're already planning our next trip back here."

Their words warm my heart. "I'm glad to hear that. That's exactly what we hope for—to give people a chance to disconnect and experience something entirely different." I pause and inhale deeply as I gaze over the landscape. "By the way, you might be in for a surprise tomorrow morning. As you probably know, we had a storm here last weekend. I noticed dormant seeds have just started to sprout, so the surroundings will suddenly look a lot greener."

"Oh, I've heard about that," Hank says. "That was lucky timing. It's—" He stops himself and laughs when Dobby comes up behind him and prods his back. "Oh, hello there. Aren't you a friendly one?"

As always, Marty, Dobby's shadow, joins him, and now they're standing there, staring at Hank, who is in stitches of laughter. "Guys, you're cute, but what do you want from me?"

"You're the one sitting closest to the treat box," I say, pointing at the big, metal tin on the buffet table behind him. I tend to let them out of the pasture when we've finished eating, as they love the attention they get from the guests. "Feel free to give them some," I continue, amused when they both start prodding him.

Hank chuckles as he reaches for the treat box. "All right, you two. Let's see what we've got here." He opens the tin, revealing an assortment of small, dehydrated pieces of carrot and apple.

Marty and Dobby's ears perk up at the sight, their eyes following Hank's every move. He pulls out a piece of carrot, holding it flat on his palm. Dobby, ever the gentleman, gently takes it with his lips, crunching happily.

"Well, aren't you polite?" Hank says, patting Dobby's neck.

Marty, not wanting to be left out, nudges Hank's arm impatiently. "Okay, okay," Hank laughs, grabbing an apple slice. "Here you go, little fella."

Marty practically inhales the treat, then prods the tin for more. The other guests laugh at his eagerness.

"They're like furry vacuum cleaners," Sarah comments, reaching for a carrot herself.

As the conversation flows and my guests fuss over Marty and Dobby, Olivia, a single woman in her forties, gets up and walks over to me. She's made her interest in me abundantly clear from the moment she arrived, and I've been struggling to find a way to deal with her. She's attractive, with long, dark hair and an hourglass figure. She's also confident and flirtatious, with a boldness that borders on aggressive.

All day, I've tried to keep my distance, to maintain professional boundaries. But tonight, it seems, Olivia has other plans. She settles into the chair next to mine, crossing her long legs and leaning in close.

"So, Frankie," she purrs, her voice low and sultry. "Tell me. Is there a Mr. or Mrs. Ranch Owner waiting for you back at the house?"

I nearly choke on my beer, caught off guard. I set the bottle down and wipe my mouth with the back of my hand, trying to buy myself a moment to compose my thoughts.

"Uh, no," I say, my voice a little rough. "No, there's no one waiting for me, but I'm kind of seeing someone."

"Kind of?" Her eyes glint with flirtation. "That doesn't sound very serious."

I shrug, feeling a flush creep up my neck. "Well, I like her very much."

"Her?" She nods, taking a sip of her wine. "Hmm...I had a feeling you swung that way." Her hand finds my knee and she squeezes it. "I have a thing for cowgirls."

I gently but firmly remove Olivia's hand from my knee. "I'm flattered," I say, "but I'm not looking for anything." It would be so easy to give in to her advances. A few months ago, I would've jumped at the opportunity to have a beautiful stranger in my bed, but I'm not even vaguely tempted. Not anymore.

Olivia's face falls, a flash of disappointment crossing her features. But she recovers quickly, her smile turning a little brittle at the edges. "Of course," she says. "I understand. I didn't mean to overstep." She sighs, draining the last of her wine and setting the glass down on the table. "Well, I guess I'll just have to keep myself entertained tonight."

I chuckle and shake my head. "I'm sure you're not short of attention."

"Tell that to the men and women in New York City." Olivia rolls her eyes. "It's easier to find a unicorn than a decent partner."

"That bad, huh?"

"Yeah. The moment I hit forty, the likes and messages on my dating apps plummeted. Age is like a disease there." She sighs. "Don't get me wrong. I did come here for the horses, but when I saw you, I won't deny I felt a little excited. You're a catch, and whoever she is, she's one lucky lady."

"Thank you." I smile and manage to relax a little. I haven't offended her, and I doubt there will be any awkwardness tomorrow. "You'll meet someone when you least expect it."

"Yeah, we'll see about that," Olivia mutters. "Is that what happened to you? Did she fall into your lap?"

I pause, thinking of Dakota and how she quite literally stumbled into my life. "Something like that," I say softly.

I look up at the stars, feeling a warmth in my chest. Dakota has changed everything for me. The nights feel less lonely and the days more vibrant, even when she's not here. It's strange how a chance encounter in the desert could lead to such a profound shift in my world, but here I am, falling head over heels. "I certainly didn't expect it."

31

DAKOTA

*A*s I drive down the familiar dirt road leading to Frankie's ranch, my heart races with a mixture of excitement and nervousness. The night sky stretches above me, an endless expanse of stars twinkling against the inky blackness.

I didn't call ahead to let Frankie know I was coming, and now, as I approach the ranch, I start to second-guess my decision. *What if she's busy? What if she has guests?*

As I round the final bend, the ranch comes into view, and I sigh. The premises are lit up like a beacon, warm light spilling from a bonfire. People are gathered around it, their laughter and chatter carrying on the night air. *Okay, so it is a bad time.*

I park my car and sit for a moment, considering whether to leave, when I spot Frankie. She's sitting by the bonfire, a bottle of beer in her hand and a smile on her face. She's wearing a fitted plaid shirt, worn jeans, and her cowboy hat, looking incredibly attractive.

But it's not just her appearance that makes my pulse race. It's the way she carries herself, the easy confidence in her posture and the huge smile on her face. She's magnetic in every sense. It's only been a few days, but I've missed her.

Then my eyes are drawn to the woman next to her. She's beautiful, with long, dark hair that falls in waves down her back. She leans in close to Frankie, her hand resting on her arm as she talks.

A sudden, sharp pang of jealousy twists in my gut. Who is this woman, and why is she touching Frankie like that?

I watch as Frankie laughs at something the woman says, her head thrown back and her eyes crinkling at the corners. I can't take it anymore. I put the car in reverse, ready to drive back to the city, but as I'm about to pull away, Frankie looks up and catches sight of my car. Her eyes widen, and a grin splits her face. She says something to the woman and then jogs over to me.

"Dakota!" she exclaims as I roll down the window. "What a lovely surprise."

I feel a flush creep up my neck, suddenly unsure of what to say. "I'm sorry," I mumble, my eyes downcast. "I shouldn't have come. I can see you're busy."

Frankie frowns, her brow furrowing in concern. "What? No, I'm not busy. I mean, I have some guests staying at the ranch, but I'm just having a drink with them. Come and join us." She reaches through the window and takes my hand, her skin warm against mine. "Please, stay. I've missed you. You're all I've been able to think about since you left."

"Really?"

"Really," she says, her thumb stroking my hand. "Now, come on. Let's get you a drink. Everyone is really friendly."

Frankie steps back as I open the door, then pulls me in and kisses me softly. Her lips linger on mine for long moments before she reluctantly pulls away. "I should probably behave in front of my guests. Can you wait twenty minutes? I need to take Dobby and Marty back to the pasture before I can go inside."

"No, don't cut your night short for me. Just enjoy yourself. I'll join you for a drink." I can feel the heat of her skin even through the fabric of her shirt, and it does crazy things to my body.

As she takes my hand and leads me toward the seating area in front of the guesthouse, the woman from before looks up, her eyes narrowing as she takes in our linked hands. Frankie smiles and nods in greeting, her grip on my hand tightening.

"Everyone, this is Dakota," she says, her voice ringing out clear and strong. "She's..." Frankie pauses and blushes as she turns to me. "She's with me," she finally settles on before kissing my cheek.

I feel giddy at the way she so clumsily introduces me to the group. I'm not a friend, I'm "with her," and it feels like a declaration.

The dark-haired woman's eyes flick between us, a slight frown marring her perfect features, but Frankie doesn't seem to notice, or if she does, she doesn't care. She gestures to her old spot on the log bench. "What can I get you?" she asks, her breath tickling my ear as she leans over me.

"I'll have a beer," I say, looking up at her with a sheepish grin. I'm so fixated on her that I have to remind myself I'm in company, and I turn to the woman next to me, who introduces herself as Olivia. "Lovely to meet you," I say. "Are you having a nice time?"

"Yeah, it's been great." She looks me over. "I love the horses, and Frankie's certainly the charmer."

"Oh?" I stare at her, and there it is again, another pang of jealousy. She's even more beautiful up close.

"Here you go." Frankie looks from me to Olivia and back

as she hands me a beer. "I'm just going to put Marty and Dobby back. They've already eaten their bodyweight in treats and they're still begging for more."

"I'll help you," I say, jumping at the opportunity to show Olivia I know my way around here. "I've missed those little rascals." It's territorial and a little pathetic, but Frankie is mine. At least, that's how it feels.

"Are you staying the night?" she asks, handing me Marty's reins.

"If that's okay with you." I follow her and Dobby to the pasture, and we linger by the gates to stroke them. "You must be tired after a full day with guests..."

"I'm never too tired for you." Frankie cups my cheek and bites her lip as she glances down at my mouth. I love the way she looks at me, like she can't wait to rip my clothes off. "Mmm..." she murmurs.

"What?"

"You look so tasty I want to eat you."

"Tastier than Olivia?" The question has slipped from my lips before I've thought it through, and I immediately regret the petty comment. "I'm sorry, that was..."

Frankie's brows shoot up and she chuckles. "Are you jealous, babe?" She inches closer and wraps her arms around my waist.

I shake my head and roll my eyes. "I'm sorry," I say again. "That was stupid. I thought you two were flirting, but we're not together, and—"

"Hey, it's not stupid." Brushing her lips against mine, she smiles. "I have no interest in anyone but you, and I can assure you, I was not flirting back." She tilts her head and regards me. "So we're not together, huh? Is that what this is? Because you seem to enjoy being together as much as I do and honestly, I'd be jealous too if I thought you were flirting with another woman."

"You would?"

"Hell, yes," Frankie says matter-of-factly. "And I think we should talk about it." She brings her hand to my behind and squeezes it. "But first, Miss Vegas...I may have to punish you for accusing me of flirting."

I feel a flush of arousal at her words and squeeze my thighs together. "Hmm. I might have to be jealous more often."

We're still in her guests' line of sight, but throwing caution to the wind, Frankie pulls me in even closer, and I reach up, tangling my fingers in her hair. She responds instantly, her mouth hot and hungry against mine.

"Let's take this inside," she murmurs, wrapping an arm around my shoulders. As Frankie waves good night to her guests and yells something about breakfast at eight, the warm glow of the bonfire fades behind us, replaced by the promise of a different kind of heat.

32

FRANKIE

*T*he first light of dawn filters through the curtains, casting a soft, golden glow over the room. I blink awake, my body attuned to the rhythms of the ranch even on mornings like this, when I have every reason to linger in bed.

Maria is making breakfast, I remind myself. She'll take care of things, and I don't need to face my guests until ten, when we're setting off for a two-hour horseback tour. It's the last activity of their stay; tonight, I'll have the ranch to myself again.

Beside me, Dakota stirs, her hair fanned out across the pillow.

Last night, I wanted to make her scream. Now, I just want to hold her in my arms and never let go. It's a strange juxtaposition.

I prop myself up on one elbow, content to simply watch her for a moment, but as if sensing my gaze, her eyes flutter open, blinking slowly.

"Morning," I murmur, my voice husky with sleep.

She smiles, stretching languidly beneath the sheets.

"Morning," she whispers back, her hand finding mine and twining our fingers together.

We lie there for a long moment, savoring the peace of the early hour, and I feel a stirring of excitement in my chest, a desire to share something special with her. I know there's a beautiful surprise waiting for us outside; I've been through enough storms to predict the aftermath with practiced precision, good and bad.

"Hey," I say softly, squeezing her hand. "Can I show you something before everyone wakes up?"

Dakota's brow furrows in curiosity, and she nods. "Of course. What is it?"

I smile, rolling out of bed and putting on my robe. "You'll see. Trust me, it's worth getting up for."

Her sleepy face is adorable as she gets up and puts on one of my T-shirts. I love it when she borrows my clothes; it makes me feel like she's mine.

We pad out to the kitchen, where I brew a pot of strong, dark coffee, and I add a splash of milk to Dakota's just the way she likes it. She takes it from me with a grateful smile, her fingers brushing against mine and sending sparks racing up my arm. She's got me and she doesn't even know it.

"Come on," I say, nodding toward the front door. "Let's go out on the porch."

We step outside, and as I turn to gauge Dakota's reaction, I see her eyes widen, her mouth falling open in a soft gasp.

The desert, which just a week ago was a barren expanse of sand and rock, has been transformed. The rainfall has coaxed forth a riot of color and life, painting the landscape in shades of green and gold and purple.

Fields of wildflowers stretch out as far as the eye can see, their delicate petals dancing in the breeze. Desert marigolds, with their sunny yellow blooms, carpet the ground in a sea of buttery softness. Beside them, the deep purple of desert sand verbena adds a rich, velvety contrast.

The usually stark and spiny cacti are adorned with crowns of brilliant flowers, their waxy petals shimmering in shades of pink and red and orange. The ocotillo, which just days ago looked like little more than a bundle of dry, thorny sticks, is now covered in delicate leaves and tipped with flaming red blossoms. I knew this would happen, but I've rarely seen the landscape come to life to this extent.

Even the air feels different. It's like the desert has awoken from a long, deep sleep, stretching and yawning and bursting forth with new life.

Dakota turns to me, her eyes shining with wonder. "How...?" she whispers, her voice filled with awe. "This is... it's incredible. I've never seen anything like it."

I smile, wrapping my arm around her waist. "It's the desert bloom," I murmur, pressing a soft kiss to her temple. "It happens every time after heavy rainfall. The seeds that have been lying dormant in the dry earth, waiting for the right conditions...they finally have a chance to sprout and grow."

She leans into me. "It's incredible. To think that it was here all along, just waiting for the right moment." Her eyes linger on mine, and I have a feeling she's not just talking about the landscape.

"That's the thing about the desert," I say softly, my eyes fixed on the horizon. "It's a harsh environment, a place of extremes. But there's a resilience to it, a strength that comes from adaptation and perseverance. You're lucky to be here. It comes fast but it never lasts long. I'd give it a few days at most before the drought drains the life out of the landscape again."

"It's still breathtaking, even without the bloom," she says dreamily. "It was the very reason you found me stranded the first time we met. I kept driving because it was so beautiful."

"And then your truck broke down," I joke. "Henry."

"Yeah, Henry." Dakota takes a deep breath and exhales slowly. "I didn't think I'd miss that old rust bucket so much. I've been missing my father too, lately. I wish he could have met you and—" She suddenly stops herself. "I mean, he would have loved to see your ranch, being a farmer himself."

"I would love to have met him too," I say.

We stand on the porch for a while, watching the desert come alive with the morning light. I noticed the slight tension in Dakota's body when she mentioned her father.

As we settle into the porch chairs with our coffees, I decide to broach the subject that's been on my mind since last night. We joked about Olivia and made light of the situation, but it was clearly a sore subject for Dakota.

"Dakota," I begin, my voice soft but serious. "We should talk." She looks at me, her blue eyes a little apprehensive, and I continue when she nods. "Last night, when you mentioned Olivia... I want you to know that you have absolutely nothing to worry about. I only want you and I hope you know that."

Dakota's cheeks flush slightly, and she looks down at her coffee. "I'm sorry about yesterday," she murmurs. "I don't know what came over me. It's not like we're—"

"Exclusive?" I interrupt gently.

"Yeah. I don't want to claim you in any way if I don't even know I'll stay in Vegas."

"You can claim me," I say. "Even if it's temporary. If the time comes that you'll leave, I'll take it from there and deal with it. I'll be fine, I promise."

"But that wouldn't be fair to you…"

"It's what I want." Holding her gaze, I hope she knows I'm sincere. "I want you, even if it's just for now."

"I want you too." Dakota smiles and her eyes carry a shimmer of hope and vulnerability. "So," she says, her voice barely above a whisper, "are we officially together?"

I cup her cheek and kiss her softly. "I'm all in if you are."

33

DAKOTA

nother day in paradise. I'm in the middle of reviewing our quarterly reports when I hear the commotion outside my office. A shrill voice pierces through the reception area of the White Spa, and with a sigh, I push back from my desk and make my way there, bracing for whatever drama awaits.

I'm met with a scene that could be straight out of a reality TV show. Serenity, her usually calm demeanor cracking under pressure, is facing off against a woman who looks like she's had a run-in with a colony of angry bees.

The client is a vision in Gucci and silicone. Her face is so unnaturally smooth it could double as a bowling ball, with cheeks so plump they look like they're trying to escape the confines of her skin. Her lips are inflated to comical proportions, muffling her speech.

"I want to speak to the manager!" she screeches.

I step forward, trying to wipe the shock off my face. "I'm Dakota, the general manager," I say. "What's the problem?"

The woman swivels to face me, her neck moving while

her face remains eerily still. It's disconcerting, like watching a mannequin come to life.

"Finally, someone in charge," she huffs, her nostrils flaring. It's the only part of her face capable of movement. "I need fillers. Now. And this incompetent woman tells me I have to book a consultation first!"

I glance at Serenity, who looks like she's torn between bursting into tears and committing murder. I give her a reassuring nod before turning back to our disgruntled guest.

"I apologize for the inconvenience," I begin, my voice sickly sweet. "But as I'm sure our highly competent beautician, Serenity, has explained, we don't inject without having a consultation first. Perhaps we could schedule you in on our next available slot?"

"I don't need a consultation. I just want fillers. It only takes ten minutes, I've done it a million times."

"Well, I'm afraid it's up to us to decide if we're comfortable injecting." I'm not sure what clinic this woman has been visiting, but I know we would never go ahead with the treatment when someone already looks like a human inflated balloon animal.

The woman's eyes narrow—or at least, I think they do. "Do you know who I am?" she asks, her voice rising an octave. "I am Vivian Holbrook-Smythe, and I have never been denied service in my life!"

I feel something snap inside me. Maybe it's the stress of the past few weeks, or maybe it's just the absurdity of this entire situation, but suddenly, I can't hold back anymore. The number of times I've heard that sentence—"do you know who I am?"—since I moved to Vegas is absurd.

"Well, congratulations, Mrs. Holbrook-Smythe," I say, my smile never wavering. "There's a first time for everything. Including being told no."

The woman gapes at me, her lips parting in shock. "I...you...how dare you!"

"Oh, I dare," I continue, feeling a strange sense of liberation. "In fact, let me be perfectly clear. We don't have time for a consultation right now, but even if we did, I can already tell you that we would not go ahead with the treatment. You are welcome to make an appointment for any treatment other than fillers in our next available slot."

"That's absurd! You can't deny me treatment. I'm filing a complaint."

"Yes, I can deny treatment," I say. "It's in your best interest. Your face looks like it's one needle away from bursting, and it's not safe."

Serenity's eyes widen, and she lets out a small gasp. But I'm on a roll now, and there's no stopping me.

"Furthermore, feel free to file a complaint through our website, or if you prefer to do it right now, I can get you an iPad."

Mrs. Holbrook-Smythe's face, incapable of showing emotion, remains frozen in its perpetual state of surprise, but her body language screams indignation as she stomps her feet and waves her balled fists in the air. "Keep your stupid iPad. I'll go straight to the top!" she sputters. "This will cost you your job."

I lean in close, dropping my voice to a stage whisper. "Go ahead. File away. But between you and me, I'd be more worried about your face filing for divorce. It looks like it's trying to escape."

The woman lets out a strangled sound of outrage, spinning on her designer heels and storming toward the exit. Well, "storming" might be an exaggeration. It's more of an awkward waddle, given how tight her dress is and how precariously she's balanced on her stilettos.

As the door slams behind her, I turn to face Serenity, whose expression is a mix of horror and awe. "Dakota," she says, "that was..."

"Completely unprofessional?" I suggest, the adrenaline starting to wear off. "Absolutely insane? Grounds for immediate termination?"

Serenity shakes her head, a slow grin spreading across her face. "I was going to say 'amazing,' actually. But yeah, probably all those things too."

I lean against the wall, suddenly feeling drained. "Oh God," I groan, dropping my head into my hands. "What did I just do?"

"You just told off the biggest pain in the ass we've ever had," Serenity says, patting my shoulder. "And it was glorious. Terrifying, but glorious, and you're my hero."

I blow out my cheeks and shake my head. "I'm so going to lose my job."

"I doubt it," Serenity says. "You just did what needed to be done and we can keep this between us."

Smoothing down my white lab coat, I'm trying to regain some semblance of professionalism. I can see Luca peeking out from behind a potted plant, and is that Zoe trying to hide her giggles in the corridor? Both our receptionist and intern are staring at me too. I sigh, resigning myself to the fact that by lunchtime, every employee in the White Spa will know about my meltdown. So much for keeping things quiet.

"All right, show's over," I announce to the room at large. "Back to work, everyone." I retreat to my office and slump into my chair, my mind reeling from what just happened. What was I thinking? That was completely unprofessional.

My phone buzzes, pulling me from my thoughts. It's a text from Frankie: *Hey, Miss Vegas. How's your day going?*

I stare at the message, a hysterical laugh bubbling up in my throat. How's my day going? Oh, you know, just casually committing career suicide by insulting a client's face. The usual.

Instead of explaining the whole sordid affair, I simply reply: *Interesting. Might be looking for a new job soon. Know of any ranches hiring?*

34

FRANKIE

*P*ulling up to the rescue center, the familiar scent of hay and horses fills my nostrils. It's a comforting smell, one that always makes me feel at home, no matter where I am. But today, there's an underlying tension in the air, a sense of urgency that has me on high alert.

I grab my veterinary kit from the passenger seat and make my way toward the barn, where Rosie is waiting for me at the entrance.

"Frankie, thank goodness you're here," she says, her voice tight with anxiety. "The bull, he's in a bad way. We don't know what's wrong with him, but he's been limping since yesterday, and he's getting more aggressive by the minute."

I nod, my jaw tightening. "Let's take a look at him. Where is he?" As the rescue center runs on donations, Rosie tends to call on me rather than one of the official veterinarians in town. I know how much she struggles, so I'm happy to do it for free—to a certain extent.

Rosie leads me through the barn, past the stalls of

horses, until we reach a large, sturdy enclosure at the back. Inside, I can see the bull, a massive, muscular creature with a gleaming black coat and sharp, curved horns.

He's pacing back and forth, his head lowered and his eyes dark with pain. Every few steps, he stumbles, his right hind leg buckling beneath him.

"Are you sure it only started yesterday?" I ask, setting my kit down and pulling on a pair of latex gloves.

Rosie shrugs. "Yesterday was the first time I noticed it. That's why I didn't let him out this morning. I thought he'd just twisted his ankle or something, but he seems to be in a lot of pain. And now, he's starting to lash out at anyone who comes near him."

"Okay, let's take a closer look. Can you help me get him into the chute?"

Rosie hesitates, her eyes flickering nervously to the bull. "Are you sure that's a good idea? He's not exactly in a cooperative mood."

I give her a reassuring smile, patting her shoulder. "I've dealt with my fair share of ornery bulls. We'll take it slow and steady, and if things start to go south, we'll back off. But I need to get a better look at that leg if I'm going to figure out what's wrong."

She takes a deep breath, nodding reluctantly. "Okay, let's do it. But be careful. I don't want you getting hurt on my account."

"Hey, it wouldn't be the first time. Remember Sahara, that pregnant mare you sent me home with a while back? Nearly took my head off when I let her into the stables."

Rosie chuckles, shaking her head. "You're never going to let me live that down, are you?"

"Nope," I say cheerfully, grabbing a rope from my kit.

She rolls her eyes and laughs, but I can see the tension

in her shoulders as we enter the enclosure. "All right, smar-tass, let's see what you can do."

It takes an hour of coaxing and a lot of gentle words, but eventually, we manage to get the bull into the chute. He's snorting and stomping, his tail swishing angrily, but I keep my voice low and soothing, my hands moving slowly and deliberately.

"Easy, big fella," I murmur, running my hand along his flank. "I know you're hurting, but we're here to help. Just take it easy, and we'll have you feeling better in no time."

I crouch down, my eyes scanning his right hind leg for any signs of injury. At first glance, there's no obvious wound or swelling, but as I run my hands over his fetlock, I feel a slight heat emanating from the joint.

"Hm, looks like we might have some inflammation here," I mutter, reaching for my stethoscope. "Let's take a listen and see what's going on." I press the bell of the stetho-scope to the bull's chest, listening intently to his heart and lungs. His breathing is rapid and shallow, a sign of pain and distress. "Definitely some discomfort," I continue, straight-ening up. "I'm going to take a closer look at that leg, see if I can find the source of the problem."

I move around to the back of the chute again, my hands gently probing the bull's leg. He flinches and kicks out, nearly catching me in the thigh, but I dodge out of the way just in time.

"Whoa, easy there," I say calmly. "I know it hurts, but I need you to hold still for me." I continue my examination, my fingers tracing the contours of his leg, feeling for any lumps, bumps, or irregularities. And then, just as I'm about to move on, I feel it—a small, hard nodule, nestled deep in the tissue of his fetlock.

"Bingo." I look up at Rosie. "I think I found the problem.

Feels like a bone spur, probably been irritating him for a while now."

"A bone spur?" she asks. "That's quite serious, right?"

I shake my head, already reaching for my kit. "Not necessarily, but it can be painful, especially if it's rubbing against a tendon or ligament. I'm going to give him a local anesthetic and see if I can remove it."

I fill a syringe with lidocaine and inject it into the bull's leg. He twitches and snorts, but the medication takes effect quickly, and I can see the tension draining from his muscles.

"All right, let's see what we're dealing with." I pick up a scalpel. "Rosie, can you hand me those forceps?"

She passes them to me, her face pale with nervousness as I prepare to make a small incision in the bull's skin.

First, I take a bottle of antiseptic solution and some sterile gauze from my kit. "We need to clean the area first to prevent any infection," I mumble, pouring the solution over the gauze. I carefully dab the area around the nodule, ensuring it's thoroughly sterilized. "This might sting a bit."

Once the area is prepped, I work quickly and carefully, my hands moving with practiced precision as I make a small incision in the bull's skin. I locate the bone spur and gently extract it.

"There we go," I say, holding up the small, jagged piece of bone. "That's been causing a lot of trouble, hasn't it, big guy?"

The bull snorts, his tail flicking lazily as the anesthetic takes hold. I clean the wound again with antiseptic and suture it closed, then wrap a bandage around his leg to keep it clean and protected.

"He'll need some rest and anti-inflammatories," I say, stripping off my gloves. "But he should start feeling better in a day or two. Just keep an eye on him, and let me know if there are any signs of infection."

Rosie nods as she lets the bull out of the chute. "Thank you, Frankie. I don't know what we would have done without you."

"Hey, it's no bother. You're doing an amazing job here."

"Thank you." Rosie shuffles on the spot. "Do you want to come inside for a cup of coffee before you head back?"

I'm about to accept her offer when suddenly, the bull lurches forward, his head swinging wildly. His horn catches me square in the face, and I stumble back, my hand flying to my eye as pain explodes through my skull.

"Frankie!" Rosie cries, rushing forward to steady me. "Oh my God, are you okay?"

I blink, my vision blurry and unfocused. "I'm fine," I say. "Just a little bump, that's all." But as I try to take a step, the world tilts and spins around me, and I have to grab on to the chute to keep from falling.

"You are not fine," Rosie says firmly, her arm wrapping around my waist. "Come on, let's get you inside and get some ice on that eye." She helps me into the house, settling me on the couch with a pack of frozen peas pressed to my face. The pain is starting to subside, replaced by a dull, throbbing ache, and I can already feel my eye swelling shut.

"Looks like you're going to have a hell of a shiner," Rosie says, peering at my face with concern. "I'll drive you to the hospital."

"No need, it's not a concussion." I chuckle, wincing as the movement sends a fresh wave of pain through my head.

"Are you sure?"

"Yeah, I'm a medical professional. I know when to be alarmed, although that was a rookie mistake," I joke. The ice pack is numbing the throbbing in my face, but I suspect I look terrible.

"You look fine," Rosie says as if reading my mind. "It's not like you were planning on going on a date tonight, right?"

"Hmm…" I shoot her a sheepish grin. "I was actually thinking of stopping by someone special on my way back, but I might have to reconsider that now."

"Someone special?" Rosie wiggles her brows. "Have you met a woman?"

"I might have." My grin widens. "She lives in Vegas and she's got the day off. I thought I'd surprise her. Well, that was until—"

"Nonsense, you should go," Rosie says. "It's really not that bad."

She's desperately trying to keep a straight face, and meeting her eyes, we both burst out in laughter.

35

DAKOTA

a knock at the door startles me, and my heart skips a beat as I leap off the couch, smoothing my hair and taking a deep breath before opening the door.

There she stands, the woman who has been occupying my every waking hour. But as my eyes land on her face, I gasp, my hand flying to my mouth.

"Oh my God, Frankie! What happened to your eye?" I exclaim, ushering her inside.

She grins, wincing slightly as the movement tugs at her swollen, bruised skin. "Oh, you know. Just a little disagreement with a big guy. I think he won this round."

I shake my head in disbelief as I lead her to the kitchen and pull out a chair for her. "Were you in a fight? Do I need to call the police or something? Drive you to the hospital?"

Frankie laughs. "No, no. Nothing like that and it's less serious than it looks. I was just doing a favor for a friend, treating a sick bull. He got a little too friendly with his horns, that's all. I've had ice on it already."

"Oh." I frown as I reach out to touch the swollen side of

her face. "You might want to ice it some more." I grab a clean dish towel and fill it with ice from the freezer, then gently press it to her eye. "Here, hold this."

She takes the makeshift ice pack from me and sits. "Thanks. You're a lifesaver."

I smile, my heart fluttering at the warmth in her voice. "I don't know about that. But I do know a thing or two about treating bumps and bruises."

Frankie smiles, a mischievous glint in her uninjured eye. "Oh, really? Well, in that case, maybe you should give me special treatment. You know, just to make sure I'm healing properly. I can put a paper bag over my head if you prefer."

I laugh. "Nice try, cowgirl. But I think you'd better stick with the ice for now. You need to keep your head upright, so the bruising doesn't get worse. We can talk about special treatment later."

"I doubt it can get worse than this." She pouts playfully, the effect somewhat diminished by the swelling on her face. "Can I at least have a kiss?"

I roll my eyes, but I can't help the grin that tugs at the corners of my mouth as I straddle her on the chair. Of course I want to kiss her. I just didn't want her to think that was the only thing on my mind when she showed up with her face all botched up.

Her free hand immediately reaches for my behind and she squeezes gently, sending a shiver up my spine. I lean in, careful not to jostle her injured eye, and brush my lips against hers. The kiss is soft and sweet, a gentle exploration that quickly deepens as Frankie parts her lips, inviting me in.

I lose myself in the taste of her, the feel of her body against mine. My fingers tangle in her hair, and I moan softly against her mouth.

"Wow," Frankie whispers when we break apart. "That really helped."

"Oh yeah?" I chuckle, resting my forehead against hers. "Do you want more of where that came from?"

She smiles, wincing again as the movement tugs at her swollen eye. "Ouch. As tempting as that sounds, I don't think I'm up for much...strenuous activity tonight. I'm a little fragile."

"Poor baby," I tease, pressing a light kiss to her uninjured cheek. "I guess we'll just have to find other ways to entertain ourselves."

"What did you have in mind?" Frankie's hand trails up my back and under my tank top, leaving goose bumps in its wake.

I climb off her lap, immediately missing her body against mine. "Well, how about I get some pillows and you sit back on the couch in the living room? And then I'll order some food. We could watch a movie?"

"A movie night?" Frankie looks amused. "Here I thought you were going to suggest something scandalous like a striptease."

"Oh, don't worry. I have plenty of scandalous ideas, but they'll have to wait until you're fully healed. Are you sure you don't need to see a doctor?"

"Positive." Frankie stands, keeping the ice pack in place. "You're bossy when you're in nurse mode," she teases, following me to the living room.

"Just wait until I break out my stethoscope." I settle her on the couch, head to the bedroom to grab some pillows, and also fetch a jug of cold lemonade from the fridge and two Advils. I'm thrilled at the idea of having her in my space and relaxing together.

"Mmm..." Frankie sips the lemonade and swallows the

pills while she takes in the room with curious eyes. "Nice place you've got here," she says, her gaze lingering on the bare walls and empty bookcase. "It's very...minimalist."

"That's one way to put it. Honestly, I keep putting off decorating because I'm not sure if I'll stay, you know?"

Her smile falters for a beat, a flicker of something crossing her face. But it's gone as quickly as it appeared. "Your balcony looks homey, though."

"It's where I spend most of my time," I say, pointing to the two comfortable reclining outdoor chairs with a little mosaic coffee table. "I got a bunch of plants at the nursery on my way back from your place last time I visited. A little green helps. My other favorite hangout is the Mexican restaurant downstairs."

"Yum, I saw that. I love Mexican food, but I rarely have it as restaurants don't want to deliver all the way out to the ranch. Are they good?"

"They're great. Gabriel's tacos are the best. Want to try?"

"Absolutely, but let me order," she insists. "I'm aware I've just come barging in here with a bruised face and a mild headache and there's not much in it for you."

"Not at all. I like having you here." I stare at her in surprise because she couldn't have been more wrong. Frankie's impromptu visit's the best thing that's happened to me all week. "What? You think I just enjoy spending time with you for the sex?"

"No..." She shakes her head. "I didn't mean it like that, I—"

"Good," I interrupt her. "Then will you stay the night? You probably shouldn't be driving far with that head of yours."

Frankie seems to ponder over that, then nods. "If you

don't mind. I can let Jose know I'm back tomorrow morning. My first tour isn't until ten. Unless you had plans?"

"I had plans with Mexican food, but I can fit you in," I joke, grabbing my phone. "I'll call down and order a bit of everything. Are you okay with that?" I wave a hand when she tries to hand me her credit card. "Absolutely not. You're my guest."

"Okay, thank you," she says when it's clear I'm not up for negotiation. "But will you let me take you out on a date when my face is back to normal?"

"A date?" I hesitate and feel a blush creep up my cheeks. "Sure. I'd love to go on a date with you."

"But?" She tilts her head and regards me. "You seem surprised."

"No...no buts, I've just never seen you outside the ranch before, until now, so it never occurred to me that we could... I don't know...go out?"

Frankie laughs. "You know I'm not actually tethered to the ranch with an invisible lasso, right? I do occasionally venture beyond the realm of hay bales and horse manure."

Shaking my head, I laugh along with her. "All right, all right. Point taken. I guess I've just gotten used to seeing you in your natural habitat."

Frankie gasps dramatically. "What am I, a rare species in a nature documentary? 'And here we see the elusive Frankie, emerging from her den of denim and leather to forage for tacos in the urban jungle.'"

I snort, nearly choking on my lemonade. "Stop it! You're going to make me ruin these pillows."

"Well, we can't have that," she says. "These pillows are the closest thing to decoration you've got in this place."

"All right, smartass." I roll my eyes. "Just for that, I'm ordering extra-spicy salsa with our tacos."

"Bring it on, Miss Vegas." Frankie rubs her hands together. "I can handle a little heat. Make it extra-extra spicy. See who wins the chili competition."

36

FRANKIE

"Okay, you win." Dakota breaks into a coughing fit, her face flushed and eyes watering as she reaches for her glass of lemonade. She's just taken a hefty bite of her taco, loaded with the extra-spicy salsa.

I laugh at her reaction, a mix of amusement and tenderness running through me as she fans her mouth dramatically. "What's the matter? Can't handle a little heat?" I tease, taking another big bite of my own taco to prove my point. The spice hits my tongue, sharp and fiery, but I manage to keep a straight face even as my taste buds scream in protest. It's so spicy it hurts, but at least it's distracting me from my throbbing eye.

Dakota narrows her eyes at me, swapping her lemonade for a glass of water she keeps refilling and gulping back. "Show-off," she mutters, but there's a smile playing at the corners of her mouth.

I wink at her with my good eye, suspecting that must look incredibly silly. "Years of eating Jose's homemade salsa have prepared me for this moment."

"Oh yeah? Does he make good salsa?"

"His wife does. I have dinner with his family now and then. Maria's an amazing cook. She also does the changeovers and prepares breakfast for the ranch guests." I chuckle when Dakota scrapes the salsa off her taco and tops it with lettuce and sour cream she finds in the fridge instead.

"Sorry. I know it's not cool, but I need something to take the heat away."

I'm tempted to do the same myself, but not one to admit defeat, I take another bite and note my palate is slowly getting used to the chili-shock.

"Are you and Jose close friends?" she asks. "He seems nice."

"Yes, we're like family. I don't think I could run the ranch without him. His wife joined the team after we built the guesthouse. She manages the morning shift at the ranch with the help of a cleaner. They have two young kids and live about two miles from the ranch. They're very close to my parents too."

Dakota nods. "Your parents are lovely. It was great to meet them, even though it was unplanned."

"Then maybe you should meet properly. They were awfully curious about you."

"I'd like that," she says with a sweet smile.

A vision of Dakota having dinner with my parents flashes before me, but I'm not sure if I actually dare arrange that yet, especially if she might leave. "So, tell me," I say. "What's happening at work? Have you heard anything about the complaint that was filed against you?"

Dakota shrugs, and I'm struck by how nonchalant she seems about it. "I have a meeting with someone higher up in the hotel this week. I guess I'll find out then."

"And how do you feel about that?" I probe, trying to read her expression.

She's quiet for a moment, her fingers absently tracing the rim of her glass. "Honestly? I'm not sure I care all that much," she finally admits. "Should I have done what I did? Certainly not. Do I regret it?" She takes another bite of her taco and ponders over that as she chews. "No. I don't regret it. It was childish and petty, and I set the wrong example for my team, but it also felt cathartic. That woman was the perfect representation of everything that's wrong with the world and someone had to put her in her place."

"Then you did the right thing for you." I study her, still finding no signs of regret. If she's trying to hide it, she's doing a good job. "Can I ask you something?"

"Anything," she says, looking up at me with a small smile.

"Did you always want to work in the beauty industry?"

Dakota lets out a short, humorless laugh. "No, actually. I...I'm a qualified nurse," she says, and I can't hide my surprise. "Growing up, all I wanted to do was help people."

"A nurse?" I repeat, trying to reconcile this new information with the Dakota I know.

"Yeah. I wouldn't be authorized to inject toxins into people's faces if I didn't have the proper medical credentials."

"I had no idea, but that makes sense. Did you ever work as a nurse?"

"I did, for two years. When I first started," she says, "I was so eager. Fresh out of school, ready to change the world. I worked in the emergency department of a busy hospital in Santa Ana." She pauses, taking a sip of her water, and I can see the memories playing across her face. "The hours were brutal. I'd often work twelve-hour shifts, sometimes back-to-back. There were nights I'd come home and fall asleep still in my bloody scrubs, too exhausted to even change."

I nod, imagining Dakota, younger and idealistic.

"There were beautiful and touching moments. Like the time I helped deliver a baby in the back of an ambulance because we couldn't make it to the hospital in time. Or when I sat with an elderly man for hours, holding his hand as he told me stories about his late wife, just so he wouldn't be alone.

"Mostly, it was tough though," she continues. "I'll never forget the night we lost a young girl to a drunk-driving accident. Her parents arrived just moments after she passed. The sound of her mother's grief haunted me for weeks." She takes a shaky breath, and I can see the toll these memories are taking on her.

"Another time, we had a man come in who had been in a terrible fire. Over eighty percent of his body was burned. We worked on him for hours, but in the end..." She trails off, shaking her head. "Yeah, it was definitely tough, but sometimes I miss the feeling of making a difference."

"Was the job getting to you? Is that why you changed careers?" I ask.

"Not exactly. It was more the temptation of something better rather than running away from something difficult that sparked the change. One of my colleagues quit her job and told me she'd been offered free training to work as a beauty consultant. She really sold it once she started working, so I decided to do the same." Dakota looks down, a faint blush coloring her cheeks. "Botox and injectables seemed more glamorous, and that attracted me when I was younger. The pay was better, and the hours reasonable. From there, I got into the spa business, and now..." she gestures vaguely around her, "here I am in Vegas, running a huge salon, in a job that I hate and get no satisfaction from."

I lean back, processing this revelation. "Why haven't you told me this before?"

Dakota's shoulders slump slightly. "I'm a little ashamed, I guess," she admits. "I'm qualified to put health first, to make a real difference, and instead, I choose to stick needles into faces and endorse unrealistic beauty standards."

"Hey…" I reach out to tilt her chin up so she's looking at me. "You have nothing to be ashamed of. We all make choices in life, and sometimes our paths take unexpected turns."

She gives me a small, grateful smile, but I can see the doubt still lingering in her eyes.

"Have you ever thought about going back to nursing?"

Dakota blinks, as if the idea genuinely had never occurred to her. "I…I don't know. It's been so long, I guess I forgot it was even an option."

I can almost see the wheels turning in her head. "It's never too late to change course," I say. "If that's what you want."

She nods slowly, a thoughtful expression on her face. "Maybe you're right. I just…I don't know where I'd even start."

"Well," I say, leaning toward her, "lucky for you, you're very smart. You'll figure it out."

"Hmm…" Dakota leans in and kisses me. "You know what? You have an incredibly positive effect on me. I don't know what I'd do without you."

"Probably eat a lot less spicy food," I quip, trying to lighten the mood.

She laughs. "Speaking of which," she says, eyeing my plate, "how are you not dying right now? That salsa is lethal."

I shrug, taking another bite of my taco for emphasis.

"Like I said, years of practice. Plus, I think the bull may have damaged my taste buds."

Dakota shakes her head in mock despair. "I've fallen for a woman with no sense of taste. What does that say about me?"

"Hey!" I protest, flicking a piece of lettuce at her. "I'll have you know I have excellent taste. Just wait until I take you out on that date."

"Smooth talker," she teases. "So, where are you taking me?"

"That's a surprise. Just let me know when you have two days off, as it will obviously include a sleepover." I smile, imagining having her to myself away from the ranch. "And you should probably pack a swimsuit too, although that's optional as you're welcome to swim however you like."

"Now that sounds like an intriguing date," she says. "I don't think I've been on anything other than a dinner date with anyone before."

"But I'm not just anyone."

"You're certainly not," Dakota agrees. "So, cowgirl, tell me more."

I run a hand through her hair and twirl a lock of the blond strands around my finger. "If I told you, it wouldn't be a surprise anymore, would it?"

"Not even a tiny hint?" she begs. "Should I be worried?"

"Nope. But I will say this: it'll be unlike any other date you've been on."

37

DAKOTA

The rhythmic chiming of slot machines and the constant murmur of voices follow me as I make my way through the labyrinth of the Quantum's casino floor. My heels click against the polished marble, each step echoing the nervous flutter in my chest. I'm heading to a meeting that could very well end my career here, but strangely, I feel more curious than anxious.

I reach the executive offices, a stark contrast to the gaudy opulence of the casino. Here, everything is sleek, modern, and intimidatingly quiet. The receptionist, a poised woman with a perfect blond updo, directs me to Mr. Thornton's office with a practiced smile.

I straighten my knee-length dress—I've taken off my lab coat for the meeting—and knock on the heavy wooden door, my knuckles barely making a sound against the thick mahogany.

"Come in," a voice calls from inside, and I step into an office that screams corporate success. Floor-to-ceiling windows offer a panoramic view of the Las Vegas skyline, the neon lights of the Strip a stark contrast to the muted grays and blacks of the office decor. A large, glass-topped desk dominates the room, its surface saved for a single laptop and a crystal paperweight.

Behind the desk sits Mr. Thornton, a man who looks like he was born in a suit. His salt-and-pepper hair is meticulously styled, not a strand out of place. His face, while not unkind, bears the signs of years spent in boardrooms and behind desks—lines etched around his mouth from forced smiles.

"Ms. Walker," he says, rising to shake my hand. His grip is firm but impersonal. "Please, have a seat."

I sink into the plush leather chair across from him, crossing my legs at the ankle and resisting the urge to fidget with my skirt.

"I assume you know why you're here," Mr. Thornton begins.

I nod, meeting his gaze. "I suspect it's about the incident with Mrs. Holbrook-Smythe."

He leans back in his chair, steepling his fingers. "Indeed. Mrs. Holbrook-Smythe is a...valued client of the Quantum. She was quite upset by her experience at the White Spa. I'd like to hear your side of the story."

I take a deep breath, deciding honesty is the best policy. "Mr. Thornton, I won't deny that I handled the situation poorly. Mrs. Holbrook-Smythe demanded immediate fillers without a consultation, and when denied, she became increasingly aggressive. In a moment of frustration, I...well, I told her that her face looked like it was trying to escape."

Mr. Thornton's eyebrows shoot up, a flicker of amusement crossing his face before he schools his features back into neutrality. "I see. And do you often comment on clients' appearances in such a manner?"

"No, sir," I reply, fighting back a smile. "It was a momentary lapse in judgment. One I regret, professionally speaking."

He nods, his expression unreadable. "And personally speaking?"

I pause, considering my words carefully. "Personally...I stand by my medical opinion that Mrs. Holbrook-Smythe should not be given any further treatments, here or elsewhere."

Mr. Thornton's lips twitch, almost imperceptibly. "I see. Well, Ms. Walker, while I appreciate your...candor, I'm sure you understand that this puts us in a difficult position. Mrs. Holbrook-Smythe is not just a client, but a friend of several board members."

I nod, a strange sense of calm settling over me. "I understand, sir."

He leans forward, his voice taking on a softer tone. "Given the circumstances, we believe it might be best for all parties if you were to accept the package we're prepared to offer. It would give you ten weeks until the end of your six-month probation period, during which time you would train a replacement and transition out of your role."

I blink, surprised by the generous offer. However, he doesn't need to know that. "I see."

"We value our employees, Ms. Walker, even when things don't work out, and we'd like to make the transition as smooth as possible for everyone involved."

I nod, a weight I didn't even realize I was carrying suddenly lifting from my shoulders. "I appreciate that. And I accept your offer."

Mr. Thornton stares at me for a beat before a look of utter surprise and relief washes over his face. He clearly expected more resistance and I know what he's thinking.

Why hasn't she denied her actions? Why hasn't she threatened with a lawyer? Why is she just letting this happen to her?

"It's fine, really," I add. "I promise I won't cause you any trouble."

He clears his throat, still stunned. "Excellent. Please take the rest of the day off. HR will be in touch with the details. Is there anything else you'd like to discuss?"

I stand and give him a smile that feels oddly genuine. It's not his fault. He's just doing his job, and he's the unlucky one who's been trapped in this business for decades. I don't understand how he's coped for so long.

"No, sir. Thank you for your time."

As I turn to leave, Mr. Thornton clears his throat. "Ms. Walker?"

I pause at the door, looking back. "Yes?"

For a moment, he looks like he wants to say something more personal, but then he simply nods. "Good luck with your future endeavors."

"Thank you. I hope Mrs. Holbrook-Smythe's face finds what it's looking for." I close the door behind me before I can see his reaction, but I swear I hear a muffled chuckle as I walk away.

Making my way back through the casino, the noise and chaos that once felt overwhelming now seem distant, as if I'm watching it all through a pane of glass. The flashing lights, the ringing bells, the excited shouts—they're all part of a world I'm leaving behind, and it doesn't annoy me anymore.

I pause by a row of slot machines, watching an elderly woman feed coin after coin into the hungry metal mouth. She's focused, determined, chasing that elusive jackpot. I wonder if she knows how much the odds are stacked against her, or if she even cares. In a way, I've been like her these past months—stubbornly feeding my time and energy into a job that was never going to pay out. But unlike her, I'm walking away from the machine.

As I step out into the bright Las Vegas afternoon to treat myself to the first real lunch I've had in months, I take a deep breath. The air is hot and dry, tinged with exhaust fumes, but underneath it all, I catch a whiff of something else. Possibility.

My phone buzzes in my pocket, and I pull it out to see a text from Frankie: *How'd it go? Do I need to come rescue you from corporate hell?*

I smile, my heart warming at her concern. *All good*, I type back. *How do you feel about dating an unemployed woman?*

That depends, she replies. *Will the unemployed woman stick around?* It's followed by a kiss emoji.

She might, I type, earning a few curious glances from passersby as I'm standing there, grinning on the sidewalk.

In that case, I'd be delighted, she types back. *Will she be homeless too? I have a big bed.*

I chuckle and type, *Possibly. Are you offering refuge?* Although our back-and-forth is playful and a little silly, I know she means it, and as I wait for Frankie's response, I realize that for the first time since moving to Vegas, I feel truly free.

A simple *Yes* is her reply, and I glance at the Quantum over my shoulder, its gleaming facade now less imposing and more like a chapter closing in my life. With a smile, I turn away and head toward El Rincon, ready to celebrate my newfound freedom.

38

FRANKIE

I step into the Quantum, and immediately, I'm hit by a wave of sensory overload. The casino floor is a mash-up of lights, sounds, and movement. Slot machines chime and whir, their flashing lights creating a dizzying kaleidoscope effect. The air is thick with the smell of perfume, mingling with a sense of excitement and anticipation. I have no interest in gambling; growing up in the area, I've seen firsthand how these casinos can impact lives, but it's interesting to be here. It's been a while since I've set foot in a casino, and this one is exceptionally spectacular.

I know I look out of place in my jeans, white shirt, cowboy boots, and hat. Around me, people are dressed in everything from designer suits to more casual tourist wear. I shake my head, grateful for the simplicity of my life on the ranch and equally, marveling at the opulence of it all.

The interactive floors gleam under the soft lighting, the tiles picking up on my steps and leaving colored footprints behind me. Near the bar area, I spot a holographic bartender, mixing virtual drinks in midair. It's so realistic that for a second, I'm not sure if it's a real person or not. The hologram smiles and winks at passersby, adding to the surreal atmosphere.

The ceiling above is a work of art in itself. It's a massive LED screen displaying a slowly moving starfield, occasionally interrupted by shooting stars or swirling galaxies. It gives the illusion of infinite space, making the already large room feel even more vast and open.

As I make my way toward the elevators, I pass by a sculpture that seems to defy gravity. It's a series of metallic spheres suspended in the air, rotating slowly around each other without any visible support. I pause, trying to figure out how it works, but the illusion is perfect. It's like a piece of magic, right here in the middle of the casino.

The Quantum is certainly worth a visit for the technology alone, but I'm not here for sightseeing. It's my first official date with Dakota and I'm excited for what I've got planned. Jose is manning the ranch, and for the coming thirty-six hours, I have nothing to worry about.

I'm early, so instead of waiting for Dakota downstairs as planned, I decide to head up to the White Spa. I'm curious as to where she's been spending her time these past months, and after everything she's told me, I'm eager to see it for myself. As the elevator ascends, I feel a flutter of anticipation in my stomach. It's silly, really. I've seen Dakota plenty of times, but something about picking her up from work, about seeing her in her professional environment, feels different.

The elevator doors slide open, revealing a world that's alien to me. The spa is a stark contrast to the energy of the casino below. Here, everything is pristine white, from the walls to the furniture. The air is infused with a subtle, calming scent—lavender, maybe? It's soothing, but almost clinically so, and it's so quiet.

I approach the reception desk, where a young woman with perfectly coiffed hair and immaculate makeup sits. Her eyes widen slightly as she takes me in, her gaze lingering on my hat and boots. I'm clearly not the typical customer they're used to seeing here.

"Hello. Welcome to the White Spa," she says. "How can I help you?"

I clear my throat, suddenly feeling a bit self-conscious. "I'm here to pick up Dakota Walker. Is it okay if I wait here?"

"Of course," one of the employees who walks past in a white lab coat, chips in. "You must be Frankie. Dakota's mentioned you. I'm Serenity."

"It's nice to meet you, Serenity. She's told me about you too."

"Oh, she did?" Serenity beams. "I'll let her know you're here. Why don't you have a seat?"

I nod and turn to the waiting area, aware of the curious glances from the other staff members. A tall, handsome, dark-haired man, also dressed in a white lab coat, is openly staring, a mixture of surprise and appreciation on his face.

"Well, howdy there, cowgirl," he drawls, sauntering over. "You're here to see the boss?"

I tip my hat, playing along, but before I can respond, I hear a familiar voice.

"Luca, are you bothering my date?"

I turn to see Dakota standing there, a vision in her crisp, white lab coat and heels. Her hair is pulled back in a sleek ponytail, and she looks every inch the professional spa manager.

"Date?" Luca gasps dramatically. "Well, well...someone's been keeping secrets!"

Dakota rolls her eyes, takes off her lab coat and hands it to the receptionist. "Not everyone gossips like you, Luca."

Underneath her lab coat, she's wearing a white summer dress. "But yes..." She lowers her voice as two people are about to enter the reception area and swaps her heels for sneakers behind the reception desk. "I'm going on a date. Lucky me, right?"

"I'm the lucky one," I say, shooting Luca a grin.

"Are you ready?" she asks, closing the distance and taking my hand.

"I think the question is, are you ready, Miss Vegas?" I retort, drawing giggles from her staff. She starts leading me toward the exit, but not before I catch Serenity giving us a thumbs-up and Luca making a throbbing-heart gesture behind us.

"I'm so sorry about that. They can be a bit...much."

"They seem fun." I chuckle, squeezing Dakota's hand as we step into the elevator. "Have you told them you're leaving?"

"Not yet. I think I'll do that in a more private setting." She winces. "I'm sorry, I should have given you a tour. I was just so surprised to see you there that I couldn't think straight."

As the elevator descends, Dakota pulls me in close. "You know what?" she whispers, her breath warm against my ear, "I've always wanted to kiss someone in an elevator.

I grin as I meet her gaze. "Well, we can't let that opportunity go to waste, can we?" I cup her face gently, tilting her chin up as I lean in. Our lips meet softly at first, tentative and sweet. But then Dakota's arms wind around my neck, and the kiss deepens. I can taste the mint of her lip balm, feel the warmth of her body pressed against mine. I'm already turned on and we haven't even left the building.

We break apart, both a little breathless, as the elevator chimes to signal our arrival at the ground floor. Dakota's cheeks are flushed, her eyes bright with excitement, and I adjust my hat, which has gone slightly askew.

"Don't they have cameras in there?" I ask, glancing up.

"Sure." Dakota shoots me a flirty smile. "But what are they going to do? Fire me?" She wraps an arm around me as we head out to my car. It's so easy with her now, so comfortable. "So, where are we going?"

"Still a surprise," I say, opening the door for her.

Dakota laughs. "Of course it is." She nudges me playfully then taps the weekend bag slung over her shoulder. "Well, I've packed clothes and a swimsuit as requested. Can you at least give me a hint?"

"I can tell you that it's about a two-hour drive with the rush-hour traffic, and where we're going, you won't need fancy clothes. In fact, you won't need any clothes at all."

39

DAKOTA

*T*he view that unfolds before us as we round the final bend in the road is nothing short of spectacular. Lake Mojave stretches out like a sheet of glass, its crystal-clear waters reflecting the late-afternoon sun in a dazzling display of blues and greens. The contrast between the vivid azure of the lake and the rugged desert landscape surrounding it is striking, creating a scene that looks almost too perfect to be real.

"Frankie," I breathe, unable to take my eyes off the view, "how did you find this?"

"I've been here before." She smiles at me, clearly pleased with my reaction. "Wait until you see where we're staying."

We pull off the main road onto a smaller, unpaved track that winds its way closer to the shoreline. The Range Rover bumps along, kicking up small clouds of dust. As we get closer to the water, I spot a small wooden structure nestled among the rocks and sparse desert vegetation.

"Is that...?" I start to ask, but Frankie's widening smile confirms my suspicion.

"Home for the night," she says, bringing the car to a stop.

The cabin is charming in its rustic simplicity. It's a single-story structure made of weathered wood that blends seamlessly with the surrounding landscape. A porch faces the water, complete with a pair of Adirondack chairs that look perfect for watching the sunset.

Frankie gets out and grabs our bags from the car. "Let's check out the inside." She steps up to a metal lockbox mounted on the wall, her fingers dancing over the keypad as she enters a series of numbers. There's a click, and the box pops open, revealing a set of keys inside. "Gotta love these Airbnb setups," she says, fishing out the keys. "Makes check-in a breeze."

I'm immediately charmed. The interior is cozy, but not cramped, with an open-plan living area that includes a small kitchenette, a dining table for two, and a sofa facing a stone fireplace. Large windows line the wall facing the lake, flooding the space with natural light and offering unobstructed views of the water. The back porch looks comfortable, equipped with a firepit and a grill.

"It's perfect," I say, turning to her with a smile. "So you've been here before?"

"Yeah. I used to come here with my brother on fishing and camping trips, and the owner is a friend of his. Most of the cabins are part of the Lake Mead recreational area, and they're commercial establishments. There are only two private ones, so we're lucky it was available."

"It's so romantic." I walk over to the windows, taking in the breathtaking view. Beyond the porch, I see steps leading down to a small dock extending out into the water, with a couple of kayaks tied up at the end. "Are those for us too?"

"Yep." Frankie opens the sliding doors and pulls me outside. "I thought we could do some exploring on the water tomorrow morning, if you're up for it. But for tonight..." She wraps an arm around my waist. "I thought we could just relax, maybe have a little cookout on the dock. I've brought groceries."

"That sounds great," I whisper, giddy with excitement. For the coming night and day, I have Frankie all to myself, and that thought sends my libido into overdrive. "I must admit," I continue, leaning into her, "when you said you were taking me on a date, this isn't quite what I imagined."

"Oh?" She grins. "Are you disappointed?"

I throw my head back and laugh, squeezing her against me. "I'm a very, very happy woman right now, although you could have taken me to McDonald's and I'd still be smiling. I just love being with you."

"I wouldn't dream of taking you there," she says.

Wrapped in Frankie's embrace, I let my gaze wander over the scenery, drinking in every detail of our secluded paradise. I only see three boats in the far distance. Perhaps the day-trippers have all returned home for dinner, or maybe this is just a quiet part of the lake.

The rugged shoreline stretches out in both directions, a tapestry of red-hued rocks and desert vegetation. To our left, the lake narrows into a serpentine channel, its azure waters winding between towering cliffs of striated sandstone. The rock faces are a mesmerizing palette of reds, oranges, and purples, their colors intensified by the warm light of the setting sun.

To our right, the lake opens up into a wider expanse, its surface a mirror-like sheet of blue that perfectly reflects the sky above. Beyond that, the faint outline of the mountains on the Arizona side rise, their jagged peaks softened by a hazy blue mist.

A pair of ospreys circles overhead, their distinctive calls echoing across the water as they search for their evening meal. Below, a school of fish breaks the surface momentarily, creating ripples that spread out in concentric circles.

Frankie weaves her fingers through my hair and pulls me in possessively. "Speaking of fast food...are you hungry? I'll unload the groceries from the car and cook you a meal. Unless..."

"Unless what?"

"Well," she says with a playful smile, "I'm feeling a little sticky from the drive. I wouldn't mind a dip in the lake. Are you up for it?"

"Only if we're skinny dipping." Stepping back, I lock my eyes with Frankie's as I lift my dress over my head and toss it behind me.

Frankie's eyes darken as they roam over my body. "I like the way you think, Miss Vegas," she says, her voice husky.

She takes off her hat and tugs her T-shirt over her head, revealing her toned abs and the simple black sports bra underneath. I watch, mesmerized, as she shimmies out of her boots, jeans, and underwear. The sight of her naked body never fails to take my breath away.

"Race you to the water," she challenges with a grin.

I laugh, quickly shedding my underwear and kicking off my sneakers. "Oh, you're on!"

We dash down the steps to the dock, our bare feet slapping against the sun-warmed wood. The late-afternoon air is warm against my skin, but I can feel the coolness radiating off the water. At the end of the dock, Frankie pauses, turning to face me.

"Ready?" she asks.

I nod, and together we dive off the dock and plunge into the cool, crystal-clear water of Lake Mojave. The initial shock of cold makes me gasp as I surface, but it quickly gives way to a refreshing sensation. I push my wet hair back from my face, blinking water from my eyes to find Frankie.

She's treading water a few feet away. "How's that for cooling off?"

"Bliss," I say, swimming toward her.

Frankie's arms encircle my waist, pulling me flush against her. The feeling of her naked body against mine is delicious, and I wrap my legs around her waist, trusting her to keep us both afloat. The water laps against our skin as we fall into a sweet kiss, and we're slowly sinking.

Frankie breaks away, chuckling. "As much as I'm enjoying this, I think we might need something to hold on to or we'll drown." We swim to the ladder, and Frankie positions herself with her back against it, holding on with one arm while the other wraps around my waist again.

"That's better," she says, her voice low and husky. "Now where were we?"

I don't answer with words. Instead, I press my body against hers and capture her lips once more. The kiss is hungry, urgent, filled with all the desire that's been building since we arrived.

I run my fingers through her damp hair, tugging gently as I deepen the kiss. Frankie moans softly into my mouth, the sound making me lightheaded, and the cool water does nothing to temper the heat between us.

Frankie's lips leave mine to trail kisses along my jaw, down my neck, and I instinctively tilt my head back.

"God, Dakota," she murmurs against my throat. "I want you."

Finding her mouth, I kiss her deeply once more. "I'm a little obsessed with you," I confess when we part. "And I can't believe you did all this for me."

"There's nothing wrong with a romantic dinner in a

candlelit restaurant," Frankie murmurs with a smile. "But I thought you might like to get away from Vegas for a bit, and sometimes, I like to escape the ranch too."

"It's so private," I mumble, brushing my lips against hers. "And private is sexy."

"Are you having naughty thoughts, Miss Vegas?"

"Always when I'm with you," I quip with a mischievous grin. "Did you bring your riding crop, cowgirl?"

"No…" She licks her lips. "But I can improvise."

"Mm…" Her comment makes me melt in her grip and fantasies take over my mind. She does that to me, every single time she as much as looks at me. "I'll be a good girl, I promise."

"Is that so?" Frankie's hand moves to cup my breast, her thumb brushing over my nipple, and I moan softly as I grind into her. Her eyes blaze with intensity as she watches my reaction. "We'll see about that," she murmurs, her voice a seductive whisper. She captures my lips in a fierce, possessive kiss, her hand slipping lower under the water to claim me in a way that leaves no doubt—I am hers, utterly and completely.

40

FRANKIE

I stand by the bed, watching Dakota squirm against the ties. Her eyes are wide, her breathing quick and shallow. She's stretched out, her naked body glistening in the dim light. It's almost too much, the sight of her like this, helpless and beautiful. Nothing turns me on more than a beautiful woman begging for my touch.

We still haven't eaten. Food is the last thing on our minds, but I intend to have her as my appetizer. We're insatiable around each other, and it's impossible for us not to be physical. My body gravitates toward her without conscious thought. A brush of hands as we walk, leaning into her as we talk, the way I orient myself to always be in her space.

When I'm with Dakota, time seems to slow down and speed up all at once. Hours can pass in what feels like minutes, and yet, a single moment of connection can stretch into eternity.

Next to me on the nightstand is a bowl with ice cubes I found in the freezer; the two glasses of white wine I was about to drop them into are still on the kitchen counter, untouched.

Dakota is eyeing the bowl with a curious and playful glimmer in her expression. "What do you have planned?"

"Don't play innocent. I think you know what I'm about to do," I say with a teasing smile, choosing the biggest cube from the bowl. "Tell me if you want me to untie you."

I drag the ice slowly along the curve of her breast, leaving a trail of cold water. Dakota gasps as the chill meets her skin, her back arching off the bed.

"Fuck," she breathes, her voice a mixture of desperation and desire. "I can't take it."

"Want me to stop?" I smile, knowing exactly how much she can take. I press the ice to her nipple, watching it pebble and harden under the icy touch.

"No..."

"See? You love it," I murmur, my own body tingling with anticipation. "Don't you?"

"Yes," she moans, her head tossing back. "God, yes."

I lean down, replacing the ice with my warm mouth, sucking the cold from her skin and feeling her shudder beneath me. She tastes sweet and cool, like a forbidden treat. I let my hand wander, the ice melting rapidly in the heat of her body, dripping between her breasts and down her stomach.

Dakota is trembling now, her muscles taut with need. "Frankie," she pleads again, but I'm not ready to give her what she wants. Not yet. I trail the ice lower, across her belly, down to the juncture of her thighs. She jerks against the bonds, her breath hitching in her throat.

I tease her with the melting ice, circling her inner thighs, knowing she's growing wetter with each pass. Her hips buck, seeking more, but I hold back, savoring the control.

"Do you want it here?" I ask, trailing my fingertip down her pussy so softly it barely brushes.

"Yes," she whimpers, her eyes locked on mine. "More."

Slowly, I press the last sliver of ice against her clit and watch as she almost falls apart. I hold it there until she clenches her jaw and groans, balling her hands into fists. Then I slide down along her body and replace the ice cube with my mouth.

At the sharp contrast between the coldness of the ice and the warmth of my tongue, Dakota jolts as I make contact, her legs spreading wider, inviting me in. Her taste is intoxicating, a mixture of salt and sweetness, and I can't get enough. My tongue circles her clit, teasing her with gentle flicks, and I can feel her tension building again.

"Frankie," she breathes, her voice a desperate plea. "Yes..."

I suck, drawing her swollen nub into my mouth, and her hips lift off the bed, her arms straining against the ties. Her responses fuel my own arousal, making me wetter with each of her gasps and moans. I slide my fingers up her inner thigh, tracing a path to her slick entrance, and she shudders as she balances on the edge.

Sliding two fingers into her, Dakota's tightness envelops me, and her hips buck wildly. She's so ready, and I thrust deeper, curling my fingers while my mouth devours her.

Her reaction is immediate, her body arching, her moans growing louder.

I increase the pressure with my mouth, my tongue flicking rapidly against her clit, and thrust my fingers faster, matching the rhythm of her rising pleasure.

"Let go, Dakota," I whisper against her.

Her body convulses, a violent tremor shaking her frame, and she screams my name, a raw, primal sound that echoes in the room. Her orgasm washes over her in waves, her inner walls clenching around my fingers as I continue to thrust. She's a sight to behold, so sensual, and I feel a rush of satisfaction. I've brought her to this point, made her lose herself completely.

I pull my fingers out gently, my mouth still working her through the aftershocks, until her body finally relaxes, her breathing slowing. I move up, kissing my way back up her body, tasting the remnants of ice and sweat on her skin. When I reach her mouth, I kiss her deeply, letting her taste herself on my lips.

Dakota's hands clench in the sheets, her body still shuddering now and then, and she looks at me with affection.

"Untie me," she whispers, and I reach up and gently release the knots, my fingers brushing her wrists as the bonds fall away. She rubs her wrists briefly, then her eyes lock on to mine with an intensity that makes my heart race.

Without warning, she raises herself and pushes me into the covers. Her strength surprises me, but I let her take control. Dakota straddles me, her thighs firm against my hips, her warmth seeping through our touch.

"It's my turn," she says, her voice low and sultry as her hands trail down my chest. She leans forward, her lips hovering just above mine, teasing me with the promise of a kiss. I can feel her breath, hot and tantalizing, before she brushes her lips against mine, not quite kissing, just enough to drive me crazy.

"Mmm..." I try to pull her closer to kiss her, but she resists and smiles wickedly as she shifts her hips, aligning herself with my center. The sensation of her wetness against me is almost too much, and I grip the sheets, trying to keep myself together.

Slowly, she grinds into me while roaming her hands over my breasts and I groan, grabbing her hips.

"I want you to watch," she whispers. "Just watch."

And I do. I watch as she begins to move, her hips rocking and her back arching in a slow, deliberate rhythm while her hair falls in wild waves around her face. Her eyes flutter closed, her lips parting in a silent moan, and I'm mesmerized by the sight of her. The way her body moves, the play of muscles, the sheen of sweat that makes her glow in the dim light.

"God, you're beautiful," I whisper, unable to tear my eyes away from her.

She opens her eyes, meeting my gaze. "So are you." She spreads her thighs farther apart and picks up the pace, and I feel her growing closer, the tension building between us.

I reach up, my hands sliding over her breasts, feeling their weight, their softness.

She gasps, arching into my touch, her rhythm faltering for a moment before she regains control. Her hands cover mine, guiding me, showing me how she likes to be touched.

"Yes..." I throw my head back and moan. "That feels..."

She rides me harder, her movements growing frantic. The coil of pleasure in my lower body winds tighter, ready to snap, and I know she's right there with me. Her eyes lock on to mine, and in that moment, we're completely in sync, our bodies moving as one when we crash together.

Our cries fill the room, while our bodies tremble with the force of our release. She clenches her thighs around me, holding me firmly in place and leaving me breathless and shaking.

Dakota collapses onto me, her head resting on my chest, and I wrap my arms around her, holding her close.

"Wow," I murmur after a while, my voice muffled against her neck. "That was..."

"Amazing," she says, snuggling closely against me as I wrap my arms around her. "Absolutely amazing." She lifts her head, her eyes meeting mine with a sweet, contented smile.

There's a warmth and softness there, something deeper and more profound than simple desire. Could this be love? The thought flutters in my mind, fragile and tentative.

Her lips part; she seems on the verge of saying something, her eyes flickering with unspoken words. Her smile widens, and she hesitates. "I uhm..."

"What?" I ask, brushing a hand over her cheek as her voice trails away.

Again, she stalls. "We're good together, don't you think? I don't just mean... uhm... physically," she clumsily adds.

"Yeah, we're great together," I whisper, sensing she's got more on her mind. I want to tell her how I feel, how deep this goes for me, but I can't burden her with my need. Not now, when she's just lost her job and has no idea where life will take her next.

Dakota nods as a shadow crosses her face. It's brief but unmistakable. Before I can ask her what's wrong, her smile returns and she plants playful kisses all over my face before changing the subject.

"How about that dinner you promised me? I don't know about you, but I've worked up quite an appetite."

41

DAKOTA

*T*he firepit crackles on the porch, and candles dot the table. Frankie has outdone herself, and the scent of grilling steak and vegetables mingles with the crisp night air. We sit side by side at the rustic wooden table, enjoying a glass of wine and the appetizers she's brought. The sourdough bread with olive oil, marinated olives, and artichokes are delicious, and I feel blissfully content and happy.

Both wrapped in the robes that came with the accommodation, we're relaxed after a long make-out session in the shower. Unwilling to be physically apart, even when we're eating, Frankie's moved her chair to sit next to me.

This is without a doubt the most romantic date I've ever had. She has a way of making me feel like I'm the only person in the world.

Frankie leans back in her chair, a satisfied smile playing on her lips as she takes a sip of her wine. She's so attractive I can't take my eyes off her.

"Thank you," I say. "This is truly special."

"I'm glad you're enjoying it. It makes me so happy to see you smile. I could live for that alone."

Her words make my heart swell, but they also bring a pang of sadness. I'm not used to women going to such great lengths for me. I've always been the one who puts in the effort, who goes the extra mile. It's a strange and wonderful feeling, but it also makes me realize how much I don't want this to end.

Frankie takes my hand in hers, her thumb gently stroking my knuckles. "What's on your mind?"

I take a deep breath, gathering my thoughts. "I don't know what to do. I have to start looking for another job soon, but I don't want to work in the spa industry, at least, not in Vegas," I confess, watching her expression closely. "I'm done with that toxic environment."

"Oh," she says, her voice careful. "Of course. I understand." She meets my eyes, and I can tell she's doing everything in her power to hide her disappointment. "I already knew there was a good chance you might move back. Of course, I'd rather you stayed here, but I want you to be happy."

"That's not what I meant," I say, shaking my head. "I started looking last week and there are a few great vacancies in California. Career-wise, that's tempting..." My voice trails off, and Frankie nods.

"There's a 'but'..."

"Yeah," I whisper and pause, struggling to find the right words. Finally, blowing out my cheeks, I decide to just say what I feel. What I've finally allowed myself to feel over the past weeks. "I'm in love with you. I love you, and I don't want to lose you."

Her grip on my hand tightens, and I feel her gaze on me, intense and searching. "Dakota," she says, her voice trembling. "I love you too."

"You do?" A smile breaks across my face as the uncertainty that's been gnawing at me dissolves, replaced by a sense of peace and belonging. "Because I want to give this a real go." Saying it out loud makes it so real and simple, and it comes with a clarity that cuts through all the confusion and doubt I've been feeling. "I've done some research into nursing jobs in Vegas," I continue. "They don't pay as well as the wellness industry, but at least we'd be together."

Frankie returns my smile. She looks emotional and a little shocked. "You have no idea how happy it makes me to hear you say that," she whispers. "But I'm worried staying in Vegas might make you resent me."

"I could never resent you," I say softly. "A job is just a job, but what we have is rare. I came here to start over, and that's what I want to do. With you."

A tear rolls down Frankie's cheek and she pulls me onto her lap to hug me. "Babe..." She kisses my cheek and holds me close. "Are you sure? Because I thought you hated Vegas and I had a feeling you missed home."

"Apart from my career, nothing is pulling me back home. My mother still lives in Newport Beach, but she's always away cruising, and as far as Vegas is concerned, it's not so bad." I feel myself blush, but I hold her gaze. "I wouldn't mind living in the desert."

"On a ranch in the desert?" Frankie asks.

"If you'll have me."

"Do you really need to ask?" She stares at me like she still can't quite believe it. "So this is happening..."

I giggle with giddiness, feeling lighter than I have in months. The weight of uncertainty that's been pressing on my chest since I moved to Vegas has finally lifted. Frankie's eyes shimmer with tears, and I'm struck by how beautiful she looks in this moment.

I lean in, resting my forehead against hers. A cool breeze blows in from the lake, making me shiver slightly. Frankie notices and pulls me closer, wrapping her arms around me. I snuggle into her warmth, marveling at how perfectly we fit together.

"It's strange," she murmurs. "Everything is different now. We don't need to take it one day at the time anymore. We can make plans. I got so used to not letting my mind go there, to not get carried away because I thought you would leave."

Cupping her cheek, I press a soft kiss to her lips. "When I lost my job, my first worry wasn't my career. It was not being near you anymore," I say, my voice breaking. "So let's look ahead together. I want to build a life with you."

A silence settles between us as we bask in the warmth of our newfound commitment. Frankie's arms around me feel like home and I breathe in her nearness.

We're interrupted by a persistent buzzing coming from my purse. At first, I ignore it, not wanting to break this perfect moment. But as it continues, a niggle of worry creeps in. *What if it's work? What if there's an emergency?*

"Maybe you should check that," Frankie says. "It sounds important."

Reluctantly, I disentangle myself from her embrace and reach for my phone. To my surprise, it's not work at all, but a stream of messages from my mother. My eyes widen as I read through them. "Oh no," I groan.

"What is it?" Frankie asks.

"It's my mom." I turn to her, still processing the information. "She's coming to visit next week—she always announces her arrival last-minute. She wants to know if she needs to book a hotel." I run a hand through my hair and sigh. "I guess I still have my apartment for another three weeks."

As I sit there, my mind racing with logistics, Frankie squeezes my thigh. "Hey, I have an idea," she says. "Why don't you and your mom stay at the ranch with me?"

I blink in surprise, not quite sure I've heard her correctly. "At the ranch?"

"Sure. You're moving in anyway, right? So why not? I'd love the opportunity to get to know your mom." She bites her lip and winces. "Unless that's too soon?"

"No... That's really sweet of you to offer, but Mom can be...a lot. She's energetic, opinionated, and has a tendency to redecorate every space she enters, even though she never sticks around for long."

Frankie laughs. "Sounds like she'll fit right in with the chaos of the ranch. Should I be worried about her giving the horses a makeover too?"

"I can't promise anything," I say with a chuckle. "But if you don't mind...I'd really like you to meet her."

"Then that's a deal." Frankie doesn't seem worried about meeting my mother at all.

"You seem so relaxed about this," I say, tracing patterns on her palm. "I was a nervous wreck when your parents showed up out of the blue after the storm and from the looks of it, you were too."

Frankie's lips quirk into a wry smile. "My parents...they worry. After Melanie left, they saw how much it hurt me. I think they're afraid to see me go through that again."

Her admission tugs at my heart, and I silently vow to never be the cause of such hurt. "And now?"

"Now it's different," she says, squeezing my hand. "I'm

more comfortable because I know what we have is real. It's not just a fleeting thing."

"Do you trust me?" I ask. "I need you to trust that I'm not going to hurt you."

"Yes, I trust you. I know this is real. I trust that you love me and want to be with me, but you need time to settle into a life that's entirely different from what you're living now."

"You still think I might change my mind..."

Frankie is silent for a long moment before she speaks. "I just think we need to see how it goes when you move in." She pinches my thigh. "Just wait until you find a tarantula in your bed. Or when you step in a giant pile of horse manure with your designer heels," she teases, lightening the mood. "I can already picture you hopping around, cursing up a storm and yelling you want to get the fuck out of there."

I roll my eyes and laugh. "Very funny. I'll have you know I'm tougher than I look."

"I know." Frankie's grin softens. She takes a sip of her wine, then sets the glass down with a soft clink. "So, do you want to tell me more about these nursing jobs you've been looking into?"

I sit up straighter, mentally scrolling through the vacancies I found. "Well, there's an opening at Desert Springs Hospital for a trauma nurse. It would be intense, but I think I'm ready for that kind of challenge again. And there's also a position at a community health clinic in Henderson," I continue. "It would be more regular hours, and I'd be working with underserved populations. There were more, but those were the ones that stood out for me. I have no idea if they'd even consider me. It's been so long since I worked as a nurse."

"But you have the qualifications and both sound like

great options," Frankie says. "How would you feel about getting back into nursing?"

I take a moment to consider that, my eyes drifting to the starry sky above us. "Nervous," I admit. "But also...excited. Hopeful. I went into nursing because I wanted to help people, and somewhere along the way, I lost sight of that. This feels like a chance to get back to my roots, you know?"

"I think you'll be amazing," Frankie says. "And I'll be here to support you every step of the way."

The grill starts smoking, and we realize we've forgotten all about the food.

Frankie jumps up to check on it and starts turning the steaks and the vegetables. "No harm done," she says, plating the vegetables that are a little charred. "I think we caught it just in time."

"I'll take over," I say, reaching for the tongs. "You've already done so much, driving and cooking." Frankie hesitates, but I snatch the tongs from her with a playful smile. "Let me help you. It's not up for discussion."

"All right. Thank you, but as long as we're clear that I won't let you help out on the ranch."

"Oh?" I prod the steaks to check if they're done. "Why not?"

"Because it's dirty work and I have enough help." Frankie passes me another plate, and I chuckle, shaking my head.

"Why? I'll be unemployed, at least for a while. You think I'm that fragile?"

"No. I just want to make sure you're happy and not overwhelmed. Moving there is a big step, and I want you to have space to adjust."

I plate the steaks and turn off the grill, mulling over Frankie's words. As we settle back at the table, I'm torn between gratitude for her consideration and a desire to prove myself.

"I appreciate that," I say, tossing the salad she's brought out. "But I want to be a part of your world. All of it. The good, the bad, and the dirty, so just put me to work."

"Be careful what you wish for, Miss Vegas." Frankie teases. "But if you insist, how do you feel about building a chicken coop with me?"

42

FRANKIE

I wipe the sweat from my brow, squinting against the late-afternoon glare as Dakota and I step back to admire our handiwork. The chicken coop stands before us, a sturdy, shaded structure of weathered wood and wire mesh nestled in the corner of the yard. It's taken us the better part of the weekend to build, and Dakota has helped me every night after work.

I have to admit, I was a little surprised at how handy she turned out to be. For a city girl, she sure knows her way around a toolbox.

My gaze wanders over to where she's standing, her hands on her hips as she surveys our creation. She's wearing a pair of denim cutoff shorts that showcase her tanned legs, and a tank top that clings to her curves in all the right places. Her hair is piled on top of her head in a messy bun, with a few loose strands framing her face. She looks incredible, all sun-kissed and glowing with exertion.

"Not bad, Miss Vegas," I say, my voice low and teasing as I sidle up beside her. "I think we make a pretty good team."

She grins, bumping her hip against mine. "Damn right

we do. Who knew building a chicken coop could be so much fun?"

"Only you would find manual labor enjoyable. Most people would be begging for a break by now."

She shrugs, her smile turning mischievous. "What can I say? I like getting my hands dirty. Besides, we're done, right? So we're due a really, really long break." She draws the words out as she pushes herself up against me.

My breath catches at the contact. "Is that so? And here I thought you were just in it for the chickens."

Dakota laughs. "Oh, don't get me wrong. I'm excited about the chickens too. But there are other perks to spending all this time out here with you."

"Oh? And what might those be?"

She leans in, her lips brushing against the shell of my ear. "Well, for one thing...I get to watch you work. And let me tell you, there's nothing sexier than seeing you all sweaty and focused, your muscles flexing as you hammer and saw and lift."

Funny," I murmur, my hands coming up to rest on her hips. "I was just thinking the same thing about you."

Dakota pulls back and raises a brow. "Oh yeah? You like seeing me get all dirty and disheveled?"

"Mmm, definitely. Especially when you're wearing those tiny little shorts that barely cover anything. I could—"

I stop myself and look up when a car pulls up the drive.

"Is that your parents' car?" Dakota takes a step back, creating some space between us. "I'm not decent," she says, looking down at herself. "I can't face them looking like this."

"Sure you can. You're on a ranch, not in a restaurant." I wave at my parents as they saunter toward us, their faces a mixture of curiosity and surprise. Dakota shifts nervously beside me, tugging at the hem of her shorts in a futile attempt to make them longer. I give her hand a reassuring squeeze before stepping forward to greet my folks.

"Mom, Dad," I say, embracing them both in turn. "What brings you out here today?"

My mother's eyes light up as she spots Dakota. "Dakota, sweetie! What a lovely surprise to see you here," she exclaims, moving past me to envelop her in a hug. Dakota looks momentarily startled but quickly relaxes into the embrace.

"It's great to see you too," she says, her voice warm with genuine affection.

My father, not one to be left out, steps forward to give Dakota a slightly awkward but heartfelt pat on the shoulder. "Good to see you again, young lady."

I catch the curious glances they're shooting between Dakota and me, but before I can formulate a response, my father's eyes scan the newly constructed chicken coop, his bushy eyebrows furrowing, then raising in confusion. "And what in tarnation is that contraption?" he asks, pointing to our handiwork.

I open my mouth to respond, but Dakota beats me to it, her enthusiasm getting the better of her nervousness. "It's a chicken coop!" she exclaims. "Frankie and I built it together."

My father's eyebrows shoot up even higher, threatening to disappear into his hairline. "A chicken coop?" he repeats. "What do you need chickens for, Frankie? You've never shown any interest in poultry before."

I take a deep breath, steeling myself for the conversation I'd been hoping to avoid for a little longer. "Well, Dad," I begin, "it's part of a new project I'm working on. I'm starting a small petting zoo here on the ranch."

The silence that follows is deafening. My father's face

goes through a series of expressions, from confusion to disbelief to something that looks suspiciously like disappointment. My mother, on the other hand, looks intrigued.

"A petting zoo?" my father finally manages to sputter. "Why on earth would you want to do that? This is a horse ranch, not a tourist trap."

I resist the urge to roll my eyes. "Dad, it's not that different from what we're already doing. The people who come here for horseback riding trips are tourists too."

He waves his hand dismissively. "That's different. Those are horse people. You can trust horse people. But day-trippers? Goat huggers?"

Dakota stifles a giggle beside me, and I have to bite the inside of my cheek to keep from laughing.

"Frank," my mother interjects, placing a calming hand on his arm. "I think it sounds like a lovely idea. Don't you remember how much fun the kids had when we used to take them to that petting zoo in Henderson?"

My father harrumphs and crosses his arms. "That was different," he mutters. "This is our family ranch, not a circus."

"Dad, you said you trusted me when you handed me the ranch," I remind him gently. "I appreciate your concern, but this is my decision to make."

"I just don't understand why you'd want to change things," he says with a shrug. "The ranch has been running fine for years. Why fix what ain't broke?"

I step closer to him, resting a hand on his shoulder. "Because sometimes change can be good, Dad. It doesn't mean we're getting rid of what makes this place special. We're just adding to it."

My father sighs and his expression wavers, his resolve

visibly weakening. "I suppose there's no talking you out of this, is there?"

"Afraid not, Dad. But I promise, we're not going to let anything bad happen to the ranch. This is just a new chapter, not a complete rewrite."

He nods, his eyes drifting back to the chicken coop. "Well, I suppose if you're going to do this, you might as well do it right," he grumbles. "That coop looks sturdy enough, but you'll want to reinforce the wire mesh. Coyotes are crafty devils and they'd love a chicken dinner."

I chuckle, relief washing over me. "Thanks, Dad. I'll be sure to do that."

My mother, who's been watching this exchange with barely concealed amusement, claps her hands together. "Well, now that that's settled, why don't we all go up to the porch? I made an apple pie, and I'm sure you two could use a break after all this hard work."

"That sounds great, Mom," I say.

Dakota nods enthusiastically. "Absolutely! Frankie's been telling me about your legendary apple pie."

"Has she?" Mom chuckles. "I hope it lives up to your expectations." Her eyes drop to our hands in between us, and it's only then that I realize our index fingers are linked. "So are you two..."

Hesitating for a beat, I turn to Dakota and I'm sure the glance that passes between us says it all. "Yeah...we're together," I finally say. "And Dakota is moving in with me."

My parents exchange a look, their expressions shifting from surprise to pure joy. Mom's face lights up like a Christmas tree as she brings her hands to her chest. "Oh, sweetheart!" she exclaims, rushing forward to pull both Dakota and me into a tight hug. "That's wonderful news!"

Dad's weathered face breaks into a wide grin, the kind I

haven't seen in a while. "Well, I'll be damned," he chuckles, shaking his head in amazement. "No wonder you two were out here building chicken coops together."

Mom releases us from her embrace, stepping back with a dramatic sigh as she takes Dakota's hand. "Welcome to the family, dear. Come on, let's get out of the sun before we burn to a crisp."

We step into the shade of the porch, and as I make coffee and watch Dakota help my mother set the table, laughing at something my father's just said, I'm struck by how right this feels. I spot Jose making his way toward us from the stables, his cowboy hat tilted at its usual angle.

"Jose!" I call out, waving him over. "Come join us. Mom's made apple pie."

He tips his hat in greeting, a warm smile spreading across his face as he climbs the porch steps. "Don't mind if I do," he says, pulling up a chair next to my father. Mom's already setting an extra plate for him, and Dakota pours him a cup of coffee.

My father leans over to him with a conspiratorial whisper that's loud enough for everyone to hear. "Jose, did you know about this petting zoo nonsense?"

"Oh, you mean Operation Swine and Dine? I've been sworn to secrecy, Frank."

Dakota nearly chokes on her pie, trying to stifle a laugh.

I shoot Jose a warning look, but it's too late. My father's eyebrows have already shot up again, his curiosity piqued.

"Dine?" he repeats, his eyes narrowing suspiciously. "What's this about dining?"

I sigh, knowing the jig is up. "I'm thinking of adding a small café to go with the petting zoo. You know, so people can have a coffee or grab a bite while their kids entertain themselves."

My father's face goes through a kaleidoscope of emotions. He opens his mouth, closes it, then opens it again, looking like a fish gasping for air.

"A café?" he finally gets out. "What's next? Goat yoga? Chicken line dancing? Pig mud wrestling?"

Dakota pipes up with a perfectly straight face, "Actually, Mr. Hawkins, Frankie was thinking more along the lines of 'Barn to Table' dining. You know, really embrace the farm-to-fork movement."

My father's eyes bulge so wide I'm afraid they might pop out of his head. He turns to my mother, his voice a mix of desperation and resignation. "Mary, quick, pinch me. I think I've fallen asleep and woken up in some kind of hipster nightmare."

My mother pats my father's hand consolingly. "There, there, dear," she says, her voice dripping with mock sympathy. "Just think of it as bringing the ranch into the twenty-first century. Who knows? You might even learn to like your coffee with oat milk and a side of avocado toast."

43

DAKOTA

*H*alf-full boxes and clothes are scattered around the living room. I pause in my packing and let out a long breath. It's strange how quickly a place can become familiar without ever truly feeling like home.

My gaze drifts around the apartment, taking in the bare walls and the empty spaces where my belongings once stood. It's a bittersweet feeling, this act of dismantling the life I thought I wanted. But as I tape up another box, I realize I don't regret a single moment of my time here. After all, it led me to Frankie.

A smile tugs at my lips as I think of her. Frankie, with her easy laugh and gentle strength, her unwavering support and the way she looks at me like I'm the most precious thing in the world. If coming to Vegas gave me nothing else, it gave me her, and that's worth more than any career advancement or fancy apartment.

My phone buzzes on the coffee table, pulling me from my reverie. It's a text from Serenity: *I'm downstairs at the restaurant!*

I glance at the clock and curse under my breath. I've lost track of time, caught up in my packing and reminiscing. Quickly, I run a brush through my hair and change into a fresh T-shirt, then grab my purse and keys.

Looking forward to seeing her, I hurry down the stairs, taking them two at a time. Over the past few weeks, as I've been wrapping up my time at the White Spa, we've grown closer, and what started as a professional relationship has blossomed into a genuine friendship.

The familiar sounds and smells of El Rincon greet me and the restaurant is bustling with its early evening crowd and the cheerful chatter of patrons. I spot Serenity at our usual table on the terrace, her face lighting up as she waves me over.

"Dakota!" she calls out, standing to give me a quick hug. "It's good to see you. I just couldn't wait to have a margarita and gossip."

"Same here." I laugh, sliding into the seat across from her. "I'm sorry if I kept you waiting. I got caught up in packing."

"Ooh, how's that going? Are you all set for the big move?"

Before I can answer, Gabriel appears at our table. "Ladies," he says warmly. "The usual?"

We nod in unison, and he chuckles. "Two zesty margaritas, coming right up."

As Gabriel heads back to the bar, I turn back to Serenity. "It's going okay," I say, answering her earlier question. "It's a bit surreal, you know? Packing up my life again so soon. But it feels right."

Serenity nods. "I'm going to miss you at work," she says. "It won't be the same without you. But I'm so happy for you, really."

I reach across the table and squeeze her hand. "I'm going to miss you too. But hey, the ranch isn't that far. We'll still see each other, right?"

"Absolutely," Serenity says firmly. "You're not getting rid of me that easily. I expect regular updates on your new life as a cowgirl."

"Actually, I've applied for a few nursing jobs," I say, feeling a flutter of excitement in my stomach. "I'm waiting to hear back, but there's an opening at Desert Springs Hospital for a trauma nurse that I'm really hoping for."

"Oh, that's right! I remember you telling me that you used to be a nurse. Dakota, that's so exciting!"

"Yeah. It's a little scary but I'm ready for the challenge."

"You're going to be amazing," she says. "Those patients won't know how lucky they are to have you caring for them."

Gabriel returns with our margaritas and a large jug of ice-water.

"To new beginnings," Serenity raises her glass and takes a sip.

"To new beginnings." Serenity has no idea of the real reason I asked to meet up, and I can't wait to tell her. "So, how was work today?"

"It was fine, nothing too dramatic," she says. "But I won't lie. I'm nervous about your replacement, whomever that will be. I've worked for some real nightmares before." She chuckles as she shoots me a pleading look. "Please don't employ an asshole."

"You won't have to worry about that," I say, leaning in. "How would you feel about becoming the new general manager?"

Her mouth falls open, and for a beat, she's speechless, which is a rare occurrence for the usually talkative Serenity. "Me?" she finally squeaks out. "Are you serious?"

I nod, my smile widening. "Absolutely. In fact, you're my first choice for the job."

Serenity's expression cycles through disbelief and excitement. "But...why me?"

I take a sip of my margarita, gathering my thoughts. "Because you're perfect for it," I say simply. "You know the spa inside and out. You have a great rapport with the staff and the clients. And more importantly, you care. You care about the quality of our work, about the well-being of your colleagues, about making the White Spa the best it can be."

Serenity's eyes are shining now, and for a moment, I think she's going to burst into tears.

"You're ambitious," I continue. "I've seen how hard you work, how eager you are to learn and grow. You've got great ideas, and as general manager, you'd have the chance to implement them."

"But," Serenity interjects, her practical side asserting itself, "I don't have any management experience."

I wave away her concern. "Experience isn't everything. Skills can be learned—I'll sign you up for a few courses—and everyone has to start somewhere. What matters is your attitude, your passion, and your willingness to take on challenges. Those are things you have in spades."

She sits back in her chair as she processes what I'm saying. "Wow," she breathes. "I didn't expect this. I don't know what to say."

"Say yes," I urge her gently. "Say you'll at least consider it. I've already spoken to the White Spa central HR department and Mr. Thornton about it. They agree that promoting from within would be ideal, and they trust me to make the right decision."

Still buffering, Serenity stares at me for a moment. "Yes,"

she says, her voice growing stronger. "Yes. Who am I kidding? Of course I want it!"

We both burst into laughter, the joy of the moment bubbling over. Gabriel, drawn by our excitement, comes over to check on us.

"What's all this celebration about?" he asks.

"We're toasting to the future general manager of the White Spa," I announce proudly, gesturing to Serenity.

"And to Dakota moving in with her cowgirl," Serenity adds.

Gabriel grins. "Ay, que bueno! This calls for a special toast. Wait here."

He disappears into the restaurant, returning moments later with a bottle of champagne and three glasses. As he pops the cork, other patrons turn to look, drawn by the festive atmosphere.

"To you both," he says, raising his glass. "Serenity, may your new position bring you as much joy as you bring to others, and Dakota, I'm so happy for you, but I will miss you, my friend."

"And I'll miss you. Thank you, Gabriel. You really didn't need to do that," I say, touched by his gesture.

"Nonsense. I've never had such a nice neighbor. You've been a bright spot in this place, and I hope we'll stay in contact."

"Of course we will," I assure him, feeling a lump form in my throat. "Once I get myself a medical job in Vegas, I'll make sure to stop by regularly for a much-needed margarita. And you're always welcome to visit the ranch."

"I might just take you up on that offer," he says. "It's been too long since I've seen the stars properly, away from all these city lights." He pulls up a chair and joins us at the

LISE GOLD & MADELEINE TAYLOR

table, pouring himself a small glass of champagne. "So, tell me about your plans. When's the big move?"

I take a sip of my champagne, savoring it. "Well, I still have to work for another few weeks to wrap everything up and train Serenity, so I'll keep my apartment until my lease runs out," I explain, giving my friend a warm smile. "But my mother is actually arriving tomorrow, and we'll stay on the ranch because I want her to meet Frankie."

"Tomorrow?" Serenity chuckles when I wince. "Are you ready for her?"

I let out a nervous laugh. "I'm not sure if I'm ready, to be honest. I've taken a few days off because we'll have a lot to catch up on. It's been a while since I've seen her, and so much has changed."

"Is she excited about your move? About Frankie?"

"She doesn't know anything yet," I admit, fidgeting with my glass. "I just said I'd made arrangements for accommodation and that I'd pick her up from the airport. She doesn't know I quit my job and she doesn't know I'm in a relationship. It's not that we're not close, but we prefer to catch up when we meet."

"Wow, that's a lot to spring on her at once," Gabriel says. "Do you think she'll be okay with everything?"

I bite my lip, a mix of excitement and anxiety churning inside me. "The question is, will I be okay with her? Ever since Dad passed away, she's become larger than life. Traveling everywhere, trying to experience everything. It's like she's constantly trying to cram a year into a week."

Serenity's eyebrows shoot up. "That sounds...exhausting."

"It is," I admit. "She's hyperactive, always on the go, always talking, always seeking distraction. I'll have to keep her busy."

Gabriel chuckles. "Well, if she becomes too much, you can drop her off here. I'm sure we can keep her entertained with margaritas and put her to work doing the dishes. Nothing like a good old-fashioned kitchen shift to wear someone out."

"Or I could give her a four-hour makeover," Serenity chips in. "By the time I'm done, she'll be ready for a nap."

44

FRANKIE

*D*akota's mother is a vision in hot pink, her outfit a stark contrast to the dusty browns and greens of the ranch. She's wearing a flowing kaftan that catches the breeze, adorned with intricate gold embroidery that glitters in the afternoon sun. Her wrists jingle with an assortment of bangles, and oversize sunglasses perch atop her perfectly coiffed silver hair. She looks like she's stepped straight off a private jet and onto our dirt driveway.

"Mom, this is Frankie," Dakota says as they approach, a mix of nervousness and excitement in her voice.

I step forward, extending my hand. "It's a pleasure to meet you, Mrs. Walker. Welcome to Red Rock Ranch."

"Oh, darling, call me Vivian," she says, bypassing my outstretched hand and pulling me into a perfumed embrace. "Any woman who can make my Dakota glow like this is family already."

I catch Dakota's eye over her mother's shoulder, and she gives me an apologetic shrug, her cheeks flushing slightly.

As Vivian releases me, she takes a step back, her gaze

sweeping over the ranch. "Well, isn't this quaint! I feel like I'm in a John Wayne movie."

I chuckle, unsure if that's a compliment or not. "I hope that's a good thing. Your outfit is stunning, by the way. I'm afraid we don't see much pink around these parts."

Vivian beams, doing a little twirl that sends her kaftan fluttering. "Oh, this old thing? I packed for Vegas nightclubs, you know. I thought Dakota and I would be painting the town red, sipping cocktails in those flashy clubs on the Strip." She leans in conspiratorially. "I even brought my sequined jumpsuit for the occasion."

"Mom," Dakota groans, but there's affection in her voice.

"I hope you're not too disappointed," I say, suddenly worried that our quiet ranch might be a letdown after the glitz and glamour Vivian was expecting.

"Disappointed? Absolutely not!" she exclaims, her bangles jingling as she waves her hands expressively. "This is even more of an adventure. When Dakota told me everything in the car— quitting her job, falling in love with a cowgirl—well, I nearly fell out of my seat. It's like something out of a romance novel."

Dakota shoots me a look that's equal parts embarrassment and amusement. "Mom, I told you, Frankie's not a cowgirl. That's just a cute nickname I gave her. She runs a horse ranch and she's also a qualified veterinarian."

"A vet? How marvelous!" Vivian claps her hands together. "So you have horses?"

"Many," I say with a chuckle. "I could teach you how to groom a horse or even how to ride."

Vivian's eyebrows shoot up from behind her enormous sunglasses. "Oh, that sounds divine! Dakota, why didn't you tell me your Frankie was so accommodating?"

"I'm sure I mentioned it, Mom," Dakota says, rolling her

eyes good-naturedly. "Come on, let's get your bags inside. I'm sure you want to freshen up after the flight."

As we help Vivian with her luggage—a matching set of hot-pink suitcases that look comically out of place—I'm still processing the whirlwind of energy that surrounds this woman. She chatters away, pointing out everything from the "charming" weathered wood of the porch to the "delightful" smell of hay in the air.

"Now, girls," Vivian says as we enter the house, "I hope I'm not intruding on your love nest. I know young couples need their space when the relationship is in the height of the physical stage."

"Mom!" Dakota exclaims, nearly dropping the suitcase she's carrying.

I feel my cheeks heat up, but I manage to keep my composure. "Not at all, Vivian. We're happy to have you here. The guest room is all set up for you."

"Oh, how lovely," Vivian coos, peering into the room. "It's so rustic, like a high-end glamping experience." Then she spots the pictures on the wall, a collection of photos showcasing the ranch's history. "Oh my, is that you, Frankie?"

I move closer, seeing the photo she's pointing at. It's a picture of me at about eight years old, sitting atop my first pony, a gap-toothed grin on my face. "Yeah, that's me. I practically grew up in the saddle."

"You know, Dakota used to ride when she was little too. Do you remember, sweetie? Those pony rides at the county fair?"

Dakota groans. "Those hardly count as 'riding.' And I was terrified the whole time."

"Nonsense," Vivian waves a hand. "You were a natural.

I'm sure with Frankie's expertise, you'll be galloping across the desert in no time."

I catch Dakota's eye, and we share a silent laugh. "Well," I say, clapping my hands together, "why don't we let you get settled in? Dakota and I will start on dinner. Are you up for a grill around the fire? I have a group of eight arriving tomorrow so it's the only night we have the firepit to ourselves. I thought we could make the most of it."

Vivian's eyes light up. "A campfire? Amazing! Will there be cowboy songs and ghost stories? Now, tell me about these guests you mentioned," she continues without waiting for an answer.

"They're a mixed group," I explain, leaning against the kitchen counter. "Some are experienced riders looking for a new adventure, others are complete beginners. They're staying for two nights and we'll be doing tours through some of the most beautiful parts of the desert. I've already arranged for you and Dakota to join us if you'd like. It's a great way to see the area. But if you'd rather spend some time in the city, that's perfectly fine too."

"Horseback riding through the desert? Please, count us in. Especially since we'll have our very own cowgirl to keep us safe." She winks at me, and I feel my cheeks flush. "Well, I'd better get freshened up quickly. I don't want to miss a minute with the two of you."

As soon as the door closes, Dakota blows out her cheeks. "I'm so sorry about her," she whispers. "She can be a bit extra."

"A bit?" I laugh. "Just kidding, I think she's great." I wrap an arm around her as we head to the kitchen. "Her enthusiasm is infectious."

"Let's see how you feel in a few days," Dakota shoots back humorously. She opens the fridge and takes out the marinated vegetables and salads we prepared earlier. While she dresses the salads, I plate salmon steaks and burgers. I like cooking with Dakota. There's always this comfortable silence between us while we constantly seek out each other's nearness. Although she hasn't even moved in officially, it's like she's always been here.

"So," I say, glancing over at her, "how was the drive from the airport?"

"Oh, it was an experience. I think I managed to cover most of the major points between her exclamations about the desert landscape and her detailed recounting of her latest cruise adventure."

"And how did she take the news about your career change?"

"Surprisingly well, actually," Dakota says, pausing in her task. "Though I think she's more excited about the whole 'falling in love with a cowgirl' part of the story."

Dakota turns, a soft smile on her face. "It's my favorite part," she says, leaning in for a kiss.

We're interrupted by a shrill scream from the bathroom. Vivian's voice echoes through the house, "There's a huge spider in here!"

Dakota glances at me, both of us suppressing our laughter. "I've got this," she says, squaring her shoulders.

I watch in amusement as she confidently marches toward the bathroom, and follow, eager to see how this will play out.

"Don't worry, Mom," she calls out. "I'll take care of it."

Vivian is standing in the hallway wrapped in a towel, her eyes wide. "Be careful, sweetie. It's huge. I think it might be poisonous."

"It's just a spider. They're harmless." Dakota steps into

the bathroom, scanning the tiles. Then she freezes, her bravado deflating. "Oh...that big."

I peek over her shoulder to see a tarantula, about the size of my palm, perched on the edge of the bathtub. It's harmless indeed, but I can understand why it might be intimidating.

"It's okay," Dakota says, her voice much higher than usual. "I've got this. Just need to...catch it."

What follows is a dance that would put any contemporary choreographer to shame. I watch, biting my lip to keep from laughing, as Dakota pirouettes around the bathroom, alternating between lunging at the spider and leaping back when it moves. Her arms windmill as she tries to corral it with a towel, all while keeping maximum distance between herself and her eight-legged adversary.

"Careful, honey!" Vivian calls out from the hallway. "Maybe you should let Frankie handle it."

"No, no," Dakota insists, her voice strained. "I'm fine. Totally fine."

I can't help but tease her a little. "You're doing great, babe."

Dakota ignores me and makes another lunge with the towel, but the spider skitters away, causing her to yelp. "Okay," she pants, her hair askew. "You're right. Frankie, honey...a little help?"

I step forward, unable to contain my grin, and with practiced ease, I scoop up the tarantula in my hands. It sits calmly in my palm, its fuzzy legs tickling my skin. Dakota and Vivian both stare at me, open-mouthed.

"See? Nothing to worry about," I say, heading toward the door. "I'll just relocate our little friend outside."

When I pass Vivian, she shrieks and runs back into the bathroom, slamming the door behind her.

Dakota follows me out to the porch, where I gently set the tarantula down in a nearby shrub, and as we watch it scurry away, she bumps her shoulder against mine.

"Show-off," she mutters, but there's a smile in her voice.

"I should have checked the guest bathroom before she went in there. It hasn't been used in a while, so I'm not surprised big boy decided to make it his home." I pull her in to steal a kiss and shoot her a teasing look. "Still think you can handle ranch life?"

Dakota laughs, shaking her head. "Ranch life, sure. But maybe we can add 'spider duty' to your list of chores?"

45

DAKOTA

*T*he desert stretches out before us, a vast expanse of rugged beauty. I'm astride Sahara, her rhythmic gait lulling me into a sense of calm. Ahead of us, Frankie leads our group, her voice carrying back as she points out various desert flora and fauna.

I marvel at how effortlessly she commands attention. Her expertise is evident in every word she speaks, yet there's a warmth and humor to her delivery that keeps everyone engaged.

Beside me, Mom sits atop her own horse. She's wearing the cowboy boots and hat Frankie lent her, but true to form, she insisted on pairing them with a flowing, floral dress. The effect is both comical and endearing—so quintessentially Mom.

"What's that grin for?" Mom asks, catching my eye.

"Just admiring your riding outfit," I tease. "I'm sure the cacti appreciate the fashion show."

She laughs. "Well, honey, you gotta dress for the occasion. And today's occasion happens to be 'cowgirl meets desert flower.' You used to love dressing up when you were little."

"I think mainly you liked to dress *me* up," I retort with a chuckle. "You used to buy me these outrageous dresses when we went shopping, but I hardly ever wore them."

"Hmm..." Mom seems to ponder over that as she gazes out over the landscape. "I suppose you're right. I just loved our occasional girls' days out, and dressing up was always a big part of that." She turns to me. "You know, it's so good to see you again, sweetie. I've really missed you."

"I've missed you too, Mom."

She sighs, fiddling with her reins. "I feel kinda selfish, gallivanting around the world instead of visiting you. I should've made more of an effort and come sooner."

"It's okay," I assure her. "I get it. After Dad passed...well, you needed your freedom. You were always tied to the farm. I figure you felt like you had years to make up for."

Mom stares at me, and she's quiet for a moment. "That's not entirely true," she finally says. "Yes, I was a little bored at the farm, and I always fancied myself more worldly than that life. But after your father passed..." She pauses. "I realized I'd never fully appreciated the beautiful life we had together, and I struggled with a lot of guilt for sometimes wanting to leave."

I reach out, placing my hand on her arm. "Mom, you don't have to explain—"

"No, I do," Mom insists. "I don't want you to think I didn't love your father. But when you went to college, it was so quiet, and I guess part of me resented him for being stuck on the farm. All he ever did when he wasn't working was fix up that old pickup of his." She narrows her eyes at me. "Do you still have it?"

"No," I say, and let out a long sigh. Every time I think of that pickup, a pang of guilt hits me, and I avoid my mother's gaze as I continue. "I sold it. It wasn't suitable for Vegas. The repairs alone would have cost me a fortune, and I didn't see the point of keeping it as I thought I'd be staying in the city."

"Of course, honey." Mom gives me a reassuring smile. "You did what you had to do, and anyway, that old truck never suited you and—" She bites her lip and stops herself. "Well, I suppose it would've come in handy now, but you never saw this coming, did you? Meeting Frankie and moving to her ranch..."

"No, never," I admit. "But it's okay. I hope someone else will love Henry as much as dad and I did."

Mom nods. "I sometimes regret selling the farm," she says. "But I tell myself the same. Some other family will be very happy there."

I'm taken aback by Mom's admission. All this time, I thought she'd been living her dream, finally free from the constraints of farm life.

"I had no idea you felt that way," I say. "I always thought you couldn't wait to leave it behind."

She shrugs. "The truth is, I couldn't be on the farm after your father passed away. That was the real reason I sold it. It was too hard being reminded of him everywhere I looked." Her eyes are glistening with unshed tears. "He was the love of my life. I see that now. And although I love traveling, it was more of an escape to begin with. I was running away, seeking distraction from feelings I hadn't processed."

I feel a lump form in my throat. "Oh, Mom..."

She manages a watery smile. "But seeing you here, so happy and in love...it reminds me of how your father and I were when we first met. "Did I ever tell you how we met?"

I shake my head, surprised by her sudden openness. Since Dad's death, Mom has rarely spoken about him, let alone shared stories from their past. "No, you never did," I say, encouraging her to continue.

"I was in my second year of university, studying literature and dreaming of becoming a romance writer. Your father was already running the farm—he was quite a bit older than me, as you know. Anyway," Mom continues, "I was at this local farmers' market with my roommate. We were broke college students, scrounging for cheap produce. And there he was, standing behind this table full of the most beautiful fruit I'd ever seen."

I can't help but smile, picturing a younger version of my father proudly displaying his harvest.

"He looked so out of place." Mom chuckles. "All rugged and tanned, surrounded by art students. But there was something about him that caught my eye. He had this quiet confidence, like he knew exactly who he was and where he belonged in the world."

"That sounds like Dad."

Mom nods, her eyes misty. "I struck up a conversation with him about his peaches. They were these gorgeous, perfectly ripe fruits—I'd never tasted anything like them. And as we talked, I found myself captivated by his passion for farming. He spoke about the land with such reverence, such love. It was…intoxicating."

I listen, enthralled. I'd never heard this side of their story before.

"We ended up talking for hours," Mom says. "The market was closing down around us, but we barely noticed. He invited me to visit the farm, see where the magic happened, as he put it."

"And you went?" I ask, already knowing the answer.

"Of course I did." Mom laughs. "The very next weekend. I told myself it was research for a story I was writing, but deep down, I knew it was more than that. When I arrived at the farm, your father was waiting for me. He gave me a tour, showing me every inch of the place with such pride in his eyes."

I can picture it clearly—the rolling hills of our farm, the neat rows of fruit trees, the old barn where Dad kept his tractor.

"By the end of the day," Mom says, her voice soft with nostalgia, "I was head over heels. We started dating, and after my graduation, I moved in with him."

"And then farm life got in the way of your career?" I ask.

"No..." Mom hesitates. "Your father always encouraged me to follow my dreams. But I suppose deep down, I knew I wasn't the most talented writer, and I used the farm as an excuse not to go down that career path." She shrugs. "Perhaps I just wasn't confident enough. I recently started writing and I'm really enjoying it."

I'm stunned by this. "You're writing? Mom, that's amazing! Why didn't you tell me?"

Mom shrugs, a hint of embarrassment coloring her cheeks. "I guess I wasn't sure if it would amount to anything. But during my last few cruises, I found myself with a lot of time to think and reflect. Once I realized I was using travel as a way to run from my emotions, I decided that writing might be a more productive way to process everything."

"That's really great," I say. "What are you working on?"

She lets out a small laugh, her eyes twinkling with mischief. "Well, believe it or not, I'm writing a romance novel. It's about a young girl who falls in love with an older farmer."

"So, basically, you're writing your own love story?"

"With a few creative liberties," she admits. "But yes, I suppose I am. It's been...cathartic, in a way. Reliving those early days, remembering how it felt to fall in love with your father."

As we continue to ride, Mom shares more details about her novel. I listen, fascinated by this side of her I've never seen before. It's like I'm getting to know both my parents all over again, through her words.

"Mom," I say, after she finishes describing a particularly touching scene, "I'd love to read it sometime, if you're willing to share."

Mom's face lights up. "Really? You would?"

"Of course. What are you planning to do with it?"

She shakes her head and winces. "Oh, I don't know, honey. For now, it's just for me. But if you think it's any good, I might consider sharing it with the world."

"That's so great, Mom." I reach out to take her hand, but Savannah has other plans. She suddenly lurches to the side, startled by a jackrabbit darting across our path. I yelp, grabbing on to the saddle horn for dear life.

"Whoa there, Savannah!" I call out, trying to sound authoritative but probably just sounding panicked.

Mom bursts into laughter beside me. "Oh, honey," she wheezes between giggles. "You should see your face right now! Some cowgirl you are!"

I shoot her a mock glare. "Hey, I'm still in training, okay?"

Frankie, who has heard the commotion, trots back to us. "Everything all right?"

"Everything's fine," Mom says, still chuckling. "Just my daughter here showing off her expert equestrian skills."

I feel my cheeks flush. "A jackrabbit startled Savannah, that's all. I had it under control."

"Uh-huh," Frankie says with a teasing smile. "Well, just remember, babe, the idea is to stay on top of the horse, not under it."

"Ha-ha," I deadpan. "You're both hilarious. Really, you should take this comedy show on the road."

Mom and Frankie exchange a look, and suddenly they're both laughing. I try to maintain my indignant expression, but their laughter is infectious, and soon I'm joining in.

Frankie reaches over and adjusts my hat, which had gone askew during my near-tumble. "There," she says, her hand lingering on my cheek. "You're doing great, babe."

She rides back upfront, pulls her horse to a stop and calls out for us to do the same. "I'm sure you've seen a few of these along our route," she says as we gather around her, pointing to a large, gnarled creosote bush. Beneath its sprawling branches, a cluster of smaller plants flourishes in the shade. "See that? That's what we call a nurse plant. That old creosote bush there? It's not just surviving on its own. It's creating a safe haven for these younger plants to grow. It shields them from the harsh sun, traps moisture, and even enriches the soil as its leaves fall. In the desert, life thrives on these small kindnesses." Her eyes find mine, a soft smile playing on her lips. "Sometimes, all it takes is a little shelter and care for something beautiful to grow."

"That's so sweet," Mom says dramatically, looking at the plants like they're newborn babies.

"I've never thought of it like that, but you're right, Vivian." Frankie shoots mom a wink. "Another example of desert kindness is the desert tortoise. These resilient creatures dig deep burrows that become sanctuaries for other animals, from small mammals to reptiles and even birds. It's like they're running a desert bed-and-breakfast, minus the breakfast part." This elicits a chuckle from the group.

As we resume our ride, Mom's flowery dress flutters in the breeze, a splash of color against the wild backdrop. She's beaming, clearly in her element as she straightens her cowboy hat, a gleam of determination in her eyes. Frankie's voice drifts back, already explaining the next wonder awaiting our discovery.

46

FRANKIE

I wipe my brow as I finish grooming Texas after our final ride with the guests. The past few days have been a whirlwind of activity—leading trail rides, answering endless questions about desert life, and trying to keep up with Vivian. Dakota's mother is a force of nature, bringing boundless energy and enthusiasm to every corner of the ranch.

Seeing Dakota and her mother bond over shared experiences, watching Vivian's eyes light up at each new discovery—it's been more rewarding than I could have imagined.

I close the stall door and lean against it for a moment, savoring the quiet. The guests have just left, but my day is far from over. In a fit of what I can only describe as temporary insanity, I've invited my parents, Jose, and Rennie and Leslie over for dinner. It seemed like a good idea at the time—a chance for everyone to meet Dakota and Vivian properly. Now, with the prospect of entertaining looming before me, I'm not so sure.

Dakota appears, silhouetted against the late afternoon

sun. "Hey," she calls, a teasing lilt to her voice. "You planning on hiding out here all evening?"

I push off from the stall door and make my way toward her. "Tempting," I admit, pulling her into my arms. "Think anyone would notice if we just didn't show up?"

"I'm pretty sure your parents might have something to say about that, but I don't think Mom would let a little thing like our absence stop her from hosting a party."

I laugh, burying my face in her hair. "Yeah, I'd better get those jugs of margarita ready."

"No need, Mom's already done that," Dakota says, pulling me toward the house. "And we prepped a grazing board while you were tending to the horses, so it's practically done." She stops on the porch, kisses me and rubs her nose against mine. "No more work for you, babe. Just sit down and relax."

"Thank you," I say gratefully, and pull her in for another kiss before settling into a chair on the porch and bracing myself for the impending chaos.

Jose is the first to arrive as he too has been hiding in the stables, grooming the horses. He tips his hat to Dakota and me before making his way to the porch. He's immediately engulfed in Vivian's enthusiastic greeting, even though she only saw him an hour ago while he helped her off her horse.

My parents follow close behind, their familiar bickering a comforting background noise as they make their way up the steps. Dad's already eyeing the margarita pitcher, while Mom fusses with a dish she's brought along "just in case." I shake my head, knowing full well our spread is more than enough, but appreciating her thoughtfulness all the same.

But it's Rennie and Leslie's arrival that really catches my attention. As they emerge from their car, I have to bite my lip to keep from laughing out loud. Rennie, usually so at home in her casual jeans and T-shirts, is decked out in what appears to be a full suit—complete with a tie. In the heat of the desert afternoon, she looks like she's about to melt.

Leslie, on the other hand, seems completely unfazed by the occasion. She's wearing a breezy sundress and is already chattering away before she's even left the car. "I brought some homemade meatballs," she yells while I walk toward them. "And a few zero percent beers for Rennie because she promised to drive back."

"Thank you, that's lovely." I give Leslie a hug and take the tray of meatballs from her before I turn to Rennie. "You dressed up," I say, suppressing a grin. "You look great."

Rennie shoots me a look that could curdle milk. "I wanted to make a good impression," she hisses under her breath. "I don't know what I was thinking. I'm boiling, but you know I'm not good with new people. I get all weird and shit."

"There's nothing to be nervous about," I assure her. "You already know my parents and Jose. It's just—"

Before I can finish my sentence, Vivian sweeps down from the porch, a vision in flowing, turquoise chiffon and jangling bracelets. "Well, hello there!" she calls out, her voice carrying across the yard. "You must be Rennie and Leslie. I've heard so much about you both!"

Rennie stiffens as Vivian approaches, but Leslie, true to form, meets Vivian's enthusiasm head-on.

"Oh, Vivian, it's so wonderful to meet you!" Leslie gushes, clasping Vivian's hands in her own. "That outfit is amazing. Where did you find it?"

And just like that, Leslie and Vivian are off, chatting away like old friends as we make our way to the porch.

Dakota gets up to greet Leslie warmly, then turns to Rennie and takes both her hands. "Hey, Rennie," she says sweetly. "I'm so glad you're here. I'll be honest. I've been a little nervous about meeting Frankie's best friend, so please go easy on me."

Rennie's shoulders relax a fraction, a small smile tugging at the corners of her mouth. "If anyone's nervous, it's me, but it's lovely to meet you too," she says, tugging at her tie when Dakota pulls out a chair for her. "If you don't mind, I might get rid of this first before I pass out from heat stroke."

"Of course. Take it off." Dakota rubs her shoulder. "You look great by the way, but if it's too warm, you're welcome to borrow a T-shirt. Do you want to come in so I can find you something? And then you can help me bring the food out." Dakota meets my eyes for a beat and a warm moment of understanding passes between us. She's so good with people, and she couldn't have said anything better to make Rennie feel more at ease.

"Really?" Rennie's smile widens. "I'd love that. This was a silly move. I thought you'd all be dressed up for some reason. Well, some of you are..." she adds with a frown, raising a hand to greet my parents and Jose.

I get her confusion; it's a strange tableau before me. Poor Rennie looks like she's going to a wedding. Dakota is wearing a simple, strappy olive-green dress. Her long hair is pulled up into a topknot and she's barefoot. She looks radiant and beautiful, but I suppose she's not the glamour babe Rennie expected. Mom and Dad don't look any different than usual, both in jeans, shirts, and cowboy boots. Jose and I are still wearing our riding attire, while Leslie and Vivian are dressed up to the nines.

While Dakota and Rennie slip inside, I pour water and margaritas for everyone. My parents are already deep in conversation with Jose, no doubt discussing the latest ranch business. Vivian and Leslie are having an animated discussion about fashion, punctuated by frequent bursts of laughter.

A few minutes later, Dakota and Rennie return, carrying a huge, stunning grazing board filled with an array of snacks and finger food. It's a work of art, overflowing with an assortment of cheeses—sharp cheddar, creamy brie, and tangy goat cheese—alongside bunches of juicy grapes, sliced apples, and dried apricots. There's a selection of cured meats, olives, and pickles, with clusters of mixed nuts filling in the gaps. Artfully arranged crackers and slices of crusty baguette border the edges.

Leslie's meatballs take center stage in a separate dish, their savory aroma making my mouth water. They're nestled in a rich tomato sauce, topped with a sprinkle of fresh basil. Alongside, there's a platter of colorful crudités with home-made ranch dip, and a bowl of Mom's famous seven-layer dip surrounded by crispy tortilla chips.

Rennie, now looking much more comfortable in one of my T-shirts, seems to have relaxed considerably as she helps Dakota arrange everything on the table before slipping back inside to get small plates and napkins.

"I think your mom just made a new best friend," I whisper when Dakota settles next to me.

She nods as she regards Vivian and Leslie, who have now moved on to the topic of cruising. "She has that effect on people. Give it another hour, and they will probably be planning their next vacation together."

"Please, not another friend," Rennie groans as she joins us. She turns to Dakota with a sheepish grin. "Sorry. No offense, your mom seems great, but Leslie has one thousand two-hundred and eighty-four friends on Facebook and she knows them all personally."

"And let me guess...you're not the most social type?" Dakota asks.

Rennie chuckles, shaking her head. "Not even close. I'm more of a 'hide in the corner with a beer' type. But..." She addresses me and nudges Dakota with her elbow. "This one seems to have a knack for making even introverts feel at ease." The genuine warmth in Rennie's voice makes me smile. It's clear that my best friend and my girlfriend are hitting it off, and I couldn't be happier.

"Well, I'm glad you said that, because Dakota's lease is up soon and she's officially moving in next week."

"I know, I'm super happy for you both. Frankie also told me you'd quit your job," Rennie says to Dakota. "That's so brave. How's the job hunting going?"

"So far so good, but I'm not holding my breath just yet. I have two second interviews lined up, so fingers crossed." Dakota shrugs happily. "I'm sure something will work out eventually, but until then, I intend to enjoy my free time on the ranch." She laughs when Marty and Dobby appear at the bottom of the porch steps. "Oh, hello there."

Catching the scent of the crudités, their noses are twitching comically. Marty lets out a plaintive whinny, while Dobby brays softly, both looking up at us with hopeful eyes.

"Well, would you look at that." Dad shakes his head. "A pony and a donkey begging for vegetables." He huffs, but I can see the pair are growing on him, despite his gruff exterior.

Marty stands up on his hind legs, front hooves resting on the porch steps. Dobby, not to be outdone, starts to sway back and forth, his long ears flopping in an almost rhythmic dance.

"Oh, aren't they adorable!" Vivian exclaims, getting up to

feed them both a carrot stick. "I can't wait to come back and see what else you've added to the furry family."

"Yeah, when are you expanding?" Leslie asks.

"I'm picking up a few chickens next week," I say, avoiding my dad's gaze. "Along with two potbellied pigs and three goats that need a home."

"Goats?" Dad interjects, eyebrows raised. "You're really going all in on this farm animal business so soon? You don't even have somewhere to put them."

"Jose and I start tomorrow," I say. "We're building an enclosure around the old shed, where the café will be. It doesn't have to be perfect. We can finish it later."

There's a moment of silence as everyone processes this information. Then, predictably, Dad speaks up. "Frankie, don't you think you might be biting off more than you can chew here? Running a ranch is already a full-time job, and now you want to add running a café on top of that?"

"I won't run it myself," I say simply. "I'll hire someone to run it for me. I'm sure there are plenty of people who would love a side hustle. They don't need to have qualifications, but they'd need to be sociable and good with animals. Oh, and they'd need to make a mean cup of coffee and be able to prepare basic food—you know, sandwiches, pastries, that sort of thing."

As I'm speaking, I notice Rennie giving me an odd look. Her eyes keep darting between me and Leslie, who's listening with rapt attention. Suddenly, it clicks. Leslie would be perfect for the job. Not only has she got all of the qualities I'm looking for and more, but her boss won't give her more than three and a half days a week at the accountancy firm where she works because her colleagues have been complaining that she talks to much. She actually needs work.

I clear my throat and turn to her. "Leslie," I begin, my voice trembling slightly with suppressed laughter, "how would you feel about, oh, I don't know...running a café?"

Leslie blinks. "A café? Me?" She looks between Rennie and me, confusion evident on her face. "I'd obviously love to but I...I've never..."

Rennie rubs her arm lovingly. "Oh, honey," she says, "you've been unknowingly auditioning for this job for years!"

Leslie's silent for a beat before her eyes widen comically. "Oh my God," she breathes, realization dawning. "You're right. I really would be perfect for the job." Her excitement bubbles over as she starts rattling off ideas. "Oh, Frankie, this would be amazing! I can already picture it—we'll have freshly baked cookies, artisanal sourdough with desert herb butter, and...ooh, how about omelets made from fresh eggs?"

Dad buries his face in his hands and groans. "Artisanal sourdough in the desert? What's next, gluten-free tumbleweeds?" He looks up to meet my eyes and I hear my mom chuckle. "Be careful, Frankie. You're creating a monster."

47

DAKOTA

I sit in the stark, white waiting room of Desert Springs Hospital, my hands clasped tightly in my lap to keep them from shaking. The smell of disinfectant brings back a flood of memories from my days as a nurse. It's both familiar and intimidating.

While I try to maintain my calm, the waiting room bustles with activity. Nurses in colorful scrubs rush past, their shoes squeaking on the polished floors. A red phone at the nearby nurses' station rings persistently, and I watch as a nurse answers it, her face growing serious as she listens.

A man in a white coat hurries by, speaking rapidly into a pager. The sliding doors at the end of the hallway whoosh open, and two paramedics wheel in a gurney. A woman is lying on it, her face pale and drawn with pain. They speak in clipped, professional tones as they pass, rattling off vital signs and injury details. It's a language I once knew fluently, and I find myself straining to catch every word.

An elderly couple sits across from me, the woman patting her husband's hand as he winces and shifts in his wheelchair. A young mother walks by, cradling a fussy infant. The baby's cries echo in the hallway, mingling with the constant hum of voices and movement that form the heartbeat of a busy hospital.

The energy, the urgency in the air, the knowledge that behind every door, lives are being saved and changed—it all calls to me in a way I'd almost forgotten. I realize how much I've missed this world, the sense of purpose and the tangible impact of the work. The sterile smell that once made me nervous now feels invigorating. I want to be part of this again—to have my hands busy with life-saving work, to feel the rush of adrenaline as we race against time, to experience the profound satisfaction of helping someone in their darkest hour.

Dr. Evelyn Chen, the head of the trauma department, emerges from her office. "Dakota? We're ready for you now."

I stand, smoothing my navy blue suit, and follow her inside. Two other people are seated at the table—a man in scrubs who introduces himself as Nurse Manager Tom Reeves, and a woman in a crisp, white coat, Dr. Sarah Patel from the ER.

"Thank you for coming back for a second interview," Dr. Chen says as we take our seats. "We were impressed with your initial interview and wanted to dive deeper into your experience and motivations."

I nod, trying to project confidence. "Thank you for having me. I'd love an opportunity to re-join the nursing field, especially in such a crucial area as trauma care."

"Very well." Dr. Patel leans forward. "It's been a while since you've worked in a hospital setting, though. How do you plan to get up to speed with current practices and technologies?"

Painting on a smile, I hope I sound convincing as I fire off the answers I've thoroughly prepared. "I've already begun refresher courses online, focusing on the latest trauma protocols. I'm also prepared to undergo any additional training the hospital requires. My experience in the spa industry has kept my interpersonal and organizational skills sharp, which I believe will help me adapt quickly."

Tom nods. "Speaking of the spa industry, that's quite the career shift. What made you decide to return to nursing, specifically trauma care?"

I pause, considering my words carefully. "While I enjoyed aspects of my work in the spa industry, I found myself missing the meaningful impact of nursing. Trauma care, in particular, appeals to me because of the immediate, often life-saving nature of the work. I want to make a real difference again."

Dr. Patel gives me a small smile and shoots off questions ranging from how I would handle specific emergency scenarios to my ability to work in high-stress situations. I draw on my past experiences, both from my nursing days and my time managing the spa, to illustrate my skills and adaptability.

As I answer, I know with growing certainty that this is where I belong. The spa world, with its focus on surface-level beautification, seems trivial in comparison to the vital, life-altering work happening all around me in this hospital. I'm ready to dive back in, to relearn, to challenge myself.

As the interview winds down, Dr. Chen asks one final question. "Dakota, trauma nursing can be emotionally taxing. How do you plan to maintain your own well-being while providing care for others in crisis?"

I think of Frankie and smile. "I've learned the importance of work-life balance and have a strong support system. I also find that connecting with nature helps me decompress and I'm positive that these strategies, combined with the satisfaction of meaningful work, will help me stay grounded and focused."

Dr. Chen nods. "Okay. And do you live nearby? What about the commute?"

"I'm actually moving in with my partner tomorrow," I say, unable to hide the grin that spreads across my face. "She lives on a ranch. It's a forty-minute drive from here, so that's totally doable."

"A ranch?" she says. "How lovely. I get your reference to connecting with nature now." Dr. Chen stands, extending her hand. "Well, thank you for coming in today, Dakota. We appreciate your time and candor. I believe our HR department has your references..." She flicks through a file on her desk. "And they seem to be in order."

I shake her hand, then Dr. Patel's and Tom's in turn. "Thank you for the opportunity. I look forward to hearing from you."

As I reach for the door handle, Dr. Chen speaks up. "Actually, Dakota, would you mind waiting outside for a little while? It's not often we get all three of us in the same room, and we'd like to discuss your interview while it's fresh in our minds."

My heart skips a beat. "Of course," I manage, trying to keep my voice steady. "I'll be right outside."

Back in the waiting area, I perch on the edge of a chair, my mind racing. Is this a good sign? Or are they just being efficient in their rejection process? I check my watch every few seconds, the minutes crawling by.

Around me, the hospital continues its relentless pace. A code blue is called over the intercom, and I watch a team of medical professionals sprint past. I try to distract myself by observing the ebb and flow of the emergency department, but my thoughts keep circling back to the interview. Did I answer their questions well enough? Should I have emphasized my management experience more? Less?

After what feels like an eternity but is probably closer to fifteen minutes, Dr. Chen emerges from her office. "Dakota? Could you join us again, please?"

The three interviewers are seated as before, their expressions unreadable as Dr. Chen gestures for me to sit.

"Thank you for your patience. We've had a chance to discuss your interview and review your application."

I nod, my mouth suddenly dry. This is it, I think. They're going to tell me the gap in my résumé is too significant, that I'm too far removed from nursing to jump back in at this level.

Dr. Chen continues, "We were impressed with your responses and your evident passion for returning to nursing. Your management experience from the spa industry, combined with your previous nursing background, offers an interesting skill set."

I hold my breath, waiting for the "but" that I'm sure is coming.

Instead, Dr. Chen smiles. "We'd like to offer you the position of trauma nurse, with a six-month probationary period. During this time, you'll undergo intensive training to bring you up to speed with current practices. After the probationary period, assuming all goes well, we'll reassess your role. Given your management experience, we see potential for you to move into a leadership position in the future, should that interest you."

For a moment, I'm speechless. This isn't at all what I was expecting. "I...thank you," I finally manage. "I'm incredibly honored and excited by this opportunity."

Dr. Chen slides a folder across the table. "This contains the details of the role, including salary and benefits. I'll ask

HR to email you the official job offer along with information on training prior to your start date. The majority of this will be online training, in your own time. Please review everything carefully, and let us know your decision by the end of the week. Do you have any questions for us at this point?"

My mind is reeling, but I manage to ask about the start date and the specifics of the training program. They answer patiently, providing more details about the intensive orientation process I'll undergo.

"We understand this is a big decision," Dr Chen says. "It's a challenging role, but we believe you have the potential to excel here."

I stand and take the folder. "Thank you all so much. I'll get back to you very soon."

Crossing the hospital lobby, I clutch the folder containing my job offer to my chest. The path to the exit suddenly feels significant, each step a preview of the journey I'll soon be making daily. I'm coming home to nursing, but this time with a wealth of new experiences and perspectives. My steps are light as I exit through the automatic glass doors and head toward the parking lot, eager to share this moment with Frankie.

48

FRANKIE

*T*he ranch is buzzing with activity as I gulp down the last of my coffee, steeling myself for the rest of the day. I've been up since dawn, making final preparations for our new arrivals—both animal and human.

I scan the premises, mentally ticking off my to-do list. The chicken coop Dakota and I built together stands ready and waiting, and the pen for the pigs and goats is secure. And of course, there's the wardrobe in my bedroom, half of it now cleared out and cleaned, ready for Dakota to move in.

Dakota. Just thinking her name brings a smile to my face. After months of back-and-forth visits and stolen weekends, she's finally moving in for good, and my heart swells at the thought of waking up beside her every morning.

When I hear Jose arrive with the animal trailer, I hop down the porch steps, giving Dobby an affectionate pat as I pass him. "Big day, boy," I murmur. "You're going to make new friends."

Jose pulls up, his truck groaning under the weight of the trailer. "Morning, boss," he calls, jumping down from the cab. "I've got them. Ready for the circus to begin?" He looks frazzled, his hair, usually pulled back into a neat ponytail sticking up in all directions.

"As ready as I'll ever be," I reply. "Let's get these critters unloaded before Dakota arrives with her stuff. How'd it go?"

"How'd it go?" he repeats. "Let me tell you how it went. It went about as smoothly as trying to herd cats. Underwater. While blindfolded."

I laugh. "I told you I'd come with you if you needed help."

"I know, but a few chickens, two pigs, and three goats... I figured it would be pretty straightforward."

"But it wasn't," I conclude humorously, reaching for the handle to open the back of the trailer.

"Wait!" Jose stops me. "Let's get organized first because the chickens are loose, so this won't be easy. Did you know the animal shelter doesn't usually keep chickens? They'd done an animal hoarder house raid and didn't expect to find them. They didn't have enough cages or pens this week, so they had to improvise." He leans against the truck, shaking his head. "Picture this. Chickens. Everywhere. In cages, on desks, even perched on the water cooler. You know what comes with chickens? Chicken shit—everywhere. And the noise? I'm not sure if you're ready for that."

I burst out laughing again. "Oh man...and you had to catch them one by one?"

"Yeah. Together with the volunteers. And that's not even the best part. Remember that rooster they mentioned? Well, turns out he's got a grudge against Curly the goat."

"What? How's that even possible?"

Jose throws his hands up. "Hell if I know! But the shelter workers had to keep them at opposite ends of the building."

I open the door a little and peer into the trailer, where I can see the animals shuffling around. "Are they okay?"

"Define 'okay,'" Jose says dryly. "It doesn't sound like they're actively trying to kill each other right now, but trust me, that's probably just because of the drive." He puts a hand on my arm. "Oh, I almost forgot. The shelter workers wanted me to pass on a message."

"What's that?"

Jose's face is the picture of seriousness as he says, "They said, and I quote, 'Thank God you're taking them. Please don't bring them back.'"

I chuckle and shake my head. "I have a feeling I may have underestimated how complicated this would be."

He nods grimly, pulling on a pair of thick work gloves. "You might want to put these on too," he says, tossing me a pair.

I slip them on, then slowly open the trailer door. "Oh boy," I mutter, surveying the scene. The chickens are everywhere, perched on every available surface; on the wooden dividers, the built-in feed and water containers, on the shelves, and even on top of the pigs and the goats. The rooster, a magnificent red-and-gold bird, is strutting back and forth on top of a crate, eyeing us suspiciously.

"Okay, let's start with the hens," I say. "They should be easier to catch than his royal highness over there."

We step into the trailer, and immediately, chaos erupts. The chickens scatter, flapping and squawking in alarm. I lunge for the nearest one, a plump brown hen, but she darts away at the last second and slips out of the trailer.

"Don't worry, she won't go far from her flock!" Jose triumphantly manages to snag a white hen. He cradles her gently, making soothing noises as he carries her to the waiting coop.

I spot a black-and-white-speckled hen huddled in a corner and approach slowly. "Easy there, girl," I whisper, reaching out. Just as my hands close around her, she lets out an indignant squawk and flaps her wings furiously, showering me with feathers.

We continue our chicken wrangling, slowly but surely transferring the hens to their new home. Some go quietly, while others put up a fight worthy of professional wrestlers. By the time we're down to the last few, we're both covered in feathers and who knows what else.

"Only the two who escaped and the rooster left," Jose says through pants, wiping sweat from his brow.

I blow out my cheeks, eyeing him warily. The hens have thankfully approached the chicken coop, but the rooster still stands there facing us, puffing up his chest.

We both approach him and suddenly he lets out an ear-piercing crow and charges at me. I backpedal quickly, nearly tripping over a crate.

"Whoa there!" I yelp, dancing out of his reach. His beak snaps at the air where my leg had been a moment before. "All right, buddy," I say, trying to sound authoritative. "Time to go to your new home."

The rooster then decides to ignore me and flies into Curly's compartment. There's a moment of stunned silence before all hell breaks loose—angry bleats and furious squawks fill the air as feathers fly in a whirlwind of chaos. Jose and I exchange a panicked look before rushing to separate the warring animals, knowing we need to act fast before either of them gets seriously hurt.

The rooster responds with a defiant crow and lunges at me again, but I dodge his attack and grab him around the middle.

He thrashes in my arms, wings flapping wildly, but I hold on tight. "I've got you now, you feathery menace," I grunt, making my way to the coop. "If you knew you'll have a much better life here than in that crammed trailer you were kept in before, you might not hate me so much."

Jose manages to catch the two remaining hens and finally, all thirteen chickens are accounted for and safely in their new home.

I turn to Jose, both of us disheveled and slightly out of breath. We look at each other for a moment before bursting into laughter.

"Well," I say, picking a feather out of my hair, "that was certainly an experience."

Next come the goats, who have collars with name tags attached. They're three Nigerian Dwarfs named Moe, Larry, and, of course, Curly. They're small but full of energy, bleating excitedly as we lead them to their pen. Curly's cute as long as he's not near the rooster and seems to be getting along well with the other two.

Their new enclosure surrounds the old shed, which I've repurposed as their nighttime shelter. Inside the pen, I've created a playground of sorts—fallen tree trunks for climbing, sturdy wooden spools for jumping, and even an old tractor tire for them to clamber through. Moe, Larry, and Curly seem delighted with their new digs. They prance around, testing out each new structure with unbridled enthusiasm.

"They're skinny, poor things," I say, watching them.

"Yeah," Jose agrees. "Let's fatten them up a little. The people from the shelter said they didn't think they've had fresh vegetables in their lives. They went gaga for the greens they fed them."

Curly, the most adventurous of the trio, has already scaled the highest log, bleating triumphantly from his perch. Moe and Larry take turns headbutting the tire, their antics bringing a smile to my face. As they explore, I can see them already establishing their favorite spots—Larry claiming a sunny patch near the water trough, while Moe seems particularly fond of a shady nook beneath an old branch. It's heartening to see them settling in so quickly, transforming this space into their new home.

Last but certainly not least are the pigs—two potbellied cuties named Hamlet and Bacon. They're surprisingly docile as we coax them into the enclosure to join the goats and immediately start rooting around in the fresh straw we've laid out.

Just as I'm about to get their food, Dakota arrives in my Range Rover. She got rid of the little furniture she brought when she moved to Vegas, but it looks like she still has an awful lot of stuff left.

"Why don't you go help her unload while I feed our new friends," Jose says, tipping his hat and giving Dakota a wave. "And then I'll call it a day. I still need to drive the borrowed trailer back to the shelter."

"Sure thing, Jose. Thanks for all your help today. You've been a trooper, dealing with this whole animal circus." I pat his shoulder. "Take it easy and I'll see you tomorrow. Oh, and don't forget to grab a cold beer from the fridge before you head out—you've definitely earned it."

I smile gratefully and jog over to Dakota. She's dressed in shorts and a white T-shirt, her hair pulled back in a messy bun. Her cheeks are red from what's clearly been a strenuous day. I was supposed to help her with the move, but then the shelter called me saying they couldn't possibly keep the animals until tomorrow. I understand why now.

"Hey there, Miss Vegas," I call out teasingly. "Looks like you've got quite the load there."

Dakota laughs when I pull her into a tight embrace. "Well, it's less than I came with, but still..." She winces. "Do you think you've got space for a few more clothes in your closet?"

I laugh and kiss her cheek. "Our closet now, and of course. I've cleared out half of it for you, but we might need to get some more storage units," I add, taking in the contents as I open the booth to my Range Rover.

We start unloading and with each trip, the reality of what's happening grows. I should be terrified—after all, ranch life is a far cry from the life Dakota's used to and I've been here before. But as I watch her, flushed and smiling despite the exhaustion, I feel nothing but certainty. Our love isn't some fragile thing that needs perfect conditions to thrive. It's resilient, like the hardy desert flowers that bloom after heavy rain. And now she's moving her belongings into my space, filling gaps in my life I didn't even know existed.

"I can't believe this is happening," she says, setting down the last box in the bedroom. "It feels surreal."

I reach into my pocket and pull out a small, silver key. "This is for you."

Dakota takes the key, her fingers tracing its edges. "My very own key to the ranch," she says with a flirtatious smile. "Does that make me a cowgirl too, now?"

"It's the key to *our* home. And the way your riding has improved lately, you're certainly getting there," I add with a wink, cupping her face in my hands. "Welcome home," I whisper before capturing her lips in a kiss that feels like a promise, like the start of something beautiful and lasting.

As we break apart, the late-afternoon sun streams through the window, catching the key in Dakota's hand. It glints, a small beacon of light. Our future starts today.

"Why don't we leave the unpacking for later and enjoy the rest of the day together."

"Sure, if you don't mind." Dakota leans into me, her smile widening. "I'm dying to meet our new animal friends."

As we step onto the porch, the new key nestled in Dakota's pocket, a profound realization washes over me. This land, which has been in my family for generations, is no longer just a legacy; it's a future.

The low sun gilds the ranch in warm light, and Dakota's hand finds mine, her grip warm and sure.

For years, I've carried the weight of thinking Red Rock Ranch would end with me. That this land, which has seen the births of countless animals, heard the laughter of guests, felt the sweat and toil of my family, would someday fall silent. But now, with Dakota by my side, I see a future stretching out before us. It's a legacy we'll nurture together, one we might someday pass on to our own children. Red Rock Ranch isn't just surviving—it's thriving.

49

DAKOTA

*M*y last day at the White Spa has come to an end and it feels surreal. The day has been a blur, the faces of my colleagues all blending together in final goodbyes and well-wishes. I won't miss the constant hum of slot machines or the smell of stale cigarettes on my way in, and I certainly won't miss our clients, but I will miss my team.

My office is already empty, the remnants of my work life packed into one small cardboard box.

I hear a knock on my open door. "Hey, you ready?" Frankie smiles, leaning against the doorpost. "Serenity said I could walk through. Thought you might need some help with your stuff."

"There's not much to carry." I pick up the box, but Frankie stops me and takes it from me. "You go do your thing. I'll put this in the car." She studies me. "Big day, huh? Are you okay?"

I laugh, though it comes out more like a sigh. "It feels weird to be leaving, but I can't wait to get out. We can go together, though. I've already spoken to everyone. I just need a moment with Serenity, that's all."

Frankie kisses my cheek. "Well, you've got a whole month before your new job starts. Looking forward to the break?"

"Hell, yes. I'm going to use the time wisely. Maybe finally learn how to ride properly."

Frankie chuckles. "You're doing just fine. But I have a feeling you might be riding something else instead."

"Oh, you're planning on physically exhausting me before I start my new job, cowgirl?" I ask with a flirty smile.

Frankie throws her head back and laughs. "Thanks for the suggestion, and I like that idea very much, but it's not what I was referring to."

I raise an eyebrow at her cryptic remark but let it slide. Frankie insisted on driving me to work this morning and picking me up, and though I still don't fully understand why as she refused to tell me, I'm going with it.

Serenity joins us, looking the part with her flawless hair and makeup, and she's wearing heels instead of her usual flats. She smiles, a mix of excitement and nervousness visible in her eyes. "So, this is it," she says. "It feels so strange to be in charge."

"You were *born* in charge," I say. I take off my white lab coat and grab the new name badge that arrived from the reception desk with the title "General Manager" gleaming beneath her name. Serenity beams as I pin it onto her lab coat. "There you go. Now every woman and her Chihuahua will be bugging you all day long."

She laughs and squares her shoulders. "I'm ready."

"If anyone is, you are. You know exactly what you're getting yourself into and you're more than capable," I say, pulling her into a tight hug. "But promise me we'll catch up soon, okay? I want to hear all about your first week."

Serenity nods against my shoulder, and I can feel her taking a deep breath, composing herself. As we pull apart, I see her discreetly wiping at her eyes. "Good luck," I say softly. With a final squeeze of my hand, she turns and walks into my old office, ready to start her new chapter.

As we step outside and into the car park, the Nevada heat hits us full force.

Frankie opens the door with a flourish. "Your chariot, m'lady."

I roll my eyes and chuckle. "You're ridiculous."

She just grins and starts the engine. Pulling away from the Quantum, I glance in the rearview mirror. The towering structure shrinks behind us, its glittering facade diminishing with each passing second. I feel a weight lift from my shoulders, like I'm shedding a skin that no longer fits. The casino becomes a mirage in the distance, shimmering and unreal, while the road ahead feels solid and true.

"So, where are we going?" I ask, watching the cityscape give way to open desert.

"We're going to Rennie and Leslie's house."

"Rennie and Leslie's?" I settle back into my seat, curious and a little apprehensive. "I thought Rennie hated entertaining? She'll have a nervous breakdown if we just show up."

Frankie smirks. "It's okay. She knows we're coming."

When we pull up to the house, Rennie is waiting in the driveway, next to a pickup. My first thought is that she and Leslie have the exact same pickup as I used to have, but then I see it—the small dreamcatcher hanging from the rearview mirror. I'd recognize that dreamcatcher anywhere; it was a gift from my father on my sixteenth birthday, the day he handed me the keys to this very truck. I left it in there when

I sold Henry; I guess part of me held some silly superstitious belief that it would help him find a good new home.

My breath catches in my throat as realization dawns. Henry, my old truck, the one I'd reluctantly sold when I moved to Vegas, has come back to me. I turn to Frankie, my eyes wide with disbelief and a surge of emotion I can't quite name. "No way..."

Frankie parks her car, turns to me, and smiles. "Surprise."

I step out, my legs feeling wobbly. It really is Henry. The rust is gone, replaced with a smooth, shiny blue coat, and the tires look brand new.

Tears prick at my eyes. "Frankie, how...?"

She wraps an arm around my waist, her smile softening as she sees my reaction. "Rennie and I have been working on it in secret. I knew how much it meant to you, and now that you'll be living on the ranch, you won't have to worry about parking."

I'm speechless as I run my hands over Henry's hood, memories flooding back. My dad's laughter, the smell of his cologne, the sound of country music crackling through the old radio. It's all here, wrapped up in this beautifully restored truck.

"Thank you," I whisper, my voice thick with emotion as I look from Frankie to Rennie and back. "I can't believe you did this for me."

"Rennie worked miracles on your engine," she says. "It should last for a good ten more years at least."

I hug Rennie tightly as she hands me the keys. "Thank you. You have no idea what this means to me."

Rennie's cheeks turn a deep pink as she steps back with a proud grin. "Let's see how it drives first. Go on, take it for a spin."

I slide into the driver's seat, the familiar feel of the worn leather under my fingers. Frankie hops in beside me, and I start the engine. It roars to life, smooth and powerful. "It sounds so good!" I exclaim, feeling a rush of excitement.

Without thinking, I steer Henry toward the main road, then onto a narrow dirt track, muscle memory guiding my hands. Frankie gives me a knowing smile, and I realize where I'm heading—into the desert, to the spot where we first met, where I was stranded that fateful night.

As we drive, I'm struck by how much has changed. The rugged landscape that once seemed alien and intimidating now feels like home. I navigate the twisting, unmarked paths with ease, no longer afraid of getting lost in this vast expanse.

We pull up to a clearing, surrounded by towering rock formations and Joshua trees. I park Henry right where my old breakdown occurred, in the middle of nowhere.

I turn off the engine and step out. Frankie joins me, her eyes scanning the landscape before settling on me with a warm smile.

"Look at you," she says, her voice filled with pride. "Not so helpless anymore, huh?"

I lean against Henry's hood, feeling the warmth of the metal against my palms. "No...I couldn't even change a tire back then. Now I can ride horses, wrangle chickens, and find my way through this wilderness." I pause, grinning. "But I still can't catch spiders. That's your job."

Frankie steps closer, her eyes twinkling with mischief. "I think I can live with that arrangement," she murmurs, her hands finding my waist.

I pull her closer, overwhelmed by the significance of this moment—the place where our story began. I capture her lips with mine, pouring all my gratitude, love, and excitement into a slow kiss that leaves me wanting so much more.

Frankie responds with equal fervor, pressing me back against Henry's hood. Her hands roam over me, igniting a familiar fire within me. Her fingers tangle in my hair as she deepens the kiss, and I melt into her. The kiss tastes of desert air and new beginnings, of home and belonging.

We break apart, breathless, only to come together again in a truth I've been searching for all along. Both of us out of breath, I rest my forehead against Frankie's. In her eyes, I see the reflection of the sunset, but also the promise of countless dawns to come.

The desert stretches out around us, vast and unchanging, and as the sun begins to set, painting the sky in the very mesmerizing hues that drew me here that night, I'm struck by the poetry of this moment. The soft pinks and purples bleeding into fiery oranges and reds mirror the journey of my heart—from hesitant beginnings to this cemented certainty.

The sun sinks lower, setting the horizon ablaze and announcing another beautiful night in this place I now call home.

EPILOGUE – DAKOTA

The wind whips through my hair, sending strands flying wildly around my face. I haven't tied it back; I like how it feels. The rhythmic pounding of Sahara's hooves against the desert sand echoes through my body, and for the first time since I started riding regularly, I feel completely in sync with her movements.

I loosen my grip on the reins, trusting Sahara to guide us home. The tension in my shoulders, a constant companion after a grueling week in the ER, is melting away. Each thundering stride carries us faster, and I lean forward, urging Sahara on without words.

My body moves in perfect synchronicity with her powerful strides, as if we've become a single entity. The boundary between horse and rider blurs, and I feel an exhilarating fusion of strength and freedom. Here, in this moment, there's only the horse beneath me, the desert around us, and Frankie riding beside me on Texas.

Glancing at Frankie, my heart flutters. She's the picture of grace in the saddle, her body moving in harmony with

Texas. There's a wild joy in her eyes that matches the feeling surging through my own veins.

We never skip our weekend morning rides. Both leading busy lives—Frankie running the ranch and me working as a full-time trauma nurse, watching the sun rise over the desert together is sacred.

As we crest a small hill, the ranch comes into view in the distance. Instead of the usual relief I feel at seeing our home, I'm struck by a pang of disappointment. I don't want this ride to end. For the first time, I understand what Frankie means when she talks about the thrill of riding.

Sahara seems to sense my mood and puts on an extra burst of speed. I let out a whoop of delight, surprising myself.

The desert flies by in a blur of muted browns and golds, punctuated by the occasional flash of green from a hardy shrub or cactus. The rising sun paints everything in warm hues, and like always, I'm struck by the raw beauty of my surroundings.

As we near the ranch, I expect Sahara to slow down, but she maintains her breakneck pace. For a moment, panic flares in my chest—what if I can't stop her? But then I remember Frankie's lessons. I sit deep in the saddle, gently pulling back on the reins while using my voice to calm her.

"Easy, girl," I murmur, and to my amazement, Sahara responds immediately. She slows to a trot, then a walk as we approach the stables. I pat her neck, feeling the sweat beneath my palm and the heaving of her sides as she catches her breath.

Frankie pulls up beside me, her face flushed with exertion and joy. "Well, look at you," she says with a grin. "I think you've found your seat."

I beam at her, still buzzing from the ride. "That was...

incredible," I manage between breaths. "I've never felt anything like it."

We dismount, and I take a moment to steady myself on shaky legs. Adrenaline is still coursing through my veins as I lead Sahara through the gates to the pasture. Now, the earthy smell of hay and horse sweat is as comforting to me as the scent of antiseptic in the ER, but there's also a cozy smell in the air—fresh coffee.

"Why don't you get us a cup while I take care of these guys," Frankie says as if reading my mind.

It's great to have Leslie here. When it's busy, she mans the café, and when it's quiet, I like hanging out with her and exchanging gossip while Frankie entertains her ranch guests.

The rustic wooden structure is charming, its weathered boards and tin roof blending seamlessly with the desert landscape, while cheerful flower boxes burst with succulents and desert blooms.

Outside, a large chalkboard leans against the wall, its surface covered in Leslie's neat handwriting. The simple menu offers a carefully curated selection of drinks and treats. "Farm Fresh Eggs" takes center stage, with options for fluffy omelets stuffed with vegetables from our garden, or hearty breakfast burritos wrapped in warm tortillas. The "Pancakes" listing promises stacks of golden goodness, topped with local honey or prickly pear syrup.

At the bottom, a "Daily Specials" section showcases whatever inspiration has struck Leslie that morning, often incorporating seasonal ingredients from our expanding gardens.

Leslie is bustling about, setting up tables and chairs on the small patio. The metal legs scrape against the wooden deck as she arranges them just so, her brow furrowed in

Epilogue – Dakota

concentration. Our motley crew of animals mills around her feet, hoping for treats or attention.

Hamlet and Bacon, our pot-bellied pigs, snuffle at the base of a table, and nearby, Moe and Larry, two of our goats, playfully headbutt each other while Curly watches from atop a large rock, king of his little domain.

"Morning, Leslie," I call out, patting Bacon as I navigate around him. "Need a hand?"

Leslie looks up, her face breaking into a warm smile. "Nah, I'm good. But stick around, will ya? I could use the company."

As she finishes arranging the last chairs, Leslie wipes her brow and turns to me. "So, how was your week? Still saving lives left and right?"

I let out a small laugh. "Oh man, where do I even start? Tuesday was absolute chaos."

"Yeah? What happened?" Leslie heads inside and removes a tray of freshly baked cookies from the oven.

"Huge pileup on the highway," I say. "We had six critical patients roll in at once."

"I heard about that." Leslie lets out a low whistle. "That must have been intense. Did they all make it?"

I nod, unable to keep the pride from my voice. "Every single one."

"No way! Dakota, that's amazing!" Leslie's eyes light up. "But God, you must be wiped out."

"Oh, trust me, I'll use the weekend to catch up on sleep," I say with a rueful smile. "But it's worth it. Nights like that... they remind me why I do this, you know?"

As we're talking, I catch sight of Mom on the porch, hunched over her laptop. Her fingers are flying across the keyboard, completely lost in her writing. "Speaking of busy," I nod toward Mom. "Looks like inspiration struck again."

"Yeah, she's been there for a while already," Leslie says. "That will be three coffees, then?"

Without waiting for an answer, she prepares three cups of coffee and sets them on the counter. Frankie joins us, taking her cup with a grateful smile and a quick kiss to my cheek.

"Thanks, Leslie. I'm going to take this to Mom," I say, nodding toward the porch. "She looks like she could use a refill."

As Frankie and I approach, Mom looks up from her screen. "Oh, sweetheart, you're a lifesaver," she says, accepting the steaming mug.

"Why are you up so early?" I ask, settling into the chair beside her.

She beams, turning the laptop so I can see the screen. "I woke up with an idea for my next novel, so I had to write the first chapter before it faded from my memory. I'm thinking of calling it *Desert Bloom: A Late-Life Love Story*."

"Sounds catchy. Can I read some?" I smile, pride swelling in my chest. Mom's first book, *Love Among the Fruit Fields*, has been doing surprisingly well since she self-published it. It seems she isn't the only one who has found her calling later in life.

"Not yet." She closes the laptop, her eyes twinkling with mischief. "It starts with a sex scene. I'll have to sensor it before I let my daughter read it."

Frankie throws her head back and laughs. "What about me, Viv? Can I read it?"

"I'll think about it," Mom mumbles, hiding behind her coffee cup as her cheeks turn pink.

It's so good to have Mom here. She's become very close with Frankie and Leslie and has visited several times this year. She still travels, but she's not running away anymore;

she's seeking inspiration, weaving the vibrant tapestry of her experiences into stories.

These weekends have become my sanctuary. After the intensity of the ER, the ranch grounds me, reminding me of the gentler rhythms of life. I have more time with Frankie, stolen moments where we can just be, without the pressures of work or responsibilities.

The café has become a hub of activity, bringing a new energy to the ranch. Serenity often pops in for coffee, her visits a welcome connection to my old life. We swap stories —hers of the spa's latest dramas, mine of the ER's chaos— over Leslie's coffee and homemade cookies.

Even Frankie's parents have become loyal customers. Her father, once skeptical of the "city folk invasion," now has a regular table where he holds court with other local ranchers. I catch him sometimes, watching the children in the petting zoo with a soft smile, though he'd never admit to enjoying it.

Frankie catches my eye, her smile warm and knowing. "That was a great ride," she says, slipping her hand into mine.

"Happy?"

I squeeze her hand, words failing to capture the depth of my contentment, but as I meet her gaze, I know she understands.

"Completely," I whisper and lean in for a kiss.

This is home. Not just the ranch or the house, but this life we've built. It's in the way Frankie's eyes light up when she sees me, in the smile on Mom's face, in the community we've created here in this little corner of the desert. This is where I belong.

AFTERWORD

I hope you've loved reading Red Rock Ranch as much as I've loved writing it. If you've enjoyed this book, would you consider rating it and reviewing it? Reviews are very important to authors and I'd be really grateful!

ACKNOWLEDGMENTS

First and foremost, thank you, Jose. Your passion for the desert opened my eyes to its raw beauty and hidden wonders. I never thought I'd fall in love with arid landscapes, but through your stories and guidance, I've come to appreciate the magic that blooms in the most unexpected places. Thank you for showing me that there's as much life in a grain of sand as there is in the depths of the ocean.

To 'Cowgirl Jess', your patience and expertise in introducing me to the world of horses has been invaluable. Through you, I've learned to understand these majestic creatures, to read their body language, and to communicate with them in ways I never thought possible. My lack of confidence around horses is something of the past!

To all the readers who've saddled up for this journey with me, thank you. May this story transport you to sun-drenched mesas and star-filled nights, and may you find a piece of yourself in the vast, beautiful wilderness of the desert.

ABOUT THE AUTHOR

Lise Gold is an author of lesbian romance. Her romantic attitude, enthusiasm for travel and love for feel good stories form the heartland of her writing. Born in London to a Norwegian mother and English father, and growing up between the UK, Norway, Zambia and the Netherlands, she feels at home pretty much everywhere and has an unending curiosity for new destinations. She goes by 'write what you know' and is often found in exotic locations doing research or getting inspired for her next novel.

Working as a designer for fifteen years and singing semi-professionally, Lise has always been a creative at heart. Her novels are the result of a quest for a new passion after resigning from her design job in 2018.

When not writing from her kitchen table, Lise can be found cooking, at the gym or singing her heart out somewhere, preferably country or blues. She lives in London with her dogs El Comandante and Bubba.

Sign up to her newsletter: www.lisegold.com

ALSO BY LISE GOLD

Lily's Fire

Beyond the Skyline

The Cruise

French Summer

Fireflies

Northern Lights

Southern Roots

Eastern Nights

Western Shores

Northern Vows

Living

The Scent of Rome

Blue

The Next Life

In The Mirror

Christmas In Heaven

Welcome to Paradise

After Sunset

Paradise Pride

Cupid Is A Cat

Members Only

Along The Mystic River

In Dreams

Chance Encounters

Songbirds of Sedona

Under the pen name Madeleine Taylor

The Good Girl

Online

Masquerade

Santa's Favorite

Spanish translations by Rocío T. Fernández

Verano Francés

Vivir

Nada Más Que Azul

Luciérnagas

Solo Para Socios

German translations by Iris Pilzer

Members Only: Nur für Mitglieder

Hindi translations

Zindagi

Made in United States
Troutdale, OR
04/27/2025

30924173R00189